THERE FOR YOU

Love & Family #1

ANYTA SUNDAY

First published in 2013 by Anyta Sunday
Buerogemeinschaft ATP24, Am Treptower Park 24, 12435 Berlin

An Anyta Sunday publication
www.anytasunday.com

ISBN 978-3-947909-30-8

Cover Design: Natasha Snow

Content Editor: Teresa Crawford
Line Editor: Lynda Lamb
Proofreader: HJS Editing

There For You

Sam:

He's solid, kind, and he's back. Luke. My next door neighbor. My best friend. My unofficial co-parent.

God, I've missed him. Really, deeply missed him.
Now he's around again? Maybe he'll help me tick my way
through my Must Do List . . .

*Swim with the **great whites**?*
*Get into crazy, nasty shape. **Lift weights** before work!*
***Date** someone ten years older.*
***Flirt**, have fun, don't fall in love.*
*Do something **sexually taboo**. (Or just have sex again.)*

I mean, I'm straight, so Luke doesn't have to help me with the
last three points.
But, what . . . what if he does?

Luke:

He's the guy I'm in love with. He doesn't even know I'm gay.

God, I'm screwed.

For my family, who knows what it's like . . .

Chapter One

SAM

MATHEMATICS. I shrink against my seat at the word. The word that stares back at me now, on a scribbled note from Jeremy. *Can you help me with my mathematics assignment?* it says. And it's funny, because that single sentence takes me back a good fifteen years to when I once asked for help too. Though, I might not have asked so much as said, "I'll flunk unless you help me, Dad."

Dad had shaken his head and told me that math was important, that understanding numbers and how they work could tell me a lot about the world and that I really should buckle down, quit trying to be a copycat Marilyn Manson, and do something that would help me in the real world.

Yeah, but like, it's just numbers.

He'd said, "Numbers that can tell you about *life*."

Well, he was right.

Numbers. They sure could tell a lot.

For example:

In **1** week—

420 dollars, give-or-take **10**, is the number I earn in wage and tips working at the *Canon Café*.

180 dollars is the number it costs to rent my house.

148.20 dollars is the amount I spent on groceries at Pak 'n Save.

18.75 dollars for phone and Internet.

18.75 dollars for power too—if it's summer.

The other **54.30** dollars goes toward things like clothes, petrol, repairing crap around the house, and a weekly movie from the video store . . .

Oh, and **-33.80** dollars is the state of my overdraft.

I flatten the note on my rickety secondhand table that's about three dinners away from collapsing. Something else I have to add to my to-do list.

But right now, all I can see is *mathematics* and goose bumps prickle down my arms and the hair on my neck rises.

The weekly numbers aren't the truly important numbers, are they? In the end, they're just money. And money is fleeting and doesn't hold much meaning at all. But there are other numbers . . . numbers that give a more macro view of my life. Numbers that have come to mean everything to me.

Like:

30

and **15**

These are the numbers that I will remember for the rest of my life.

Let's start with 30. Yes. The number that has my heart pounding second to none. The number that is the reason I'm sitting here reading Jeremy's note not with a mug of coffee next to me, but with a glass of cheap bourbon and ice.

30 is the age I'll be turning in three weeks.

Call it a mid-life crisis if you like, but it freaks me out. I still work as a waiter. I never even managed to get a high school qualification. I live in the moldiest, most ramshackle house on the block. And I haven't had a love life—if you can even call it that—since . . . well, that would be the next number . . .

I pick up the glass, the condensation wet and slippery against my palm, and take a long drink. A half-year ago, when it dawned on me that my twenties had all but disappeared, I'd written up a *20s Must-Do List* of all the things I should have done and hadn't.

I glance at the letter-writing desk Jeremy and I had rescued from Old Jones, who'd been about to make firewood out of it. I have the list somewhere in one of those drawers . . . I thought just writing it down would be therapy enough, that I'd come to terms with what I'd missed out on, but—

I take another sip of bourbon. It's warm and smoky on my tongue, and exciting too, since I almost never drink.

I sigh.

But the thing is, I'm not okay about it. I want to do all the things on that list.

I laugh. Why the hell not? I have three weeks left before the big **30**. Maybe I can reclaim a little of my youth?

Out the window, a familiar truck rolling into the driveway next door catches my eye. I shuffle back in my seat and slap the table. "Luke?" The devil's back?

I jump up. For a second I'm on a buzz that my neighbor and friend has finally arrived home after six months up in Auckland. I put my glass down and it lands on the note. Through the side of the glass "mathematics" is magnified.

Dad's voice is back. "*. . .can tell you about life.*"

In my mind, I see him shaking his head and sadly closing the door.

I'd been **15**.

He hadn't kicked me out; he'd begged me to stay, but I couldn't.

He visits every few months and sends me a card every year. December **15**th. My birthday. He always puts money in it too, which helps me climb out of overdraft. But every time I touch the cash, I think how right he'd been. How I wish I'd listened.

I watch over the green wooden fence that divides our places as Luke empties his letterbox—something I was supposed to do while he was gone and had only remembered half the time.

I will him to turn around so I can glimpse his signature dimpled grin as he waves to me, like he always used to when he came home from work. But the guy is lost in thoughts, hurrying into his house hunched over that rather large armful of mail . . .

I might have to apologize for that. In fact, he couldn't have had time to go to the supermarket, so better yet, I'll be neighborly and make him spaghetti and meatballs.

I glance at the clock. Quarter past three. I laugh, because that damn number follows me everywhere I go.

15. It is the number that says everything important about my life.

Why?

Because on my **15**th birthday on the **15**th of December, my girlfriend Carole went to the hospital and gave birth to our son, Jeremy.

Jeremy turns **15** in three weeks.

Chapter Two

JEREMY

This is the reason I don't eat bananas.

I look at the table in front of me and wish the next five minutes were already over. Every second week since I turned fourteen, my mum makes me practice putting a condom on a banana.

It's one thing to imagine doing that in a Sex Ed class at school, where you can smirk and talk shit about it with your friends. It's a totally different thing to do it in front of your freaking mum.

I have to be as red as the reddest freaking fire truck. I tear the foil and hurriedly roll the condom over the spotty yellow banana skin.

Of course she likes to give me the soft mushy ones. *No matter how hard it might be to get it on, that's no reason not to use it. There's no naked tango—never, ever—unless this thing is on. Got it?*

I'd gotten it the first time she said it. The sheer mortification of having that conversation with my mum in awkward detail was enough to make me remember. But it is never enough. She needs bi-weekly proof I haven't suddenly and magically forgotten the Golden Condom Rule.

When it's time to take the condom off the banana, I can feel her staring, making sure I do it right. I have to hold the rim tightly and carefully slide it off, tie it in a knot and trash it in the bin.

So yeah, there is a reason I don't eat bananas anymore. My mum just laughs and says I'll get over it. But I'm pretty sure I'm going to be traumatized the rest of my life.

No more banana cake for me. Ever.

And if it weren't for sweet-faced Suzy, my sort-of girlfriend, I might forego the sex part too.

Except, not really. Because although I tell my dad I don't have any girl I like—his bi-weekly version of the How-Not-To-Get-A-Girl-Pregnant-At-Fourteen = no girlfriend at all—I do. I really like the way Suzy moves. And how she grooves. Her brown curls that bounce on her shoulders. And that plump bottom lip that she lets me suck on behind the wood workshop at school.

Her hot tongue in my ear made me jizz a little in my pants just last month. It was sticky and sort of gross, and I had to stay like that for the rest of the day, but oh God was it worth it.

At the school dance last week she'd gone further, groping me, and there was a wicked sparkle in her blue eyes that suggested maybe we go further than that . . .

Yeah, this summer is going to be awesome.

Or it will be as soon as I finish this last week of assignments and school officially ends for the year.

I wash my hands, twice, as if it will miraculously get rid of my embarrassment too.

"Oh, hon," mum says, coming over and pulling me into a

side hug, "you're so cute when you blush. You look just like your dad did at your age."

"Doesn't mean I'm going to make the same mistake as he did," I say, grabbing a dishcloth and drying my hands. Even with the apple-scented detergent we have, I still think I can smell the rubber.

I never say it, but of course I'm glad *they* made the mistake. It would suck not to have been born. My life is great.

I mean, my parents can really be downers sometimes. They make me do chores, finish all my homework, and read at least one book a month or they take their respective televisions away —like seriously, they unplug them and heft them to the loft— and of course there is the banana thing . . . but I have it good, too.

Like Dad lets me play video games late on Fridays and Saturdays and when I don't have school the next day, and Mum can bake the best non-bake cheesecake ever, and she takes half of my soccer team in our van to all the competitions we have around the city and up North.

And at Dad's it's cool because most of the time there's Luke and I fucking love Luke.

He likes to take Dad and me all over the place, where we have all sorts of adventures. We go on camping and kayaking trips, biking trails, and rock climbing expeditions . . . And yeah, he's just cool. Like, I know he pays for all the stuff and pretends it doesn't cost as much so Dad doesn't have to worry about it. When I found out, I promised not to say a word, and I haven't. I won't. But it makes me like him even more.

But there's another reason I love having two homes, two rooms, two routines . . . it means I can get away with shit.

I say to Dad that Mum says it's okay if I go to Steven's house to study after school on Wednesdays. I tell Mum the same thing. *Dad says it's . . .*

Wednesdays are the days Suzy and I go on our sort of

dates. Mostly we hang out at KFC in one of the corner booths and make out. Sometimes we go to the local park and hang behind some well-placed bushes—

"What are you thinking about, Jeremy?" Mum asks, grinning as she grabs a banana from the fruit bowl and peels it.

I shrug, looking away before she stuffs the thing in her mouth. "Nothing. I have to get over to Dad's. I have a math assignment he's going to help me with."

Mum snorts. "Good God. Sam? Math?" She kisses my temple. "Good luck, dear. You want me to drop you off?" The phone rings.

"Nah, it's a nice day. It'll take twenty minutes."

Mum nods and answers the phone. "Oh hey, Debbie," she says, moving away from me into another room.

I run upstairs and pack my bag. When I come back down to say goodbye to Mum, I pause. I can hear her from the hallway and she's talking in hushed tones.

It puts me on alert, because over the last few months I've been noticing a few strange things at home. Like finding a large T-shirt in the wash that I'd never seen before. And the mouthwash that suddenly showed up half-used in the bathroom cabinet . . .

I think Mum is hiding something from me. And I refuse to acknowledge what it likely is. If I'm ignorant enough, it won't be true. Those things won't be happening. There will be no sudden and big changes to my life.

Even though I don't want to know, I strain to hear what Mum is saying. I want to resist, but I can't help it.

I swallow in relief as I catch her just gossiping about me.

"Yeah, Jeremy's great. But, you know this age." She laughs. "Exactly. Sometimes I just wish he was gay, you know? So I wouldn't have to fear him getting some girl pregnant. Sure would make me feel more relaxed."

At first I frown.

But then the wheels in my head are turning, and any and all secrets are forgotten, because boy am I grinning. I hitch my bag strap higher on my shoulder, then make a ruckus as I round the corner into the living room. Mum instantly stops talking.

"You off, love?"

"Yep." I give her a wave and leave.

I use the walk to Dad's to ring people. First I talk to Suzy. I learn that after the last day of school on Wednesday, there's a party Simon is having in his garage. Her voice is husky at the edges, and I don't even think about the *how*, I just say I'll be there.

Then I ring my best friend Steven.

"What's up?" he answers.

"I need your help with something," I say. I tell him my plan and he hangs up on me. I laugh; I know Steven will come around.

In under a week, I'll have my plan in action.

Chapter Three

LUKE

This sounds stupid, especially coming from a thirty-six-year-old man, but I'm nervous to say hey to my neighbor again. I've only been away six months, but those six months felt like forever.

The saying goes something along the lines of: you don't know what you've got until you've lost it. Well that's exactly what Auckland was for me. It was six months of being in the Lost and Found box, and it's the reason I couldn't even glance up at Sam's place as I came inside.

I was never meant to stay in this place. When I first moved here, seven years ago now, it was meant to be temporary until I found something better. I imagined living closer to work, somewhere in central Wellington. But then . . .

Well, then the boys next door happened . . .

I sit on the same spot at the end of the couch and stare over the coffee table at the black screen of the television. The mail is spread out next to me, a lot of swimming words that aren't making much sense right now, and they're not the words I care about.

I lean back, arching my torso to reach my pocket, and pull out a folded piece of paper. It's worn and grey at the edges from my constant re-reading. The paper used to crackle, sharp and fresh the first few times I opened it, but now it unfolds soft and silent like a handkerchief.

This is why Auckland was like being in the Lost and Found box. This is why I'm nervous to say hey to Sam.

Before I left six months ago to help out with a family crisis, I'd gone over to give him my keys. He'd called out from his room that he'd be there in a second, and while I waited in the dining room, I chucked my keys on his writing desk. I threw them too hard and they slid over the top, taking down a pile of paper with them.

I gathered them up, and a list caught my eye. I don't know what possessed me to read it—an overabundance of curiosity, perhaps. But I reached out and scanned the list, and once I'd gotten to the end I sucked in a sharp breath and with shaky hands hurriedly folded the paper and stuffed it in my pocket.

It's been on me ever since.

It was there when I helped my mum through her breast cancer surgery and recovery.

It was there when my sister told us she was getting a divorce.

It was there when we all drove up to Orewa and strolled the beach side-by-side.

It was there when we went out for morning coffee and our afternoon walks.

It was there when I finally came out to my family.

It was there when they all told me I was a fool for waiting so long.

It was there when they asked me if I had someone special

in my life, and I said yes without hesitation, without even thinking.

It was there when they demanded I bring him home so they could meet him.

It was there when I couldn't say that my special someone didn't know he was my special someone.

It was there when I realized he and his son were the reason I'd never moved from this place.

It was there when I caved in to my mum's persistent nagging and blurted out that I'd introduce the boys from next door at Christmas.

It is there now as I wonder how on earth I can live up to that promise.

I smooth the paper over my thigh and read Sam's *20s Must-Do List*. These are words that mean something. They jump out at me, grab me, beg me to come and play. They are words that make me smile, make me sad, make me excited, and make me nervous.

Read *the books I should have read in school.*
Stay up the whole night **dancing***.*
Have a **hangover***, wear shades, and eat mince pies.*
Go out with someone and **go to the bathroom when it's time to pay***.*
Date *someone ten years older.*
Flirt*, have fun, don't fall in love.*
Do something **crazy with my hair***.*
Swim with the **great whites***?*
Try a **sport***.*
Take an **interest class***.*
Understand **Kanye West***. Who the fuck is Kanye West? Find out.*
Get into crazy, nasty shape. **Lift weights** *before work!*

I have my fingertips resting on the last line. If I don't, I can't seem to read the rest of the list. This last line is the one that is the loudest, the one that makes my insides somersault, the one that makes me feel like I'm jumping off a bridge and free falling. The one that makes me plot, plot, plot . . . the one that gives me nervous, hopeful energy.

I slowly pull my fingers back and my gaze goes directly to it.

*Do something **sexually taboo**. (Or just have sex again.)*

I run my thumb over the line again and chastise myself for thinking the way I do. For plotting in detail how I could convince Sam to be sexually taboo—with me. We can make it a game. We can call it experimenting. Later we can brush it off as something wild he did in his twenties . . .

I sigh. It's all a ruse. I want it. I *don't* want it.

I brush the edge of the paper over my frown, as if it will erase it. It's better to have and lose than never have at all, right?

Seven years we'd been friends, neighbors, *bros* . . . and it took only a week on my own in Auckland missing him so damn much to realize what I had here. I love him, Jeremy, our routine together.

I love *us*.

I know it's ridiculous to think that if Sam just tried the taboo with me he'd magically fall in love. I know things don't actually work that way in real life.

But I just can't help that niggling thought in my head. What if he *does*?

It's this little thought that reassures me it's okay to plot. That it's okay to tease . . . I want to try. Want to know for sure.

A hearty knocking on the front door jerks me to my feet. I quickly refold the list, slip it back into my pocket, and answer the door.

There, cradling a pot with a dishtowel and an oven glove, is my someone special.

He turns his dark, thick-lashed eyes on me, just as a breeze blows a bang over his forehead. "Luke!"

I push aside any nerves I have and breathe out. "Hey."

Chapter Four

SAM

"Hey." Luke smiles, dimples deepening, and beckons me in. It's immediately easy between us, almost as if he never left at all. Almost.

"Sorry about the mail," I say, and motion to the pot. "Figure I owe you. Spaghetti and meatballs." I make my way inside to his kitchen and rest the pot on the fake marble bench. I open the cupboards and pull down some plates. Over my shoulder, I call out, "Jeremy's home. He's got this assignment to do, and I"—*am no good at math*—"I told him to bring it here. That all right?"

There are footsteps, and then I feel Luke's presence behind me. I turn around and he's leaning back against the wall, arms folded, nodding. "Of course it's all right."

"Good, because we've both missed you, Luke, and we want to catch up. Also, I barely know what Trigonometry means."

He laughs. "Math, eh? Shouldn't be a problem. When's he coming over?"

"He's on the phone to a friend. After that." I turn back to the plates and serve us both some pasta. "How's your mum doing?" I ask quietly. The metal serving spoon clunks heavily on the pot in the silence that follows.

"She's fine." He clears his throat. "I, uh, told her a lot about you guys."

"You did?" I pass him his plate and we move across the hall to the dining room. "Good stuff I hope."

"Yeah. Good stuff." He sits down and spears a meatball. He's still prodding it after I've inhaled my first one.

"Something up?"

Luke rests his fork on the side of his plate. "I, uh, I—she wants to meet you. Both of you. I said we could go up at Christmas?"

"She wants to meet us? You must have talked us up a bit too much." I laugh, but Luke goes back to prodding his dinner.

I lean back in my chair, taking in Luke's navy long-sleeved T-shirt, and his metal watch gleaming with the light from above us. He's a touch taller than me, definitely stronger than me, older than me in that "big brother" sort of way, but right now his expression looks lost and a touch . . . *something else*. It's like he's swallowing a smile. It's endearing and . . . *new*.

There's something I know for sure. Luke's my best friend, and if his mum wants to get to know his friends, I want to be on the top of that list. Number *1*. That's math I can do. "I want to meet her too," I say, "but the thing is, I don't know I'll have any holidays at Christmas. I . . ."

I laugh. There is a small trace of bourbon still working. I scratch the back of my head. "Thing is, last week I told my boss I was taking the rest of this year until Christmas off. As of tomorrow."

Luke's head snaps up. "Your boss was okay with that?"

"He said it was about bloody time, so long as I worked the Christmas rush."

He finally takes a bite of dinner, and murmurs that it tastes great. I sense he wants to say something else, but he keeps hesitating.

I lean over and punch his arm. "Just say it."

His dimples are back for a second, and then they disappear. "Are you going somewhere? What about Jeremy?"

I shake my head and twist spaghetti on my fork. "Nah. I just . . ." *want to live the last of my 20s.* "I'll still be here. Just doing other . . . stuff."

He raises a brow and I glimpse a smirk. "Other stuff, eh?"

"Yeah. Hey, you wouldn't happen to have any weights around, would you?"

"I do, somewhere." His brows knit together.

"What? Don't think I can buff up?"

"That's not it at all. But honestly, I don't think you need to buff up. You've got a good runner's build."

"Well, regardless, give me some tips, coach, because I want to get crazy, nasty fit."

Luke leans back in his chair, balancing it on two legs. His dimples are back and this time they look like they're staying. That *something else* is in his gaze again. And I'm going to figure out what it is . . .

"Dad? Luke?" Jeremy calls down the hall. His steps follow, dragging lazily over the carpet. I want to tell him to lift his feet, but I know this stuff goes in one ear and out the other. I've learned to pick my fights, and though the *chrr-chrr* sound bugs me, I try to ignore it.

I grit my teeth a lot.

"In here," I say and drum on the tabletop.

He comes in slouched over a couple of textbooks and a

frayed notepad. Like me, he's wearing a brown T-shirt and jeans, and I am thankful he has Carole's button nose and thin lips because otherwise it would be like looking at myself at fourteen. And I'm not sure I'd ever let him out of my sight then.

Jeremy glances between us, lips quirking into a grin that I just know will get him in trouble with the girls sooner or later. His face is glowing like the time he scored the winning goal in his soccer finale.

"Fuck, Luke, you're back!"

"Watch the language," I growl, using my great, deep rumbling voice, cultivated from necessity after a few short years of parenthood. Like always he straightens and nods. But it doesn't wash out the smart-ass in him.

"Freaking eh, Luke, you're back!"

I mask a smile and stand, clapping my boy on the shoulder. "How hard was that?" Then I ruffle his hair, which at some point over the last year he's come to hate, but I'm still locked in the habit.

He leans his head out of my reach with a scowl and drops his books on the free end of the table.

Luke has a secret buddy smile going on with Jeremy. "Shoot, man, you've grown. It's been too long." They do a funny high-five, pull-like handshake move.

"You can say that again. Dad was miserable without you here. It was a"—he looks at me—"*freaking* long winter."

I slide back into my seat. Luke blinks fast a few times and his swallow is audible. From the way he grips the tabletop, I know that he's missed us too. "Yeah, the longest."

"I wasn't *that* miserable," I mumble, though it's complete and utter rubbish. "I read a lot."

For some reason, this really sparks Luke's interest. He levels his green gaze on me and folds his arms. "What'd you read?"

I pick up my fork and gesture toward his plate. "Your spaghetti is getting cold."

He starts shoveling down his dinner, and I know he's hurrying through it to ask his question again. I shake my head and focus on Jeremy, who has sat down and flicked open his books. He bites his lip as he reads what looks like the assignment sheet.

I don't know which question I want to avoid most. The math one that will make me look like an uneducated fool of a dad, or the books one that will make me seem like I'm trying to be a pretentious prick.

Maybe they'll balance each other out?

Luke winds the last of his spaghetti on his fork and the grin he gives me as he brings it to his mouth helps me make up my mind.

"So, what was it you needed help with, Jeremy?" I quickly jump up and move behind Jeremy's chair. Over his shoulder are a lot of numbers and triangles. The word "sin" comes into focus, and for a second I think this could actually be interesting, but it is short- lived.

Luke's chair makes the same *chrr* sound as he pushes it back. He comes over and peers over Jeremy's other shoulder. It takes a few moments, but Luke glances over at me with the same blank *What the fuck is this?* expression. I laugh and shrug, then I pull out a chair close to Jeremy and Luke does the same on his other side. I split the textbooks between us.

"I think I sort of get it," Jeremy says, scribbling something on his pad. "No, wait. That can't be right."

Luke and I look up at each other and I know we're thinking the same thing. This is going to be a *long* night. We open the textbooks and begin.

We finish at quarter to eleven, and unless the word "sin" works really, deliciously hard to redeem itself, I don't ever want to see it again.

Jeremy tosses his pencil onto the table and leans back, stretching. "I so don't get the point in math."

I hear my dad's words coming out before I can censor them. "Math is important. Understanding numbers and how they work tells you a lot about the world. Trust me."

He mumbles something inaudible and then rips out a yawn. When he drops his arms back to his side, he says, "Hey, Luke. Can I ask you something *actually* important?"

I growl and Jeremy smirks.

"What's that, Jeremy?" Luke asks, his lip twitching as if he's suppressing a grin.

"So, like, us Hutt Penguins drew with the Oriental Lions in the soccer finals last month 'cause it got cancelled. But me and the team want to do a match against them anyway. Would you be able to help set up a game for us? We can so beat their asses."

Luke lights up, his smile coming out in full force. "It won't reflect in the official results—"

"We know that. But those guys practice on the field next to ours and show off all the time. Trust me. They want this as much as we do." Jeremy beats a fist into the air. "We're so gonna take 'em down a peg."

I shake my head. "Hmm, maybe I should root for the Oriental Lions. It'd be nice to see you taken down a peg or two."

"Dad!"

I laugh. I want to reach over and ruffle his hair, but refrain.

"So?" Jeremy looks to Luke. "Could you?"

Luke pretends to think about it, wincing like it's going to be hard to do. When Jeremy leans over and whacks his arm, he laughs. "Sure thing. I'll get permission to use our school field and locker rooms for the game."

"Score!" Jeremy's beaming. He looks down at his math

books, but I can tell by the way he bites his lip and grins that his thoughts are so far away from his assignment.

Jeremy leans back in his seat and folds his arms. He says, without looking up, "Dad?"

I know this tone. It's soft and careful. He wants something from me he's not sure he'll get.

Luke knows this tone too, because he's looking at Jeremy with one brow raised.

"Yes?" I say.

"You know how it's the end of school on Wednesday?"

Get on with it . . . "Yes."

"Well, Simon is having a sleepover, and I'd like to go. Can I?"

There's something wrong with this request, and it takes me a moment to pin-point it. I laugh. Usually Jeremy is more confident when he asks to stay at a friend's place. He says it like it's no big deal. This time though, the way he ambled toward the question . . . this time it was a bigger deal. I'm immediately suspicious.

"End of school sleepover? Will there be girls there?"

He stutters and his eye twitches and I know the answer already. Luke does too. He must, because he shakes his head. "No can do, Jeremy. Your dad told me that he wants to take you out to a movie that night and celebrate the end of the school year with you."

"That's so totally lame, Luke," Jeremy says. "Dad so did not organize anything." My boy looks over at me, brow arched like he knows what Luke said is a lie. He sighs and picks up his pencil, using it to doodle on the end of his note pad. "I mean, yeah, there will be girls there for a bit, but they're just the ones from my class."

The ones from class . . . the ones he saw everyday and no doubt spent hours fantasizing about . . . yeah, because they're nothing to worry about . . .

"Luke wasn't lying," I say, feeling a need to defend him. "I got some holiday lined up and I wanted us to go out. Sorry, Jeremy, but the answer's no to the sleepover."

Jeremy looks ready to argue, but he slumps back and nods once. "Fine." Then he hurries to gather up his things, not looking at either of us. "Night," he mutters and leaves.

I stand up, suppressing a sigh, and try to think of something to explain it to him. But Luke is up too, skirting around the table; he grabs my arm and stops me chasing after him. His fingers skate off my skin and leave goose bumps behind. It reminds me how goddamn long it's been since anyone has been close enough to touch me.

But that will change soon. I have a *20s Must-Do List* to fulfill. . .

"So what did you read?" Luke asks, and his voice is all smirk.

I shake my head and collect our dishes. "You don't know when to give up, do you?"

He takes the dishes off me; our fingers brush, and he jerks them back. "I'll do that," he says. "You cooked, after all."

I hate dishes, so I quite like the arrangement. When he tugs the plates, I realize I haven't let go. I quickly remove my hands.

"You want to play a board game or something?" Luke calls out from the kitchen.

I shake my head at the empty table. "It's probably a bit late for that." Then I tell myself off for being so reasonable. I want to let loose for the next few weeks. "I mean, what do you have in mind?"

"How about Taboo?" he says, so close behind that his words bounce off my neck and I jerk to the side.

"Taboo?" I repeat, and I'm not thinking of the game, but . . . something else.

And then Luke bends over to wipe down the table,

reaching to clear the spaghetti splatters that somehow made their way to the middle.

I curse myself for making spaghetti. Why couldn't I make something that guaranteed no mess? Like . . . like . . .

Under Luke's T-shirt his back muscles bunch and his ass is jiggling. I blink, scratch my head, and inch toward the hall. Suddenly going home and being sensible sounds like the best idea ever.

"Ahhh," I say. "Don't you need more players for that game?"

He finishes, turning toward me, shrugging. "Why not just us two guys? We can work around the rules a bit."

My mind literally blanks, and I hear my nervous laughter. Tomorrow morning I am going to work. Not to actually work, but to finally ask Hannah out. "Um, actually"—I yawn, hoping it doesn't sound too forced—"I think I'm gonna call it quits for tonight."

Luke nods. "Okay. You said you're free tomorrow?"

"Yeah."

"I want to try that new Chinese place I saw on Queen Street," he says, following me as I move into the hall.

"That might be a touch expens—" I gulp down the rest of that sentence. "Actually, yeah, that sounds good."

I hurry to the front door, trying to remember all that math stuff to keep me bored and not thinking about . . . Jesus, I need to find a fling, and soon.

Just before I escape from Luke's place, he catches me. He holds the door open and in the porch light I catch that *something else* in his gaze again.

"Okay," I say, leaning on the outside of the doorframe and crossing my ankles. "What's up with that look of yours?"

He scrubs his face as if he can get rid of it, but the *something else* just deepens as his dimples do.

"Seriously, what aren't you telling me? You look like you're hiding the news that you won the lottery."

His smile widens. "Maybe I'll tell you about it at lunch tomorrow."

I leave him watching me as I make my way home. Jeremy's room light is on and I can hear the soft beat of music through the door. I knock and tell him to get to sleep. He has school in the morning.

Once the music is off, it's quiet and I don't know what to do with myself. I can't concentrate on *Mill on the Floss*, the last on my to-read list.

I pour myself a bourbon and pace. What I'm really doing is trying to figure out why Luke is so freaking happy. And the thing is, I think I know, and I'm not sure how I feel about it.

He must have met a woman in Auckland. That *something else* . . . yeah, but damn, that something else looked an awful lot like being in love.

I finish my drink and pour another. I've been expecting this since the beginning. I know our friendship can't last forever— I'm lucky it's lasted as long as it has. But Luke is . . . well he's amazing. Of course he's found someone.

And tomorrow he's going to tell me about her.

I drink.

I don't think I can handle hearing it. It makes me so fucking sad thinking of losing him. I know we'll still be "friends," but it'll never be quite the same. There'll be someone else around him. His attention will be on her. Then he'll move. Have kids. We'll see each other a few times a year at first and then it will wind down to the occasional email, maybe birthday and Christmas cards . . . and then, it'll be nothing but memories.

I finish my drink.

Until I get used to the thought, I'm going to navigate

around his attempts to tell me about her. I just need . . . just a little bit of time.

Buzzed and needing to distract myself, I move to my writing desk and pull apart my drawers, searching for my *20s Must-Do List*. I haven't touched it in months, but I'm pretty sure it's here somewhere . . .

I take everything apart. The list is not there.

I sigh. Maybe I chucked it out.

Shaking my head, I pull out a notepad and write the list again. The clock is ticking. Tomorrow, I'm beginning it . . .

Chapter Five

LUKE

It's seven thirty in the morning when I drop off a set of weights to Sam. I start to put them on the table, but it groans and I shift them to the floor in the corner of the room, under the windows.

Sam crashes through the door, back from a run. Sweat is dripping down the sides of his flushed face. He wipes his brow with the back of his hand and leans against the kitchen bench catching his breath. "You do this every day?" he wheezes.

I laugh and go into the kitchen to pour him a glass of water. He guzzles it down.

"But I do feel revitalized," he says after finishing his water. "I think I could get used to this not having to work thing."

I snort. "Yeah. Feel you there."

He looks at me over his empty glass. I stand across from him not doing anything except leaning back against the bench as well, watching him. "When does your sabbatical end exactly?" he asks.

"I'm going in to talk to my boss this morning. She knows I'm back in Wellington now. I think I'll start with the new school year."

"Makes the most sense." Sam peels off his wet T-shirt and moves out of the dining room toward the bathroom. I follow, just to the door. He dumps the T-shirt in the wash hamper and looks at my reflection in the mirror. "You think we'll get sick of each other if we're hanging out days *and* nights now?"

I catch the breath that has rushed out of me, and smile. *Hell no, absolutely not.* "Guess we'll see."

He laughs and hooks his thumbs into the waistband of his shorts. "All right. I gotta shower. You mind getting Jeremy's lazy ass out of bed?"

I pull the bathroom door shut, and stand there smiling stupidly to myself. Like I'll get sick of spending more time with him. This is what I've wanted for a while now. Some him-and-me time that wasn't constantly interrupted by, well, life.

I hear Sam hum a tune and I stay a little while longer to listen, feeling his voice vibrate through the door and into my skin. With a shiver, I reluctantly pull away and stroll toward Jeremy's room. The lazy bum, he should've been up a half hour ago to get to school on time.

The door is slightly ajar and I push it open. "Wakey-wakey, time to—"

Holy crap!

I grab the door handle and yank the door shut.

Jeremy is cursing like a sailor and I feel like doing the same. I hurry down the hall and into the kitchen. Crap. There are just some things you should never, ever walk in on. And your best friend's son spread out on top of his bed having a morning wank is one of them.

Almost the very tippy-top of the heap of what *not* to walk in on.

I yank open the fridge. I don't care that it's seven-freaking-thirty in the morning, I want a beer.

Unfortunately, the fridge has barely anything in it except for a half carton of milk and some cheese and eggs. I take the milk and drink it right from the carton.

Two minutes later, Jeremy sulks into the room, dressed and blushing. He doesn't look at me, and I don't look at him.

The quiet between us is so tense, I can hear Sam humming. Suddenly this shower he's having feels like it's taking forever even though he can't have been in there for more than a couple of minutes.

"Uh, so, you want scrambled eggs?" I ask after an awkward stretch.

"Fuck," Jeremy says, and I think this is one of the occasions where a swear word is just fine. He slumps further down on his chair and half looks up at me. "Could you, like, not tell dad?"

"Scrambled eggs it is," I say. I put a pan on the stove, and drizzle some oil on it.

This is the worst kind of awkward. For the both of us, no doubt. And I'm not really sure of my role. What I can or should say. I want to opt for saying nothing, but I don't want Jeremy to think what he was doing is wrong.

"Look, man, we're all guys here. We all do it, okay?" I crack an egg, but the pan is not hot enough. "Just lock the door next time, alright?"

He mumbles something and turns to look out of the window, where clear skies promise a sunny day.

When the eggs are done, Sam finally struts into the room. He's dressed in brown slacks and a tan shirt, his sleeves rolled up to his elbows. He looks good. *Very* good. "Why're you dressed up this morning?" I ask, shoveling egg onto three plates.

He shrugs, but I catch a glimpse of a blush. "You just rarely see me in the morning without my work clothes on. But, um, I look alright?"

So much so, I want to nip every part of your body with kisses and taste you. "Sure, man."

Sam grabs the toast that's just popped, smears it with butter and adds it to the three plates. "Careful," he says to me when we are all sitting at the rickety table eating, "I could get used to my mornings like this."

A stream of sun comes into the room and warmth floods over me, and I wonder if I'd have felt the warmth even if the sun hadn't been there.

Jeremy scoffs his food, and barely looks up when he shoves back from the table. His dishes clatter in the sink, and then he scuffs his feet over the floor, which makes Sam's jaw twitch.

"Clean your dishes," Sam starts, but I stop him.

"I said I'd do them this morning."

Jeremy is relieved. I see it in the way his shoulders drop. "Yeah. Thanks, Luke," he says. Then to his dad he says, "I'm going to be late back after school—Steven and I are stopping by Mum's place. I left an assignment there we've been working on."

Sam nods at him. "Sure." His arms twitch, as if he wants to ask Jeremy for a hug but doesn't dare to anymore. It makes me want to take hold of his hand, twine our fingers together and squeeze. "You need me to give you a lift in?"

"Nah," Jeremy says, and leaves.

I look at Sam and lift a questioning brow.

"It's uncool," he explains with a shrug. "He'd rather take the bus."

"He's grown into a real teen since I left."

Sam rests back in his chair and looks up at the ceiling, sighing. "Yeah. And I have no fucking idea what to do with him half the time." He peeks at me out the corner of his eye, and his lips twitch into a smile. "But you're around now. You'll help me out, right?"

I want to lean over, cup his face and kiss him. I want him to know I'll always be there for him. That I'm here as long as he wants me to be—and that I hope that's forever.

I shake off the fantasy, stand up instead, and take both our plates to the kitchen. "I'll do whatever I can, but teens elude me too, most of the time. It's why I like working with *pre-teens.*"

Sam watches me as I wash the dishes. I wonder what he's thinking about, but don't want to ask and break his concentration on me. I like that he unabashedly gazes at me the way he does sometimes.

Finally he looks away, glancing toward the corner of the room. He spots the weights and jumps off the chair. "Awesome!" He picks one up and drops it back down again. "Damn, that's heavy."

I laugh. "You did say you want to get nasty fit."

He waggles his brows. "That's right."

I wipe my hands on my jeans and come over to him and the weights. Crouching, I take off the extra rounds and give him something more suitable. "Start with this, okay?" He tries it. "Do you want to do something before we go for lunch? We could go for a swim." I hear the nerves in my voice, and try to temper it by clearing my throat and shrugging. "Or whatever."

Putting down the weights, he shakes his head. "No can do, Luke. There's something I've got to do this morning."

I hide my disappointment behind another shrug. "Lunch then."

We are both crouching, staring at the equipment at our feet. "Can't wait," Sam says, and then I feel his gaze lift up to me. I can't bring myself to meet it. It's too intense to look at him when we are so close. I might not be able to pull back from making my fantasies happen.

I'm just about to stand when Sam does something he's never done before. He casually rests his hand just above my knee and uses me to push himself up. I feel his touch linger on my thigh and my pulse doubles.

"This is going to be the start of an awesome holiday," Sam says. I nod, the only thing I am capable of doing.

AT KRESLEY INTERMEDIATE, THE SCHOOL WHERE I TEACH, I find the principal and we talk about reinstating me in the new school year.

I wait until the very end before I open up to her about my sexual orientation. I've hidden it long enough, and I don't want to anymore. She takes the news with barely a blink and assures me it's no problem. She consoles me with the knowledge that there are a few other gay and lesbian staff members.

I know one of them is Jack. *Know* because we used to be together.

It's first break, and I find Jack in his wood workshop. Despite him leaving me seven years ago—because I didn't want to come out to my family—we remained friends. Sometimes with benefits. Although that has gotten less and less over the years.

Jack is stacking some planks of wood at the back of the room when I show up.

I knock on the open door.

When he sees me, he straightens and flashes me a shit-eating grin. "Well, look what the cat dragged in."

We meet halfway inside the room and I reach out and pull him into a hug, hitting him lightly over the back of his sawdust-colored hair like I used to. "Hey, man."

"Hey yourself," he says gruffly. "Been too long, Luke."

"Yeah," I say. "Mum's stable now, so I'm back. I start again next school year. I can't wait to get back properly." Well, actually, considering this holiday I'm sort of sharing with Sam, I *can* wait. But generally, I'm excited to be coming back to work, teaching physical education and health.

"I'll make sure we get our co-coaching positions again," he says as he sits on a workbench.

I lean back against the bench opposite, and I give him a run down of my time in Auckland. When I get to the part about coming out to my mum and sister, he straightens and blinks.

"So," he says, and his grin is growing, "you *finally* met someone that means enough for you to step out of the closet. He must be a real charmer." He shakes his head, and there's the briefest moment where he winces, but he quickly schools his face. "So everyone knows now, huh?"

I dig both hands into my pockets and tap my thumbs on the outside of my jeans. I feel Sam's list over my right palm, and swallow.

Jack sucks in a breath. "So who haven't you told?"

I laugh, but I'm berating myself at the same time. "The charmer."

"The guy you came out for doesn't know you're gay? Hmmm, now why do I get the feeling that spells disaster?"

With a wince, I push away from the bench and pace the aisle. "Because it does. He's straight. And my neighbor."

"Oh Christ. The friend you've been talking about for the last decade? I should have seen this coming."

"So should I. And seven years. Not a decade."

He shakes his head. "It just gets worse."

I look around for something to toss at him, but there's nothing. I sigh instead. "I'm going to tell him. I just have to find the right moment."

Jack jumps down from the bench. "There's never a right moment. You up for getting coffee?"

"Sure." I follow him out. On the way, I pass his student noticeboard and a flyer catches my attention. "You're running carpentry courses for adults?"

Jack glances at me over his shoulder. "Every Saturday."

"That's new."

"Yeah, well, I don't have a neighbor-friend to keep me otherwise occupied." His laugh echoes around the corridor between classrooms as we leave the workshop.

"You not refurbishing old houses and selling them for a good buck anymore?"

"Haha, yeah. Actually I'm working on a cottage in Rory Street. But running the workshop is great. I can get a lot of shit done at the same time. Last week I managed to make the new skirting boards for the kitchen."

"Does it get easier, selling them once you're done?"

He shakes his head. "And this one, she's a real beauty. I'm tempted to keep her, but I need the money. Still saving to buy my dream villa one day."

"Does this mean you'll be busy refitting kitchens or what-not on Sunday?"

"That depends. What's on Sunday?"

"A soccer game, if you'll help me set it up."

Jack lets loose his shit-eating grin again. "I'm sure I can squeeze that in. But only if I get to meet your charmer first."

Chapter Six

LUKE

I wait for Sam at a table in the corner, next to the windows overlooking the busy street. It's ten after twelve when he crosses the road with a ridiculous smile on his face. His hair is fashionably mussed and I swear his eyes are laughing. He's practically skipping, and it makes my heart skip too.

I want him to be as excited to see me as I am to see him.

I stand up when he comes in and beckon him over. I'm nervous though, and I can feel it in the clamminess of my hands and the way I knock over my water glass as I sit.

Sam is on to it. He already has serviettes in his hand and is wiping up. Then he does something he's never done before, and it goes right to my groin. He winks. "My waiting experience pays off for once."

He laughs and I stumble over a "thanks."

"What has you so cheerful today?" I ask, opening the menu and scanning over it without seeing a single thing.

He doesn't say anything, just shrugs and smiles wider.

I look up at him and raise a brow.

He swallows, the smile still there, and focuses on the glass I tipped over. He spins it in circles. "I'm on holiday. I feel . . . so *free*."

Boy does he deserve it too. I'm so happy for him, I can taste the freedom myself, and that wonderful free-fall feeling comes over me again. "And what are you going to do with your time?"

The waitress comes over and we order. When she's left, Sam leans over the table conspiratorially. I lean in too.

"I have a list."

I try not to smile, but I know it's slipping out of my control. Even though I'm not touching it, I can feel his *20s Must-Do List* in my pocket, warming me through my jeans. "Oh yeah?"

"Yeah. I'm going to make my way through it. Also, so long as you're still on a sabbatical, we should, I don't know, do more stuff together. Catch up, you know. Hey how do you feel about sharks?"

Truth? I'm not a fan. In fact, they scare the crap out of me. I don't say that though. I shrug. "Oh yeah, you know. They're just animals." *Animals that can freaking tear you apart with their massive, killer jaws.*

"Want to swim with them with me?"

Leave the "with them" part out, and I am all there. "Hell yeah."

He smiles, and I know swimming with sharks will be worth it.

Leaning back, he looks out the window and squints. "You wouldn't happen to know who Kanye West is, would you?"

"Yeah, I do."

"You do? How do you know this stuff?"

I lean back in my chair, feeling a glint of hope as I say, "I *am* almost a *decade* older than you are." I hope my emphasis on decade hits him the way it's meant to, and I think it has, because he flushes and glances toward the kitchens.

"What's taking them so long?" he says, and begins fidgeting with his placemat.

It hasn't been long at all, and I like knowing he's just as nervous as I am. I want to reach out and take his hand and say *I want to be your summer fling.*

For all our summers, always.

But it's too much at once, and I have to break into things more gently. I have to tell him about me—"Sam," I say, shifting on my seat and looking down at the placemat in front of me, fingering the dragon indentations. "There's something I want to talk to you about—"

I hear him sucking in a deep breath and I look up. He's suddenly tense, gripping the table.

I frown. "What?"

"Nothing." His gaze skips over mine to look at the wall behind me, and then out of the window. "I mean"—he rings out a nervous laugh—"did I tell you I scored myself a date for Friday night?"

I laugh, because surely I've misheard. And focusing on laughing helps me not feel the roughness of the hand that's clawing at my chest. "Date?" It comes out as strangled as I feel. "Was that the 'something you had to do' today?"

I want the food to get here so I can pay for it and leave.

"Yeah," Sam says, still not looking at me. "There's this woman at work. It's taken me a while, but this morning I finally gave her my number. She asked me out right away. We're going dancing on Friday night."

"Woman?" I ask, the word sour enough to bring tears to my eyes. I blink them back. What was I thinking with my teasing? How stupid am I? Sam is a straight man. There is no sense crushing on him and letting fantasies get the better of me.

I'm a fool. A little bit of taboo won't change him.

He swallows and nods. "Uh, her name is Hannah."

He breathes out slowly just as the waitress comes over with our food. We wait until she's left before we continue.

"Okay," Sam says, still gripping the table, his knuckles whitening. "I'm sorry. Your turn. What were you going to say? I'm ready to listen."

I can't say it. I should. He—and Jeremy—are the only ones who don't know the truth about me. I want them to know. I want to be completely out of the closet. But the words are trapped under the same claws that have my heart. Because if I tell him I like other men, and he's cool about it and waggles his brows and asks me if there's a special someone like my mum and sister did, I think I'm going to break. Maybe even cry.

And crying is not something I do, really. The last time I cried was when my mum told me she needed surgery, and before that, it was when dad left when I was fourteen.

I sniff, and quickly dab a fresh serviette to my nose. "It's spicy," I say, and silently will myself to get over it. I haven't lost Sam. We are still friends.

I eat.

He eats.

The silence between us is awkward and the clatter of our utensils against the plates sounds too loud.

Then he looks over at me for the longest time, until it becomes a game of who turns away first. And when I break away and he chuckles and knocks my foot with his under the table, I want to reach over, clasp a hand behind his neck and kiss him.

Which I don't think I will ever get to do now. It'd been nice to daydream, but destructive too. I've got to stop.

We finish eating. I didn't taste anything.

"That was great," Sam says, patting his stomach. Then he glances at the cashier desk, and stands abruptly. "I'm, uh . . .

just going to the bathroom," he says, and there's a nervous excited glint in his eye as he turns and walks off.

And it makes me love him more.

I fucking laugh because it's either that or sob. And then I go pay.

Chapter Seven

SAM

I can't hold back a cheeky smile when Luke and I leave the restaurant. I should probably feel ashamed at making him pay my **18** dollars, but I don't. What I feel is, well, *naughty*. And there's something liberating about that.

It feels like the Dad in me is on vacation, and this new Sam is being allowed to run rampant for a while.

I laugh for a beat, and Luke gives me a funny smirk back. He pulls out his keys and motions to his truck, parked at the curb. "That's me."

"My Honda is parked two-streets down. Shall I meet you . . . wherever we're going next?"

"Next?" Luke looks at me quizzically, his gaze dipping to the hands I'm stuffing into my pockets.

"Yeah. I thought we'd be hanging the rest of the day. Or something. Unless you're busy?"

He shakes his head. "Nah. That sounds good. Leave your car here and jump in with me."

I do as he says and in **15** minutes we are driving around the coast. Luke is such a confident driver and is always in control; I like that I can sit next to him and feel safe enough to doze off, despite the perilous blind corners that make up half of the drive.

I look from his hands on the steering wheel to the steep climbing hills peppered with houses out his window. Then I look out my window to the sea, edging the road in turquoise. "Jeremy will want to do his learner's license soon."

"He's old enough for that already?" Luke gives me a small shake of the head and focuses back on the road, his thumbs rubbing the wheel. "He's growing up so fast." I detect a sigh in his words and I understand exactly.

"He is. I can't believe he's the age I was when I *became* a dad. It's . . . eerie."

A few beats go by and, resting my head against the window, I let out my own sigh. There's a sudden need to get this thing off my chest. To explain why I need to cut loose these next few weeks.

"The thing is," I say, "being a Dad has never come as first nature to me. I've been faking my way through the first fifteen years of Jeremy's life. Half the time I have no clue what I'm doing."

I laugh at myself, but it sounds as hollow as it feels. "And the other half . . ." I drift off. What I want to say sounds . . . *sappy*, no matter how true it is.

Luke changes gear. "The other half . . .?"

I straighten and look over at him. I offset my words with a shrug, as if it will rub some of the sappiness out. "The other half I have you to help me."

A soft whoosh of breath leaves him, then Luke checks the rearview mirror. Suddenly, he's pulling the truck off to the side, into a wide bay used for turning on the narrow roads. He puts the handbrake on, and then faces me. "We all fake it. I'm sure it's the same for Carole." His voice catches as he adds more quietly, "I feel clueless most of the time too."

I nod, but his and Carole's "faking it" always seems so much better than mine. "One day I'm afraid Jeremy will look at me and see me for what I am. A fraud."

Luke goes to say something, but I raise a hand and stop him. "I'm just so nervous. I don't know what to expect. My experiences at fifteen and his are going to be so different. I'm afraid I won't know how to relate to him and will mess it all up."

"And . . ." I feel the prickle of tears at the back of my eyes. I blink them down. "The honest truth, Luke? I'm a bad Dad."

"Fudging your way doesn't make you a bad Dad," he says, and the way he leans forward, it looks like he wants to comfort me. I want to let him too, but I'm afraid it'll make things more awkward. And added to that, I don't think I deserve it.

I say it quietly. "It's not just the faking. Shit, I hate that I feel this way, but sometimes I can't help it. I'm jealous of him, Luke."

Luke shifts back in his seat and blinks.

I rub my forehead with the back of my thumb. Then I shrug. "I never got these years he's going to have now. I should have made some great friends, done a few minor stupid things that I could have laughed about now, you know, thrown a party when my parents weren't around or whatever."

I shake my head. I was only **14**. "All I got out of my teen years was a first time with Carole. We weren't even dating! I never got to do that. It was only the one night. It wasn't even everything I thought it was going to be. That's it. That's the last teen thing I got to do. Then Jeremy was there, and—*bam*—I'm a dad."

I laugh again, but it's the nervous kind. "I just wish . . .

wish I'd done things differently. I see him now and I want to know what it's like to not have to care about stuff so much. Sometimes I just don't want to have to be responsible."

I look away from Luke's gentle, non-judging gaze and back out to the sea. "There's a reason for this list I have. A reason I snuck off back at the restaurant to let you pay. . . ."

Sneaking a peek at Luke, I'm surprised his lips are twitching into a smile. When he catches me looking, he says, "Is that the worst you can do? Come on, Sam, consider this holiday your time to cut loose. Get really wild." His tone sours a fraction. "Asking Hannah out is something, but it's a little . . . vanilla, isn't it? There are other things out there to try and do."

His voice fades into something more serious. "I get it, though," he says. "And I don't think you're a bad dad. And, you know, for your peace of mind, I'm happy to take care of the responsibility stuff for a little while. You know, maybe I could pick Jeremy up like I used to?"

I nod, and the relief at having Luke behind me has me sinking into the seat. "He usually takes the bus now. Except for Tuesdays after practice. But I'm in town anyway, so you don't have to."

"When it comes to doing things for Jeremy," Luke says, restarting the car, "it's not a matter of *having* to do something, okay? I want to."

I laugh for real this time. "Well I hope you'll still *want to* when you start teaching him to drive! Because I'm sure as hell going to have a coronary if I do it."

Chapter Eight

JEREMY

Steven shakes his head for the fourth time that afternoon. "You so owe me for doing this," he says, but there's this little glint in his eye that makes me think he's sort of okay with what we're going to do.

I open the door to Mum's. She's not home yet, but she'll be home any minute.

"So," Steven says, going straight to the fridge and grabbing the carton of chocolate milk. "We're just holding hands, right?"

"Exactly. On the couch. When mum comes in we're going to separate like we're trying to cover it up."

Steven pours a glass for him and me and shoves one over the bench. "Wouldn't it be better if we're making out?"

I laugh out loud. "Hell no." A small flush creeps up my friend's cheeks. Huh. "You want to tell me something, Steven?"

A deeper shade of red gives him away.

"Seriously?" I say. "Are you for real? Dudes?"

He just picks up his milk and drinks. When he sets his glass in the sink, he shrugs. "You've never been curious?"

"Can't say I have. You don't have a crush on me, do you?"

Steven rolls his eyes. "You really are an arrogant prick."

I grin.

"But, uh, I mean, if I were into guys . . .?"

He needs me to say something about it. I've known him most of my life, and I can sense when he's uncomfortable. I sip the milk. "I don't really give a shit who you dig," I say. "Just don't start falling for me or anything. This is just a ruse, okay?"

"Fuck you," he says, smiling again. "No way on Earth would I go for you anyway. I've seen your dick and it's tiny."

"Shove off, you pervert. And I'm not tiny."

"Oh really?"

"You just want me to show you my wang, don't you?"

He laughs. And then I can see his mind ticking. I almost know what he's going to say next. "No fucking way," I say, backing out of the kitchen.

An evil grin quirks his lips, and he prowls forward. "You *do* owe me for doing this with you."

"My tiny dick is out of bounds to you. So just . . . kept yours in your pants, okay?"

He laughs as we enter the lounge. "I'm kidding with you, man. Except for the tiny part."

I fall back onto the couch and Steven follows. He grabs my hand and gives it a little squeeze. Then says seriously, "Thanks man. For being cool."

I'm not going to squeeze his hand back, but I nod. "Less competition with the girls for the next four years. What's not to like about that?"

The front door lock snaps. Mum's home. I bunch closer to Steven. I suddenly wonder if Mum will even see our hands together like this.

Ah shit. "Okay, fuck it," I whisper. "Kiss me okay. No tongue. Consider it payment."

Mum's footsteps come down the hall. I nervously glance at the doorway and at Steven. I hope I don't make a face when we kiss and give myself away.

But I don't get a chance to worry further. Steven grabs my shirt and crushes me against his lips as he leans back to the arm of the couch, so we're lying on each other.

I don't know whether I want to swear at him or be impressed at the scene we're giving.

My mum's footsteps slow, and that's when I mutter a soft—but hopefully audible—"Oh fuck, Mum's home."

We scramble apart just in time for Mum to see the hurried retreat. Then I act nonchalant, like nothing's happened. "Hey Mum," I say.

She frowns. "What are you two up to?"

I meet her frown with a shrug. "Oh, you know. Nothing much."

"Thought you were staying at your dad's this week?"

"Yeah, we were just grabbing our assignment I left here."

She looks from me to Steven and the surprise on her face almost makes me laugh. But I can't do that, or she'll know something's up that's not quite right.

Steven looks super uncomfortable, and I wonder if it's an act or if he really is feeling weird about this. And then I notice the bulge in his pants and the way he's trying to twist away from my mum.

It's perfect, in a way. Mum has to have gotten it now. But in another way, I feel a little bad for Steven because my mum has known him since he was a kid too, and he is sort of coming out to her for real. Ish.

I move over to him, grab his arm, and move past Mum into the hall. "We're off to Dad's now," I say, heading down the hall.

I stop when she calls out, "What about your assignment?" Her arched brow says she knows there's no such assignment. But she doesn't know that's the point. And that I've won this round.

"Oh yeah," I say. "Steven, you go wait outside. I'll be down in a tick."

It takes me only a minute to race upstairs, grab something that looks like it could be an assignment, and head back down. I nip into the kitchen where Mum is standing, resting against the counter eating a banana.

"Bye," I say, and wave.

I leave, praying as I do that this will lighten mum up.

And that maybe it'd even stop the bi-weekly banana condom practice.

Chapter Nine

SAM

I look at the box of dye in my hand, and then pour the contents into the bathroom sink. Plastic gloves, a tube of dye, and instructions—it looks pretty straightforward.

I run a hand through my light brown hair. "It's going to be goodbye to this for a while," I say to the mirror me.

I slip on the gloves and pick up the tube—

There comes a knock from the front door. "Just a second!" I drop the dye and shove on a shirt as I go to answer the door. I realize I'm still wearing my gloves when they make a noise as I twist the handle.

Morning sun stretches into the hall, smelling of perfume and outlining Jeremy's mum. Carole looks at my hands and smirks. "Can I come in?"

"Jeremy's left for school already."

She nods and walks past me toward the kitchen, her heels

clopping over the floor. "Yeah, I know. I wanted to wait until he was gone."

"Is something the matter?" I ask, now concerned. I try to think back to when Carole has come to me to talk about Jeremy and cared whether he was around or not. I can't think of a single time.

"Nothing's wrong, exactly," she says, slipping into the chair Jeremy always uses.

I sit opposite her. She points to my gloves. "I hope you're not dyeing your own hair."

I hurry to peel them off.

"Get someone else to do it. I once tried those packets and my hair was splotchy for months because I didn't do it right."

"Maybe I'm going for splotchy."

She laughs. "What color?"

"Black."

She groans. "Don't let Jeremy get any ideas. Didn't you get over black back in school?"

"Why are you here, Carole? You're making me nervous. Is Jeremy going to be okay?"

She laughs. "Um, yeah, he's going to be okay, alright."

"Then—"

She must see my frown because she sighs. "Look, I just thought I should talk to you about something I saw. I want you to be prepared in case Jeremy wants to tell you someday soon."

"Prepared for what?"

"The possibility our son is . . . gay."

I scratch the back of my head. Carole isn't making any sense to me. "Gay?"

"And this is why I wanted to talk to you. We need to be sure we have the right reaction, Sam, not sound like we've never heard the word before. We have to show him that we support him one hundred percent. That we love him just as we always have."

"Carole, get back to the gay thing. Jeremy's gay? How do you—"

"I accidently caught him and Steven making out on our couch. I don't think they know I saw them though. They did move apart like lightning on speed."

I don't know what to say. I'm surprised, mostly. It was the last thing I expected to come out of Carole's mouth.

"Get the gaping mouth thing out of your system. You can't do that in front of Jeremy. He won't know what to think. He'll worry you don't accept him."

"What? Of course I'll accept him! He's my son. I'll always love him." I push back my chair and pace into the kitchen. Blindly, I grab **2** cups and heap **4** teaspoons of instant coffee in each.

"Good," Carole says. "I didn't think you'd have a problem with it. I just want you to be ready."

I stare at the instant powder in the cups. "Should we . . . I don't know, say something to him?"

Carole shakes her head. "Let him come out in his own time."

Suddenly, I laugh, thinking of how I'd worried about that end-of-year party Jeremy wanted to go to. Carole looks at me curiously, and then I tell her my thoughts, "Guess it's not the girls we have to worry about anymore."

She laughs. "I thought it'd be more of a relief than it is. Now I'm scared of him getting hurt by anyone for his choice of lifestyle. I guess there's no end to the worrying."

"I doubt it."

"Sam?"

"Carole?"

"There's something else I want to mention. It's . . . well I've told you a little about it in passing before, but now . . ." She looks up at me and her face is glowing with a smile, eyes dancing in the light. "You know how I've quietly been seeing Greg?"

"Guy from work?"

She nods. "Well, I don't think it's going to stay quiet much longer. Greg, he, well, he's made it known he wants a future with me. I'm ready to tell Jeremy about him. Get them to meet each other."

"So you're really moving on with your life," I say, reaching over and touching her hand. "Good on you, Carole. If he makes you happy, you deserve it."

"Thanks, love." She looks out at the garden and grips my hand back. "And I'm sure there's someone amazing out there for you too."

I think of Hannah from work. I like her and she's fun for sure, but would she be that someone? I shrug. "We'll see, I guess. How are you going to break it to Jeremy?"

Carole bites her lip. "I don't know. But soon."

CAROLE LEAVES **5** MINUTES LATER, AT THE SAME TIME LUKE arrives.

I pull him into the kitchen, still somewhat hazy with my surprise over Jeremy. I lift a finger to tell him not to say anything. Then I pace in front of him. I'm bursting to share this new revelation with someone because I want to make more sense of why I suddenly feel off-kilter about my son being gay.

It's not because I'm upset about it. It's something else inside that squirms a little bit.

Luke folds his arms and watches me carefully. "You okay?"

I nod. "Yeah. I'm fine. Really. I am."

"You sound it."

I stop pacing and laugh. Then, taking a breath to calm myself, I offer him a cup of coffee.

He shakes his head. "Not until I know what's up with you. Is it something about Carole? Has she met someone? Is she getting married or something?"

I move over to the counter where he leans, and I do the same. "Nah, it's not that." I swallow and look at him from the corner of my eye. "Jeremy might be into guys. Carole just told me she caught him making out with Steven."

Luke stills, and for a second I wonder if I should have said anything at all. "And," he says slowly, "is that a problem?"

Ineloquently, I try to get to the root of the jumbling feeling in my stomach. "No. I guess not. I just . . . I don't know." I scrub my face with my hands and then give a half-laugh. "Maybe I don't really get it, you know? I mean, I love him and whoever he's into is fine by me. I just . . ." Something. I just *something*.

Luke slowly pushes away from the bench and turns on the jug. His back is to me as he talks. "I think I get it. It's just nothing you've ever considered before and it seems . . . foreign to you."

I'm not sure that's entirely it, but it's close enough for now. "Maybe."

I watch the way Luke reaches into the cupboard and brings down two mugs. There is gracefulness to the way he moves, and comfort in the way he knows my kitchen better than I do. I am thankful he is reacting well to my news. I'm so thankful I can trust him to be open like this.

It's not really something we do—we have an unspoken bro-gap rule—but sometimes I want to hug the guy and tell him how much he means to me. I always leave it at a thought though, and hope somehow he can just sense it.

"How come you're so calm about all this? Do you have kids come to talk to you about it in school sometimes?"

Luke looks at me over his shoulder; his voice seems a little rougher than usual. "Something like that."

He finishes making me my second coffee in **30** minutes, and we drink it together at the table. Luke sees my discarded plastic gloves lying to the side and picks one up. "What are these for?"

His face lights up as I tell him my plans to dye my hair.

"I like your hair the way it is," he says. "But I do admit to being curious how this will look."

"Will you maybe help?" I suddenly ask as I pluck up the second glove. "Could be a lark."

He looks up at me, and for a second he worries his bottom lip like he's not sure if he wants to.

"Come on," I say, getting up and inclining my head for him to follow me into the bathroom. "Let's make it a memory."

"In that case . . . "

Close behind me, Luke snaps on the one glove he has. We enter the bathroom and I grin at him in the mirror as I dangle up the other glove for him to grab.

He nabs it and slides it on. "You know, of the two of us, it should be me dyeing my hair."

I turn and look at his hair. It's thick and dark, and if it were my hair, I might not consider dyeing at all. "No way."

He comes closer, touching one spot near his temple. "See that?"

"See what?"

"There are, like, five strands of grey there."

I look, but I can't see anything. "You're imagining it."

"Well, there will be some soon anyway."

He's only **36**! "Come on, you're not that old." I shrug out of my T-shirt and check out my stomach in the mirror. But it's too soon to see if the running and lifting weights have done anything. I still look a bit too lean. I shrug it off and glance back up to Luke and his hair. "Besides," I say, "you'll pull off grey. It'll be hot on you."

Luke frowns and looks down at his gloved hands. "You think that?"

"I think *everyone* will think that. Now . . . how should we do this?"

I decide to flip the toilet seat down and use it as a stool. I'm wearing only shorts, and the base of the toilet is cold where it touches my skin. "I think you have to smother that tube all over my hair. Then we wait half an hour before I can shower it off."

Luke takes the tube, opens it, and is about to squeeze some onto his fingers, when I lift a finger in warning. "You might want to take off your shirt first. I wouldn't want the dye to ruin it."

He hesitates a second, his Adam's apple bobbing as he swallows. Then he rests the tube on the edge of the sink and slowly peels off his top.

His stomach is gently defined with muscle and tapers nicely from his broad shoulders to his waist. "I want your body," I say.

Luke makes a choking sound and I glance up to his reddening face. "You okay?"

"You want my body?" he repeats.

"Yeah. Trust me, I'm working on it."

Luke just stares at me, his eyes darkening in the dim bathroom light.

I flick on the light, which I can reach from the toilet. "How long do you think I'll have to use the weights before my abs show?"

He shakes his head suddenly and looks away over my shoulder and then toward the slightly tilted window. A breeze brushes his hair and little goose bumps pepper over his arms. "A while," he says and snaps up the tube once more. He gives me a sharp smile. "Okay, let's do this." He squeezes some of the grey paste on his fingers. "God this stuff smells strong."

I get up, open the window wider and then sit back down.

Curling a finger at him, I say, "Come on then, you. Lather me up."

He lets out a strangled laugh that makes me want to ask him if he's okay, and he moves over to me.

He hesitates before lowering his hands onto me, and I wonder if he also realizes this goes against that weird bro-gap rule we have. That's not to suggest we've *never* touched one another before because we have, but I can count the times on **2** hands—and **1** foot. It's just that . . . well, *I can count the times*.

I shrug, as if to tell him it's no big deal. Not on my part. I don't care.

A clucking sound escapes him, and then his fingers are in my hair.

His first touch, working the paste onto my roots, sends a shiver through me—one that's noticeable, because Luke asks if I'm cold.

"No," I say. Because I'm not. It just feels nice having someone run their fingers through my hair and over my scalp. It's been a while since I went to the hairdressers, but it's always been my favorite part to have my hair washed.

Luke adds more paste and gently starts to comb my hair with his fingers. I let out an involuntary moan. I think about being embarrassed by it for a second, but then Luke does the same move again, and I don't care what the hell I murmur. Luke won't care anyway. He's heard me do worse. Like the time I got stung **3** times by a wasp and I whimpered all the way out of the park.

"It feels good," I say to Luke. "I could fall asleep. Or drool."

He chuckles, and though I know he's used all the paste, he continues to massage my head.

"Has to be in a half hour, right?"

I hum as he teases the tips of my hair.

"Is there a clock in here or something?"

"There's a cooking timer in the cupboard," I say, and grumble when his hands come off me.

He takes off the sticky gloves and drops them into the trash bin. Then he finds the timer. "Should I even ask why you keep this in the bathroom?"

I laugh and shrug. "Hot water isn't cheap. Jeremy and I set it to five minutes so we know how long we've been in the shower, and when it's time to come out."

Luke blinks, startled. "Five minutes? That's it?"

I sigh, and Luke mutters a "damn." He washes his hands, and he looks upset. "Sometimes," he says suddenly, eyeing me in the mirror, "I just wish you two would live with me. You could save on rent and most certainly have a longer shower. You wouldn't have to work yourself crazy through the year, either. I don't care how you justify it, working double shifts on the weeks you don't have Jeremy and working the weekends he's not here . . . it's just too much."

"It's what pays the bills," I say. "And thanks for the offer, but you wouldn't want us as flatmates. We'd take up too much room. Besides," I think of the mystery woman Luke hasn't yet told me about up in Auckland. "I don't think your girl would like that."

Luke twists around, frowning, and folds his arms across his chest. "My girl?"

I look down at my hands resting on my thighs. I've been afraid of this moment, of hearing Luke admit that he met someone up in Auckland. I want to keep putting it off and ignoring it, but now I let it slip. "You'll want to move somewhere else, start a family."

Luke says nothing for a moment, and I can't read his face. Coming over to me and crouching by my side so our faces are almost level, he says, "What the hell are you talking about, Sam?"

I suddenly wonder if I got it all wrong, and a warm thread

of hope tingles somewhere in my gut. My breath comes out relieved. "You mean you're not going to leave? Then what else was it you were trying to tell me?"

His eyes are laughing as he reaches out and touches my knee. His touch only lingers a second before he draws away again. "There's no girl. And I'm not going to leave you."

"Oh thank fuck for that," I say, and reach out to grab his arm. I want to rest my head against it, but remember the dye in my hair just before it touches him. "Guess I've been worrying for nothing."

"You were worrying?"

"Since the night you came home. I thought . . . but I guess you were just happy to be back here then?"

Luke laughs nervously. "Yeah, you have no idea."

I look into his eyes, trying to work out why he's so nervous. "You do have something to tell me though, don't you?"

"How did you know?"

"I didn't, it was just a feeling. But now I know for sure—something's up."

Luke stands. "I think it's time to rinse out your hair."

I stand too. "The cooking timer will tell me that." He darts his gaze away from mine when I step closer. "Now tell me."

"Fine." He swallows, and then opens his mouth to speak, but shuts it again. He tries again. "Thing is . . . you know how I said my mum wants to see you? And maybe we could go up at Christmas?"

"Yeah," I say slowly.

"Actually, I sort of promised her you'd come. It just slipped out, and now she's making plans."

Oh. "Damn. Luke, I really want to meet her too, but I don't think I can get Christmas off."

The timer goes off then, and Luke quickly twists to turn it off. "I should never have promised her to begin with. No big deal. My fault."

I reach into the shower and turn on the spray. "Yeah, but I want to meet her too. It's just when I asked Hannah out yesterday, I also talked to the boss. Putting a feeler out, you know. But he kept saying he can't wait for his best waiter to be back. It's barely been a day without me and he's regretting giving me so much leave."

I hook my thumbs into my shorts and push them down with my underwear. Luke turns around just as I do, and keeps going until his back is to me again.

"Sorry," I say, laughing as I hop under the hot water. "Didn't mean to give you an eyeful—I just want to jump in quickly. The dye is starting to make my head feel numb. I want black, not bald."

"It's . . . fine."

Dye water runs into my mouth and I splutter to get it out again.

"You good in there?" Luke asks, and through the foggy glass, I can see him sitting on the toilet.

"Hope this dye looks better than it tastes." I massage the dye out of my hair, and it feels nowhere near as nice as when Luke had done it. "Back to your mum for a sec," I say, moving on to scrub the rest of me while I'm at it. "What if . . . I mean, maybe we could go up earlier? Or . . . or hey, why doesn't she come down here? I haven't really thought about how to celebrate the big **3–0**."— I cringe as I say it, and scrub harder —"But being around family sounds good. Maybe I'll invite mine too."

Luke hums. "You want *my* family at your birthday party?"

I open the door and poke my head around it, dripping water onto the floor. "Hey, Luke, sure I do. I really want to meet the rest of you."

I feel for the tap behind me and turn it off. "Mind passing me a towel?"

Luke grabs me one. Before he lets go of it though, he asks, "You sure?"

I tug the towel out of his grip. "'Course." I wrap the towel around my waist and step out.

"That's . . . yeah, that'll be great." He lifts a hand to my hair and messes it. "I think it's going to take some getting used to."

I hair-dry it and then spike it up toward the middle with some product. "Does it look crazy?" I ask, turning to find Luke smirking and snapping photos with his phone.

"Crazy?" He laughs. "You're going to be embarrassed looking at these photos in a few years. Jeremy will piss his pants."

And I smile. Because that's the reaction what I want.

Another thing I can cross of my 20s Must-Do List.

Chapter Ten

LUKE

Ambivalent. That's the word. The perfect word to describe my state of mind as I walk with Jack while he's on lunchtime duty. Actually, it's the perfect word to describe me since being with Sam that morning.

Maybe I don't really get it, you know? I mean, I love him and whoever he's into is fine by me, I just . . .

I swallow a sigh and linger back when Jack moves to break up a scuffle.

Yes, Sam was accepting. I should be happy about that. But . . . it wasn't as warm as I'd hoped. Of course, I'd have been disappointed with anything that wasn't Sam coming out of the closet himself.

Why did it have to be Jeremy to figure out he's gay?

I dig my hands deep into my pockets, as if I'll find some peace of mind in there. There's nothing but the feeling of paper scraping over my right fingers. Sam's *20s Must-Do List*.

It tingles my skin as I pull my hand out, and it's the same feeling I got as I'd threaded my fingers through Sam's hair and he'd moaned. Except that tingle had shot straight to my cock, and I had to focus on some nasty images to keep myself from boning up in front of him.

It barely worked. I was almost a gonner when Sam almost rested his head on me. I wanted to curve a hand around his neck and pull him to me, dye or not.

Jack says something to the bigger boy and sends him on his way. He looks over at me, rolling his eyes and chuckling. Before he can make his way back to me though, a girl taps his arm and asks a question.

I can't hear them from where I stand, and even as I watch them interact, I'm still thinking about that morning. The moment Sam said we were family. The simple, sweet words keep coming back to my mind. They make me smile. Make me frown. We are a family. We've been one for seven years. We've just lived in separate houses.

"What are you scowling about?" Jack asks, nudging my arm.

"Nothing." But that's not true. Thinking of separate houses jumped me to another thought. The one when I told Sam I wish we lived together, and he'd somehow brought up the whole secret-girl thing.

At that moment, I wanted to laugh and cry at once. Laugh since I was happy Sam wasn't keen on the idea *at all*. And cry because Sam obviously didn't see me in any other light than as a close friend. Flatmates! There I thought I'd practically confessed my feelings, and Sam had completely misunderstood.

"Yeah, if that's nothing," Jack says, chuckling and motioning for us to continue walking toward the back paddocks, where kids kiss and hold hands behind the bushes, "I don't want to know what *something* is."

We walk quietly for a couple of minutes. The jingling of

coins in Jack's pocket and the kids in the distance make comforting background noise. I breathe in the scent of freshly cut grass and glance at Jack, who's staring ahead, waiting patiently for me to say something.

I slow my step, and he mimics me. "I couldn't say it to him." I can tell from his nod he knows I'm talking about telling my neighbor I'm gay. I continue, "I don't know why. I had the perfect opening."

Jack hooks his thumbs into his pockets. "I know why."

"You do?"

"Yeah." He pauses, and then gives me a small smile before going on. "You're scared you'll know for sure how he feels and that it's not the same way, and then you'll have no more excuses to let you keep hoping."

I let the words sink in, and I hate that they're spot-on. "That's exactly it. How do you know?"

He shrugs, and I think he's not going to answer. He swivels as if to walk off in another direction, but then he stops. He looks at me instead. "Because I thought the same once."

The way his gaze meets mine, I know he's talking about us. This truth is both flattering and awkward, and I don't know what on earth to say. Luckily, I don't have to. He unhooks one of his thumbs from his pocket and slaps my arm. "But I moved on. Like you might have to as well."

At four thirty, I find myself rolling the truck into the parking lot at Jeremy's school. I figure since he has soccer practice, I can watch him for a bit and then talk to the team about the plans for the game on Sunday.

I walk to the field at the back of his school. The team is huddled together, some of the guys high-fiving one another. Jeremy says something to one of his mates, and then laughs before lifting his drink bottle and pouring water over his face. The soccer coach is chatting with Steven and gesturing toward the goal.

I take slower steps, feet crunching over the recently mown grass. Déjà vu hits me as I raise a hand and wave to Jeremy. It's as if I never left for Auckland and this is just any other day I'd rock up to help out with the boys' soccer practices or games.

"Luke!" Jeremy calls out, and his face breaks into a grin. He waves me over to him and the guys. "So, we still good to play the game against the Oriental Lions?"

I incline my head. "How's Sunday at noon for you?"

"Wicked!"

Simon and Darryl, the team's defensive players, grunt and punch each other's shoulders. "We'll thrash them."

A soccer ball rolls out of the net next to Jeremy, and I hook it onto my foot and balance it. "It's just a social game," I tell them.

"Yeah, we know," Simon says. "But we have a wager going."

I kick the ball up, catch it, and tuck it under my arm. "Wager?"

Steven strolls up to us then, hooking his arm around Jeremy's neck. It looks like he goes to hook his other arm around Simon and thinks better of it, keeping his arm at his side. Friend dos and don'ts. It seems like there's a whole political thing to it. "The losing team pays for the winning team to eat all they want at Pizza Hut," Steven says.

"They'll *so* be paying for our dinners," Darryl chimes.

Jeremy shrugs. "I think we have a shot." He looks over toward the chain-link fence that separates the schools' playing fields. "I have their captain's number, so I'll tell them the deal."

I nod toward the coach, and say to the guys, "Twelve o'clock at Kresley Intermediate. Excuse me for a sec." I weave through the team and shake the coach's hand. I should know all of Jeremy's teachers—but his former teacher/coach left around the same time I did.

I introduce myself and tell Mr. Charleson how I usually help out and that I'd like to start doing that again for the next school year. "I'm also happy to ref social games or practice."

"I'll take all the help I can get." He laughs as he moves to grab the cones they used for drills. "Simon! Help me and take these and the balls back to the lockers, would you?"

I throw Simon the ball I'd picked up. Except Simon seems to be lost in his thoughts, gazing over toward Jeremy and Steven, and the ball hits his chest and thumps to the ground. He startles out of his thoughts and hurriedly picks up the ball.

The coach grins, points to Jeremy and says, "That's your boy, right? He's talented that one. A little cocky on the field, but his footwork is impeccable."

My chest swells with pride as I nod. Yeah, that's my boy. "He's always been good at center and left wing."

Mr. Charleson nods. "He has a great rhythm when he works with Steven. They know each other so well, they can zip around the field like no-one's business."

I'm smiling so much on the inside, I can't respond. I glance over at Jeremy who's juggling the ball I bought him just before I left to help my mum. "Those two have been friends forever." And are maybe more than that now. I shake that thought off. It still doesn't feel right to think of Jeremy as anything more than a kid. "They know each other well and have practiced together forever."

"Hey, Luke," Jeremy calls out. "You wanna see if you can still take the ball from me?"

To the coach, I say, "Seems I've been challenged. I gotta show the boy he's still got tricks to learn. Let's see if I can't scrub some of the cockiness out of him, eh?"

He laughs. "Well I'm outta here. Sorry I can't make the game on Sunday."

Steven is suddenly next to me. "Thanks for running another training today, Mr. Charleson," he says. "We won't let you down, promise."

"You're good, kid," Mr. Charleson says. "Just remember it's about having fun in the end."

I clap Steven on the shoulder. "I'm sure I'll see you around before Sunday."

"Try tomorrow, Mr. Luke." Steven spots a loose ball under the heap of bright orange practice pinnies, scoops it up and jogs after Simon, who's halfway across the field.

I move over to Jeremy, whose arms are balanced out as he uses his head to control the ball.

"Give it here," I say, and he lets the ball drop between us, but before I can snatch it with my foot, he's snagged it back and is rolling the ball around me.

"Cheeky boy. Yeah, you're smiling now. Just you wait."

I race after him as he dribbles toward one of the goals. For as far back as I can remember, this has been our game. The first few years, I didn't have to work that hard to take the ball from him, and even made myself lose on occasion.

Now, though—now it's tougher. I know I'm going to have to pull out some serious stunts to take and keep the ball from him.

"First to score," I say as I nip the ball with the outside of my foot, just enough away from Jeremy that I have a chance to get control of it. If I'm fast enough.

I almost manage. But Jeremy takes back his advantage and does a hip swivel, reversing direction and taking the ball with him. It's a well-executed move, and I want to tell him so—I'm about to tell him so—when he says, "Come on, old man. Is that all you've got?"

Game on.

He's not getting away lightly with that. "I'll give you old."

We play at this for close to twenty minutes. Soon it's just us on the field and the evening sun is dipping low at our backs.

I've managed to steal the ball from him twice, but before I managed to score, Jeremy blocked me. But it won't happen a third time. . . .

I can feel the sweat rolling down the back of my long-sleeved T-shirt, and I shove up the arms. Jeremy is holding the ball under his foot and grinning at me. He's just outside the goal area.

"Don't look so smug. You haven't scored yet."

"Yeah, but I will. You'll see." He does a fake pass with his instep, pulling the ball back with his sole. This time I am ready for it.

"That was just lucky, Luke," Jeremy says, scowling as I roll the ball away from him.

It's my turn to smirk. "You see who's still got it? This old man." I dribble up to the penalty arc and then head toward the goal again.

I have to shield the ball as Jeremy marks me close. I scissor over the ball in an attempt to throw him, but he's too good. I'm not about to say that to him though. I can see what his coach meant by being a little cocky on the field.

"If I can get that ball from you and score in the next five minutes," Jeremy says, "will you buy us fish and chips for dinner?"

"Tell you what," I say, making it a few more feet toward the goal. "I'll get you your fish and chips if you win, but if *I* score you're making dinner tonight. From scratch. I got a whole bag of dirty potatoes that need peeling for a Shepherd's Pie."

I know for a fact the boy hates peeling potatoes, and I laugh at his groan. But all too soon the cockiness is back. "You're on, Luke. I'm gonna order fish, a spring roll, and a corn fritter. And a deep-fried Moro bar."

I pull a vee around him in a sharp, well-timed move.

Jeremy is taken by surprise, and swears under his breath.

I take off toward the goal. I yell out as I hook the ball and score. "Yeah!" I run up to the goal post and high-five the top of it. "And that's how it's done, boy!"

He's clutching his hair and groaning as he catches up to me. "Crap. That shouldn't have . . . how'd you . . . damn."

I grab him into a hug, rubbing my knuckles over his hair. Then I pause and lift my nose into the air. "Do you smell that?"

"Don't say it's the smell of victory. That's so lame."

I shake my head and pick up the ball. "Nope. But I smell shepherds pie."

"Double or nothing?" he tries, pulling a hopeful face.

I shake my head. I'm done for the day. Plus it would be stupid of me to risk it when Jeremy had the upper hand for most of our session. "It's only potatoes. You should be thankful you don't have to rub my sore, old feet."

His nose wrinkles. "Ugh. Gross."

I laugh and shift the ball to my other arm. "Let's—"

Go. The rest of my sentence is lost as I look up. Across the field is Sam, standing at the sidelines with his hands shoved into his pockets, smiling at us. The sun is hitting the side of his face, bathing him in a warm orange. He pulls both of his hands free and claps. "Nice show, boys."

"What. The. Frack?" Jeremy comes to a halt, then hisses to me, "What is that thing on Dad's head?"

"You mean his hair?" I say, unable to pull my eyes away from Sam and his lithe grace as he moves toward us with long strides.

"What happened to it?" He starts laughing, and gets louder the closer we get. His eyes glisten with tears. "Holy Moly. No freaking way. A mohawk?"

I smother a grin. "Not *quite.*"

"Close enough!"

"Luke," Sam says, catching the ball I throw to him. "Should have guessed you were going to pick him up after practice. Came here and saw your truck in the parking lot."

"Thought I'd tell the team the plan for their big game."

Sam throws the ball up and tries to catch it on his foot to juggle, but it drops. "You guys make it look so easy," he says with a sheepish grin.

Jeremy snorts, picks up the ball and starts showing his dad how it's really done. "You look ridiculous, Dad."

Sam seems pleased with that, but I snag the ball mid-air and bounce it off Jeremy's head. "He looks just fine, kiddo."

It's hard to tell with the light, but it looks like Sam's blushing. I have an urge to hook an arm around both my boys and hold them close to me.

I let myself daydream about what it would be like to have nothing to hide, to lean over and kiss Sam on the lips in front of Jeremy.

I get lost imagining the feeling, and miss what Sam has said. "Sorry?" I try not to let my gaze dip down to his lips.

"Looks like you scored this round," Sam says, hooking his thumbs into his jeans.

I steal the ball from Jeremy again. "Sure did." Then I move with Sam, shoulder-to-shoulder, toward the parking lot. "Jeremy's making us dinner, by the way."

Jeremy groans.

Chapter Eleven

SAM

W hen Luke rings to tell us to come over and do dinner, Jeremy grumbles and moves reluctantly. His feet *chrr* against the floor and it makes my teeth ache. "Lift your feet," I say. "It's hard to believe you're so good at footwork when you can't even seem to walk over carpet."

Jeremy blinks up at me. "Huh?" Then he shrugs and we head out the door.

At Luke's I don't bother knocking; I push open the door he's left ajar and we walk in. "Luke?"

"Dining room," comes the answer.

There's a familiar smell in the air, and I follow it to the table where there are **2** big bundles of fish and chips. Luke isn't there, but I hear him crashing about in his kitchen.

Jeremy whoops in delight. "Damn, Luke's the best." Then louder so Luke hears him. "You're the awesomest."

"I know," he calls back.

Jeremy pulls out a chair and immediately starts unwrapping to get to the deep-fried goodness. Just as I take my place, Luke strolls in and I pause halfway to the seat. He's changed since getting home: low-slung jeans, a singlet, and sandals.

I've always wished to have a body like Luke's, so tight and defined without appearing too bulky, but now I'm really wishing for it. He just looks so good. Not that that's something I could ever tell another guy. But damn.

Before anyone starts to wonder why I'm ogling Luke's corded arm muscles, I focus on a piece of crumbed fish lying on top of crinkle-cut chips.

But my mind goes blank again as Luke reaches out and takes some chips. Even his hands are perfect—

I jerk out of the thought, blurting the first thing that comes to my mind. "So how did Jeremy get out of making dinner? I was looking forward to watching him suffer through it." I wink at my boy, who rolls his eyes like I'm the lamest thing around.

I sigh, and grab for some chips.

Luke looks from Jeremy to me and shakes his head. "Next time I'll tough it out. Maybe potato peeling would be good for his character growth." He dips a chip in a puddle of tomato sauce he squeezed onto the paper. "But I missed doing this with you. When I drove past *Fins* I got all nostalgic." He laughs at himself, and then gestures to the fish and chips. "And there you go."

His dimples grow fainter, but they're still there when he looks at me. Our gazes meet, and it's like we have an unspoken conversation, where I'm telling him I've missed this too and I'm glad he's missed it just as much.

He nods and sucks in breath, forcing his mood into something more upbeat. "So, last day at school for you tomorrow, Jeremy. That'll be nice." He turns a smirk on me. "And what crazy shenanigans do *you* have planned?"

"Nothing much." But that's not true. Tomorrow, I'm going off-the-charts crazy. And I'm looking forward to it.

My fingers are greasy from the chips and I wipe them on my pants before grabbing some crumbed fish. I bite into it and it's like I've gone back in time, to the first time we all ate fish and chips together on the Petone foreshore and got half-mauled by seagulls.

I chuckle at the memory. Luke had freaked out, sending Jeremy and I into hysterics. My laughter only abated when Luke reached over and covered my mouth with his palm, scowling like no one's business.

When I think back to it, I can still feel the firmness of his hand against my lips. The action had taken me and him by surprise, and if it'd been something guys could do together, I would've licked his palm to make him jerk it away.

But that would have come across weird.

"What are you thinking about, Sam?" Luke asks as he squirts more tomato sauce onto the paper.

Heat suddenly creeps up my neck and I try to shrug it away. "Oh, just, stuff. How we used to do this."

Jeremy pipes up. "I remember the time you guys left me in the fish and chip shop. I still can't believe you forgot you had a kid with you."

More heat blooms over my cheeks, and I'm glad Luke is getting red as well. "We're sorry about that," Luke says. "Your dad and I just got caught up in our conversation."

"We only drove half a block before we realized," I say, wincing as I do.

Jeremy gives us a droll stare. "Must have been some conversation."

It had been. Actually, it was more bantering, really. I can't really remember what it was about exactly, only that I kept laughing and shaking my head and telling Luke he had it all wrong, which he insisted wasn't true. And the **20** minutes or so we'd talked had only felt like **3**.

"Of all the awesome things you could remember of your childhood," I murmur, "you have to remember that one."

Jeremy shakes his head at me. Then he turns to Luke. "Your turn, what fish-and-chips story do you remember?"

Luke leans back in his chair, and then he eats another chip without comment. But his lips twitch at the corners and his dimples deepen. He picks up some more chips and focuses on them as he speaks. "I remember the time you got food poisoning, Jeremy. You'd eaten something funky in the morning and when I brought home dinner, you took one look at it and ran to the bathroom to throw up."

He throws a chip into his mouth. "Your dad and I spent the night taking turns to clean up after your bouts in the bathroom. It wasn't pretty."

"Gross."

I laugh at Jeremy, but I can't pull my gaze away from Luke. Thinking back to that night a couple of years ago, there is another memory that arises. Luke resting on our couch, twisting and turning to find a comfortable position. I'd stumbled from my room to get a drink of water and had seen him squirming on the couch, bathed in milky moonlight coming though the windows.

I'd stood in the doorway to the lounge and watched him. I wanted to tell him to get up and share my bed. I'd even stepped into the room to do it too. And then Jeremy had his next bout and Luke jumped off the couch in an adorably sweet daze and stumbled over to me. "Need help, yeah?" he said, assuming that's why I'd come in.

I'd just nodded, and together we got Jeremy's bed sheets changed and the bathroom wiped down.

Luke glances up at me. "Now it's your turn, Sam. Tell us your memory."

And with a laugh that unleashes something tender inside, I tell them. But I face Jeremy as I describe how the birds had pecked at Luke's fingers when he stubbornly tried to save his chip. I face him because if I look up at Luke right now, I'm going to blush—and I don't want any questions to come out of *that*.

Chapter Twelve

JEREMY

Dad's been acting weird. Yesterday his black mohawk-ish thing sent me into fucking hysterics. I actually had tears in my eyes.

I thought it was a joke, or that the dye would wash out. But then I found the permanent-dye box in the bathroom trash and the honey-scented hair gel he'd spent ten whole dollars on. That was stretching it for a joke.

But, okay, the black hair I can write off as Dad trying something new. Whatever. Sweet—it doesn't hurt me any.

Today though . . . today things are actually starting to worry me.

I blink at Dad, who's making something with chocolate in the kitchen. "Dinner will be ready soon," he says.

But it's not the chocolate thing that gets me—though eating dessert for dinner is a first for me. No, it's the metal ring in his right ear, glinting under the kitchen light.

"What the freak?" I say, dropping my shit on the floor and moving to the opposite side of the kitchen bench. "Tell me that's not real. It's a clip-on, right?"

Dad winks at me. "Nope. Got it pierced this afternoon. Just felt like trying something different."

I want to tell him it looks bloody ridiculous, but then I have a thought. What if this is him trying to tell me in his own way that he's cool with me being gay? He doesn't know that I'm not. Yeah, maybe Mum has spoken to him about it, and this is his way of showing acceptance or some shit like that. I mean, the earring? How gay is that?

And I have to say, weird though he looks, it's kinda fucking awesome that he does this to make me feel accepted.

I shake my head. "You look like a punk gone wrong," I say, and then I grin. "But somehow, you're still cool."

Dad stops stirring the chocolaty batter in the bright yellow mixing bowl. "I'm sorry," he says, "I think getting pierced damaged my ears. I thought I heard you say I'm cool."

I blush and shrug. "Maybe you should have thought about permanent damage before you went and stuck a needle through your ear." I reach over and dunk a finger into the mixture and lick it off. It's gooey and chocolaty with a hint of caramel. "Mum's gonna freak though," I say, trying to scoop some more mixture, but Dad slaps my hand away. "She'll think you're being a bad influence. What if I decide I want a few holes in my ears as well."

Dad pours the mixture into a baking tin, murmuring something under his breath about not thinking that far.

"What's that?" I say.

He looks up at me. "Your mum doesn't have to know everything. And you don't get to put holes in your ears until you're sixteen. At least."

"I wouldn't do my ear anyway. Eyebrow maybe. Or nipple."

Dad sucks in his breath, laughing. "Trust me, don't do the nipple. It hurts like a—" He stops, but I'm pretty sure he was going to say a bad, bad word.

I grin. "How would you know, anyway?" And suddenly I don't want to hear it, because Dad touches his chest and I *know*. "No fucking way. You got pierced *there*?"

That's the moment Luke strolls into the room.

A couple of things happen at once. Dad goes beet red and stammers, telling me to watch my mouth, and Luke comes to a comical halt and says "There?" all confused, like. And then he sees my dad's ear, because he blinks hard a couple of times. "Okay. This one sure takes me by surprise." Then his voice drops as he looks from me to my dad to me again. "There?" he says again, like now it's starting to dawn on him there's more.

I flick my nipple through my T-shirt. "He's gone nuts, Luke." Dad beams like I've given him a freaking compliment. "Like, seriously. Nuts."

"Anyway," Dad says, smiling at Luke as he moves into the kitchen, "what I want to know"—he turns back to me—"is how your last day of school was? And how did you do in that math assignment?"

"B+. And it was okay, I guess."

Actually, it was pretty damn fantastic. The good grade was only a bonus. The real treat was Suzy parting her legs under the desk when I ducked under to pick up a pencil I dropped.

She wore these white undies with tiny sunflowers on them, and the way her hand traveled up her leg had me close to panting. When I picked up my pencil, I brushed the eraser end on the inside of her thigh just part of the way up . . . She made out with me good at lunchtime after that, which sorta makes me want to know what would happen if I went *all* the way up.

Maybe I'll find out tonight at Simon's end-of-year party.

"What are you grinning at?" Luke asks as he moves to my side and rests his elbows on the bench like I have mine.

"Um. Nothing."

He raises a brow at my Dad like he doesn't believe me one bit.

I thump him on the back. "Nothing you want to know," I amend, and then I start on my plan to get me to that party. "Dad, Steven is coming over in a bit. Can he stay for dinner?"

My dad blushes and is flustered as he puts the chocolate dessert into the oven, almost dropping the tin and then burning his hand. He shoves it under cold water. "Sure. Yeah. Steven. Dinner . . . Awesome."

Luke is shaking his head next to me, and I wonder if the news of my supposed gayness has spread. For a second, I have a bad feeling in my gut, like what I'm doing is really wrong. And, yeah, it *sort of* is. But I never outright told a lie—and I won't. It's all their assumptions making fools of them in the end.

Still, that queasy feeling isn't going away.

It's tempered just enough by the thought of seeing Suzy's undies once more, though. So I don't blurt out I'm not actually gay.

I can feel Luke's gaze on me. I turn to find him watching me carefully. "How is Steven?" he says.

"Good? But you can ask him at dinner yourself." I glance over at the oven. "Or should I say dessert?"

"Assuming I'm invited," Luke says, staring once again at my punk dad.

"Like, when are you not invited? And, like, when was the last time we didn't eat together?" I move to answer the door when I hear Steven knock and shyly call out if anyone's home.

"Come in," I say and grab his arm to haul him inside. "Just, don't freak when you see my dad, 'kay?" I lower my voice. "He's got a strange way of showing me he's cool with the gay thing."

"Dude," he says, toeing off his shoes—something I hadn't

bothered to do myself— "*both* your parents are good with it? Damn, you're not even gay. This is so unfair."

"Yeah, wait until you see my dad before you decide you want him as yours."

Steven waggles his brows, looking hopeful as he asks, "So, can I shove my tongue down your throat this time?"

"Shove off. There'll be none of that." Then I hook an arm around his neck and drag him to where Dad and Luke are.

"Hey Mr. Sam. Mr. Luke." That's something I like about Steven—he's real good with parents. Dad and Luke have been telling him for years to call them by their first names, but Steven says he feels rude every time he does it. After a year of this, they compromised on Mr. Sam and Mr. Luke. Sometimes I call them that too for shits and giggles.

"Mr. Steven," Luke says, like always.

Steven nods, but he's focused on my dad's semi-mohawk and earring. "New look, Mr. Sam." I can tell he's thinking something else, but I don't learn what it is until we escape to my room.

And then I wish I'd never learned it.

"Now he's a DILF."

I throw a pillow at him where he's lounging at the end of my bed. "Gross. Never, ever, ever say that again! That's just disturbing."

Steven laughs. "But seriously," he says. "It's sorta cool that I can shoot the shit with you like this. No one else knows. But I think I might say something to my parents soon. Hey . . . you wanna help me by making out in front of them?"

I use my last pillow on him. "My tiny dick shrivels up inside of me just thinking about it."

"Awww, harsh. You still trying to get into Suzy Livingston's pants?"

"As much as she's trying to get into mine." I catch the

pillows he throws back at me. "But about that—so, over dinner, you know what to say right?"

He rolls his eyes. "I remember. You're a bad boy, Jeremy."

Chapter Thirteen

LUKE

At dinner—*dessert*—I don't know what to focus on. My first instinct is to stare at Sam's ear and chest, and wonder if the second ring will turn me on as much as the first does.

But a very close second instinct is to watch Jeremy and Steven for any clues. It's not like I have the best gaydar in the world, but I'm surprised I've never picked up on anything from Jeremy before.

On closer inspection, there are a couple of things that Steven does that make me see it. One of them was the way his gaze slowly scanned over Sam, and then the way he blushed when *Mr. Sam* smiled at him.

But he got zilch from Jeremy, and something nagged at me about the whole thing. Shouldn't Steven be checking out his *boyfriend* at the table, when he thinks he can get away with it?

"I'm going to Simon's end-of-year party tonight," Steven

says when Sam asks what his plans are for the rest of the week, now that school is out. "Then just hanging with my . . . friends, I guess." Steven looks at Jeremy then. "You coming tonight too?"

Jeremy shakes his head. "Nah. Dad wants to take me to a movie, if I recall."

Sam jumps in his chair, and it's obvious he's forgotten all about his fake plans. "Oh yeah, well . . ." He looks at his son and Steven. "I guess if you want, you can go."

Jeremy lights up. "For real?"

"Um, yeah," Sam says. "Just so long as you're safe." I swallow a chuckle at the way he blushes as he says that. Then he adds, "And I don't want you to sleep over. Be home at eleven."

"So, he's not allowed to sleep over, eh?" I say after Jeremy and Steven leave and Sam and I are settled on the couch. We turn on the television and there's some movie on with a woman vigilante blowing up stuff.

Sam stares at the screen, and his face lights up blue and green. "It's not because I have a problem with gay sex, if that's what you're thinking."

"Oh, you don't?" I say, raising a brow.

He blushes as he shrugs and then he manages to scowl at me. "He's just too young for *any* sex."

"Yeah." I get what he means. It's terrifying thinking the boy I've helped raise is sexually active. "I shoved a couple of condoms in his hand before he left," I say, focusing back on the screen. "I just . . . It's not that I want him to go out and do that. I'd just rather he be safe, you know?"

I hope I haven't crossed the line doing this. I let out a relieved breath when Sam says, "Thank God. I totally didn't even think of that." He shivers. "It's really weird thinking about it. It should be the other way around, you know? Me, the adult, having the sex life."

"Well . . ." I feel sick inside as I force myself to say with a smile, "maybe things will work out for you on your date this Friday." Then I add (with a truer smile), "She might dig your hair and metal."

Sam flushes and steals the blanket I draped over my legs. "It's not really me, the look, but I don't mind it. Just for a while."

"I think you work it."

He closes his eyes and smiles, resting his head back against the couch. "I so work it, don't I?"

And it's the smile, in combination with the way he's stretched out, his feet propped up on the coffee table and the blanket pooled in his lap, T-shirt stretched over his chest showing a bump over his nipple, where the plaster is over his piercing—it's all this and then the sigh he gives that sends a traitorous signal to my cock.

It's turning super hard and aching in my jeans, and the bulge is becoming more than obvious. No amount of nasty thoughts can keep me from seeing the beautiful sight in front of me though.

I pinch the edge of the blanket and drag it back over me. Only once I've arranged it, Sam opens his eyes and with a cheeky grin, yanks the blanket back over him.

As he does, the blanket tickles over my sensitive bulge and it feels so good I want to link my hands behind my head and moan, thrusting my hips up so he will do it again.

I don't. Of course. I hunch forward, resting my elbows on my knees, and clasp my hands together. "You know, I should probably head back over." I slowly stand, facing away from him slightly.

Sam laughs. "Unless you have some hot date you didn't tell

me about, sit your ass back down. You're not leaving me here undistracted."

I glance down at him, and he's biting his lip.

"I'm going to be sitting here and worrying pretty much until Jeremy comes back home," he says. "I'd like it if you'd worry with me."

I let out a breath and sit back down. I worry too. Always have, always will. "Only if I get the blanket," I say, trying to tug it back.

He shakes his head. "How about we share it?"

I have to sit closer to him than before to do that, and even though there's still an inch between us, I can feel his heat caressing my side. It's hot enough to bring tears to my eyes as I try to gather up the courage to give up on my hope, and just tell him, finally.

But every time I open my mouth, nothing comes out and I have to shut it again.

After a while, Sam grows restless. He picks up the remote and turns off the television, drowning us in navy darkness. "The movie's boring," he says and then stretches up from the couch. "I have a better idea."

"What's that?"

Sam beckons me out of the room and I follow to the kitchen, where he pulls out a bottle of bourbon. "Let's drink. And we can play board games or something."

I take the bottle, open it, and sniff. The stuff is nasty.

"Leave that crap here. Come on." I jerk my head toward the door. "Grab your keys."

We trek over to my place where I find whiskey that's half decent. I pour us a couple and we take it to my solid dining table. "What game you want to play?"

Sam blinks rapidly and downs half of his drink in one mouthful. "How about Taboo?"

I freeze as I think of his list, and wonder if he's thinking the same thing, and why he's mentioning this game of all the games I have here.

"Or . . . uh, I don't know. We could just play some cards?" He shrugs.

I drink all of my whiskey. Then I leave, coming back when I have a dusty box of Taboo in my hand.

"Been a long time since it's been played, huh?"

"You have no idea."

He looks at it for a while. His eyes slowly light up, eager, and there's something almost excited in the way he glances up from it to me. But then he frowns, shakes his head at something he's thinking, and drinks the rest of his whiskey.

"Have you ever . . . thought about it?"

"About what?" I say as I pick up the bottle and pour us both another shot.

"What it's like with another guy, not a woman?" Sam turns his dark, thick-lashed gaze to the table between us.

I swallow, because this is the moment, and I can't push it off any longer. "Sam," I say. "I have to make something clear to you. I'm—"

But he cuts me off, laughing. "You don't have to tell me you're straight. I know. I was just wondering if it ever crossed your mind. Once, maybe."

I don't know how to continue. It feels like the world doesn't want me to tell Sam the truth. Well, maybe that's not the case —but I know I'm using it as an excuse anyway. It's stupid and ball-less of me, but I can't help it. "You know I'm straight?"

"'Course," Sam says, laughing. "I never once for a second actually thought otherwise. It was just a question, you know?"

I'm quiet. And then, "Sure. I've thought about being with a guy." Every day of my life. "You?"

He blushes, and that combined with what he says next has me lost to another hard-on.

"I don't know. Not really. Maybe."

"Well, if you wanna try it. We can definitely try it together."

Shit.

I did not just say that out loud. Please don't let me have said that out loud. It was the whiskey talking. Must have been.

I pinch myself hard on the thigh and tell myself to shut up and stop letting my dick control my mouth. But it doesn't want to listen to me. Even as I sink into my chair, it's stretching, eager to hear Sam's answer.

"You're kidding, right?" he laughs, and then he slowly sips his drink, looking at me over the rim of his glass, gaze traveling down my face and over my chest. Whiskey misses his mouth and runs down his chin and onto the table. "Shit. Sorry." He wipes it up with his sleeve, doing everything he can to not look up at me again.

I wish he would. Maybe then he'd see the truth on my face without me having to say it.

"It's okay," I say and pick up my own drink, willing myself not to say anything more. But I can't help it and they pour out. "And I wasn't kidding."

Chapter Fourteen

JEREMY

I t takes until I'm at Simon's place for my embarrassment to go away at Luke handing me condoms. Steven asks why I'm so flushed, but I shrug it off, step out of the bus with him following behind me, and make my way up the road.

When Simon lets us into his garage with a grin, we're ready for a few hours of fun. Well, *I'm* ready for fun. Steven just looks nervous. He can't even look Simon in the eye.

And then it hits me. *Oh.* He can't look *Simon* in the eye.

When it's just the two of us, I find a corner to lounge in while Simon goes and gets us both drinks. I elbow his side. "Simon? Seriously?"

Steven shrugs.

"But he's so large and . . . *man*ly. He could probably bench press you."

Glancing at the way Steven is practically drooling, I've probably just described his wet dream. I so don't get it.

Get tits, though. *That* I get.

I search for Suzy, but she's not here yet. I hope she comes soon because I want to do some wicked things with her, but I don't want to miss my curfew. Not because I'm a stickler for rules, but if I get home like I say I will this time, Dad's likely to be more flexible in future.

Simon is slowly making his way through the crowds of punch-drinking classmates, and Steven is eye-fucking him none-too-subtly.

"Just ask to see his room and suggest wanking off together. See where it goes from there."

Steven shakes his head and says quickly, just before the guy reaches us. "I'll give myself away."

"Here you go Jeremy," Simon says, handing me a drink. Then he gives the second one to my gaping friend. "Steven."

"Thanks," he says, and it sounds so breathy I choke on a sip.

He glares at me and I mouth a sorry.

And just then *she* walks in.

Her hair is dancing around her face in the breeze coming in from outside and her skirt is flying up to show her upper thighs. Suzy.

As soon as I think it, she's found me. She giggles something to her friends and struts her way over to me. Her mouth moves slow and sexy as she says hello and her lips curve into a smile that whispers for me to hurry up and start sucking on them.

She reaches out and takes my drink and rests it on the windowsill behind her. Steven pauses in his conversation with Simon to look at me and raise his brow.

I sling an arm around her shoulders and ask if I can get her a drink.

"Nah," she says, and cuddles closer to my side. "I'm so glad you could make it, Jer." Then she pushes up on her tippy-toes and gives me a long, slow kiss. The way she rubs against me as she kisses is giving me one hell of an erection, and I untangle us. Not because I don't like where this is maybe going, but I'm aware we have an audience.

Suzy blushes when she sees Steven and Simon bug-eyed and watching us, but it disappears quickly. That's what's so cool about her, she's hardly ever fazed by anything. She pulls the two other guys into a conversation about our school rugby team, and how she doesn't think we have the strongest team this year. This gets Simon worked up, and before we know it, a couple of hours have passed.

Somewhere in the space of that time we moved to sitting down on some chairs. Only Suzy chose to sit on my lap, shifting every now and then as if she's making sure I'm still hot for her.

And I so am.

When she does this little move for the tenth time, I'm about to come in my jeans. I slide her off me. She laughs and gives me a small pout. I kiss it off her. "Simon, where's the bathroom?"

"Upstairs across from my bedroom."

Steven swings his head away from me to Simon. "You live above the garage? That's awesome. I wish I had so much privacy."

Simon grins. "You wanna check it out?"

And so we all traipse up the stairs, Simon and Steven turning left to his bedroom, and me and Suzy turning right.

It surprises me—and turns me on more—when Suzy pushes her way into the bathroom with me. For some reason, I thought she was going to hang outside until I'd sorted myself out.

She locks the door behind us and snags me into another deep kiss. Just like the one at the beginning of the night. My hands slide down her back to rest on her bum. She must like that, because she rocks against me. I think I'm hard enough to cut through all the porcelain crap in this bathroom.

"Think we have enough time to get to second base?"

"We'll *make* time," I say and slip my hand up over her hip and under her shirt. It takes me a painful amount of time fiddling with the clasp of her bra, but soon both of her tops are in a heap on the floor. My hands are freaking out, shaking as they roam over her breasts.

When she presses me through my jeans and rubs, I know two things: 1) This is the best moment of my life so far 2) I'm not gonna last a minute.

Unfortunately, I don't get proof on the last one. Someone starts banging on the door telling us to hurry up.

Suzy rolls her eyes. "Mood killer," she calls to the door and picks up her tops. As she puts them on, I dash a bit of cold water on my face. "Another time, Jeremy, yeah?"

She leaves and shuts the door behind me.

I count to ten and follow.

Bumping my hip against Simon's room door, I'm ready to grab Steven and give him all the details as we head back. But I stop as soon as the door swings open, and Simon's rips his hand off Steven's knee.

Gah! Fuck. I want to make a joke about putting a sock on the door, but the way Steven is leaping off the bed and coming toward me, I save it. "Curfew time's approaching, huh?" Steven says.

"Yeah," I say, glancing between the two of them.

Steven waves at Simon over his shoulder without turning to look at him. I barely have a chance to say bye to Suzy, and before I know it Steven and I are striding to the bus stop.

"So it looked promising back there," I say to him.

"It's *not* what it looked like," Steven says and sighs. "He was just showing me where his brother got a tattoo."

Huh? "Then why did you fly outta there like that?"

"Because it was turning me the fuck on, okay? I couldn't have him see that. You saved me."

"Good thing I held my tongue on the putting a sock on the door comment I thought of saying."

He blushes. "Very good thing."

Chapter Fifteen

SAM

I *wasn't kidding.*

Luke's words roll around my head all of Thursday and Friday. I've sort of skipped around seeing him since then too. I keep making excuses and lunch dates with friends that don't exist. The only time I see him is when Jeremy's around.

It's just . . . Jesus, I must really need to get laid.

At least I have a date tonight. Maybe just spending time with a woman will help me get rid of these random, intrusive, somewhat taboo thoughts.

After trying on three different T-shirts, I settle on the one Jeremy gave me last year. It's an awesome turquoise color, and I figure if conversation between Hannah and me goes really badly, at least I can tell her the story behind it.

I spike up my hair with honey-scented hair gel and I'm just about done when my phone rings.

My hands are greasy and I hurry to wash and dry them before picking up the call.

I miss it. Carole was calling.

I stroll out of the bathroom and move into the kitchen, where Jeremy is raiding the fridge. He pulls out the chocolate milk I bought yesterday and starts drinking from the bottle.

"Oy!"

He jumps, managing to spill milk down his front. "Jeez, Dad, now look what you made me do."

"Serves you right. Only I'm allowed to drink from the bottle."

His face scrunches up as he looks at the chocolate milk he's still holding. "Ugh. You don't do that, do you?"

"I will if you don't stop."

I pick up the landline phone and hit Carole's home number. She doesn't answer, and I try her cell.

"Sam, thanks for calling me back."

"Sure, what's up?" I hear voices in the background. "Where are you?"

"That's the thing," she says. "I got caught at work. The boss has called a spontaneous meeting. He's upset about something. Look, can you have Jeremy stay with you this evening?"

I tap my fingers over the bench as I look to the ceiling in frustration. I have always been as flexible as I can with Carole on days when I look after Jeremy, and she is flexible with me too. I shouldn't be annoyed. This is just life and all. But . . . it's the first time I've had a date in years. I don't want to cancel. "I sort of had plans tonight," I say, and Jeremy comes round to my side and calls out, "He has a hot date."

Carole laughs. "Oh really? A date, Sam?"

I swat Jeremy over the back of the head and he smirks as he scampers out of the room. "Yeah. A date."

"Ah, crap," she says. "Maybe I can call Sarah to see if she can babysit."

I shake my head. Jeremy *is* almost **15**. Old enough to be the babysitter himself. "Jesus, Carole. Can't he stay here alone for the night?"

She sighs. "I guess."

I cover the mouthpiece and yell out down the hall. "Jeremy, you good for hanging here tonight?"

There's a scuffle of his footsteps, and then he pops his head around the corner. "Sure. Can I invite a friend over for a movie or something?"

Carole must have heard the question, because I hear her asking me to ask Jeremy if it's a guy or girl friend.

I ask Jeremy. "Who?"

He shrugs. "Maybe Steven—but, damn, no, he's busy tonight. Suzy might like to watch something though."

"Suzy?" I say at the same time Carole says it down the line. "Who's Suzy?"

"A friend."

"A friend?"

"Yeah," he laughs. "Trust me, Dad, she's just a friend."

"What do you think?" I ask Carole. There's a pause, and then someone is speaking to her on the other end. She says quickly, "Sure. That's fine. So long as Suzy has a way to get home safely afterwards."

I glance out the front window toward Luke's. "Yeah, I'll make sure she gets home safely."

I know he'll say yes. And he's a lifesaver for it. Because I *really* need to get out on this date tonight.

Hopefully by the end of it, Luke's offer will be sufficiently drowned from my mind.

Chapter Sixteen

JEREMY

I haven't seen Suzy since Simon's party. I'm really ready to see her again.

My plan showed just how well it's working when Dad and Mum said I could have Suzy come over here.

Alone in my bedroom, with the door locked, I ring and tell her I'm going to be home alone tonight and ask whether she wants to come over.

Her voice purrs down the line and vibrates through my ear right to my major. I have to rearrange myself when she says, "I'll come alright, but . . ." she pauses and then adds, "But we can't fuck tonight. I got my days."

"Oh, um . . ." Too much information! "That's cool. I wasn't expecting . . . that."

The word *fuck* seems to have magnified and is still ringing in my ears; it makes me shiver with nerves at the same time as making my dick weep a little in excitement. I press against it and glare. *Not happening tonight buddy. Calm it down.*

Suzy laughs lightly down the line. "Come on. I know you want to get laid before you turn fifteen. And anyway, I want to before I'm sixteen, so . . . it'll happen soon. Just not tonight."

I don't think I contribute much more to the conversation, just a couple of hums and murmurs. When she hangs up, I high-five myself in the mirror. But it shakes and falls to the ground. I catch it with my hip, just in time to save myself from seven years bad luck.

I set the mirror back on its hook in the wall and ring Steven. "Hey man, you'll never believe the call I just had with Suzy . . ."

Chapter Seventeen

SAM

The date.

Well. Turns out it's *not* a date.

I laugh at my idiocy as I drink my **4**th Jack and Coke in a sweaty bar in Wellington City. Hannah and the **2** girlfriends she brought along to go dancing are chatting up the bartender. It's all fucking awkward. It has been since I showed up at her place to pick her up and **3** girls—tiddly and giggling—bundled themselves in my crappy two-door Honda.

Hannah had slapped me on the shoulder, said I looked good, and asked if I was ready to dance the night away. I just blinked at her and said, "Sure."

I thought for a brief moment that maybe there still might be a chance she liked me, and maybe had brought her friends along for moral support or something. That thought went away when she pointed to the bartender and whispered, "He's hot, don't you think?"

I have no idea how I was supposed to answer that. In the end, I just shrugged and got started on making the most of the night—which included getting myself drunk.

"Hey, Sam," Hannah says, nudging me in the side. "Do you want to dance with us?"

I shake my head. Actually, I do want to try dancing, but I'm nervous and I need at least one more drink before I brave getting out there. I scan the crowd for any girls that look single that I may be able to dance with—or at least next to. But as I look at the crowd, I don't feel any thrill to get out there and get sweaty.

Still, it's on my *20's Must Do List*, and I'm going to do it. I drain my drink and order two shots of tequila.

The **1**st one burns going down, the **2**nd may have too, but my throat is too numb to feel it. When I get off my barstool to weave my way through to the dance floor, my head spins. The beat of the music pulses through my entire body and I laugh as I feel myself letting go.

Hannah and her friends wave at me and I sidle through jumping bodies to reach them. They pull me close to them and we dance. Suddenly, I'm the center of their attention and they are all almost pressed against me, grinding and laughing.

I like the attention, and my heart is beating hard. I spin Hannah. "You're such fun," she says in my ear. "It's so nice to go dancing with a guy and not have him want to get into my pants."

And I realize I really *don't* want to get into her pants. Just dancing is enough. I dance my way through the crowd and I'm not feeling anything for anyone. Maybe it's the alcohol that's making me lose interest in the impressive display of womanly flesh in here. Or maybe the scene just doesn't do it for me. It's fun, dancing, but that's about it.

Hannah catches up with me at the bar. "Me and the girls are going to bar hop. You gonna join us?"

I sip the water I ordered and shake my head. "Nah, I prob-ably shouldn't."

"Oh, come on. Let loose a little more, Sam."

Isn't that the whole point of this? A voice inside my head says.

Yeah, but . . . I murmur back to it, but it interrupts me.

You're thirty soon. How do you want to look back on your twenties?

So I look up at Hannah and nod.

And so the barhopping begins.

Chapter Eighteen

JEREMY

Suzy is cuddling into my side, her weight warm against me. We watch the film saying very little, and I don't think I've paid attention to it at all. I'm still caught up on her call about us *doing it* soon. I breathe in Suzy's fruity-scented hair.

When the movie is over, I switch off the TV with the remote and look at Suzy in the darkness. The light in the hall is on, so I can see her enough.

She nips my ear and her hand travels up my thigh. My head is saying this isn't a good idea right now—what if Luke comes in for a random check in? It's telling me I need to stop.

But it's hard to listen to my head when my dick suddenly starts screaming for me to get closer to Suzy. It still remembers the promise made to it earlier that day, and it seems to want to tell Suzy how much it likes the idea.

My mouth finds hers and I suck on her lip as she strokes me through my slacks. Now that I've started, I can't pull away.

It goes on and on and her petting gets firmer in direct proportion to my dick getting harder.

"I so wish I could do it with you right now," Suzy says as she dips her fingers into the waistband of my briefs and skims over the sensitive head of my major. "Guess we'll just have to settle for me sucking you off."

With that she pulls down my pants and underwear just enough to expose me. I'm overtaken by a rage of hormones and I whimper. Suzy looks at me and smiles. All I can think of is how large and wide her mouth is and how it's gonna feel having it over me.

But then she dips her head, and my head starts hammering something about protection. Suddenly my mind fills with bananas and with a superpower I didn't know I have, I gently push her away from me.

"What?" she says, blinking.

I reach into my pocket where I have a condom.

"I'm just giving you head, you sure you need one of those?"

It's the hardest thing I've done, but I nod and tear at the foil. All my practice has paid off, because I slide it on effortlessly. Even Suzy looks impressed at my swiftness. No fumbling about for me.

Guess I should be thankful for those bloody bananas after all.

She gags a lot as she bobs up and down on me, but I don't care. I'm lost to the pleasures rolling through me. Oh God, if a blow job feels this good, what was the real thing going to be like? Suzy sucks harder, her cheeks sallow and sunken around my dick. I lose it then, crying out as I come in hot waves.

Suzy pulls off and quirks her lips at me, pleased with herself.

"That was amazing," I say and lean in to give her a kiss. But I don't linger long. I remove the condom, tie it up, and then scrunch it in some paper before throwing it in the bin. I don't want anyone to see the evidence.

I'm feeling pretty damn good when I stroll back into the lounge where Suzy is waiting.

"Next week's going to be fun," Suzy says with a cheeky twinkle in her eye.

I swallow and lean over to kiss her some more. But now that my dick has gotten what it wants for today, my head starts up again and I'm more careful about maintaining a reasonable amount of space between us, should Luke walk in.

Chapter Nineteen

LUKE

Jeremy looks like he's glowing when he comes to my door telling me I can drop off Suzy now. I ask him what's up, but he doesn't say anything. His jaw slacks with a smile though.

"You gonna come along for the ride?" I ask as I snag my keys and make my way to the truck.

He shakes his head. "Nah, she's good. I'll send her out."

And that's it. He turns and heads back to his place. By the time I've reversed out of the driveway and am idling in front of the house next door, a pretty girl wearing too much makeup comes out.

She looks older than the fifteen she says she is when I ask. I quickly get the feeling she doesn't want to chat, though, so I turn on the radio and listen to that all the way to her place.

Once we're there, she gives me a quick thanks and hops out of the car. I wince as the girl walks up the path of a rundown house with rusting car parts in the front lawn, which is so overgrown it's almost impossible to see the concrete path running up the middle.

I wait until she's safely inside before I pull out from the curb and drive back toward home. Halfway there, my cell rings. It's midnight, a strange time for a call, and so I immediately worry something's happened. Maybe Jeremy is really sick . . . or did something happen to my mum . . . or—

The caller name flashes on my screen, and I hurriedly answer, pulling over to the side of the road. "Sam?"

"Luuuuke."

My heart beats faster just at hearing his voice. "Hey, man. Are you okay?"

"I'm drunk, eh!"

I smile. "Yeah, I can hear that. What's up? Are you still with your date?"

"Date?" Sam's slur sounds confused, and then he lets out an *ohhhh*. "Nah. Turns out it's not a date. I think she thinks I bat for the other team, know what I'm saying? Yeah, didn't get it for a while, but her and her friends kept asking what I think of the guy bartenders."

He sounds adorably perplexed by this, and I can't help but smile. I lean back in my chair and reflexively rest my free hand on my pocket. "And?" I said, going for the joke. "Were they?"

"Nowhere near as good as you, my friend."

I know it's the alcohol talking and he's probably just joking, but my chest tightens anyway. It takes me a second before I can speak again. "So . . . why'd you ring? Miss me, did ya?"

He laughs, and the sound is cheerful and free. "It would have been better if you were here to even up the male side of the night." His voice gets quieter as if he's not speaking into the mouthpiece anymore. "But actually, I rang because I'm in a pickle."

I make out the word pickle and sit up straighter. Sam's voice comes down the line clearer again. I hear cars honking in the background and guess he's outside somewhere. "Thing is, I'm way too drunk to get home and I can't afford a taxi. My card just declined at the ATM. I don't get paid till Monday and I've only got ten in cash. Also, I sort of lost Hannah and her friends."

"No worries," I say. "I'll come pick you up."

His breath crackles down the line. "You will?"

"Of course."

He sighs. "You're my lifesaver, you know that?"

"You can thank me later. Just tell me where to find you." I'm already pulling out and doing a U-turn.

"Um, I'm close to Vivian Street." He gives me the name of the bar he's standing outside of.

I don't like the idea of him standing in the windy streets waiting for me, so I tell him to go inside and I'll find him.

It takes me twenty minutes to get into the city. I park the truck and run a hand through my hair before I get out and walk into the packed bar. It smells of stale beer and sweat as I push my way through the crowds searching for Sam. It doesn't take me long to find him, casually leaning back with his elbows on the bar. He keeps glancing at the door, and I grin.

"Sam!" I call out, but my voice is drowned out by the blaring music.

Just before I reach him, his eyes finally latch onto me and he immediately pushes off from the bar and comes over. "Luke!"

I'm surprised by the hug he gives me, but I go with it, squeezing him back. His fingers press firmly against my back and tickle as they skate off me again when he pulls away.

There's a dopey, drunken smile on his face, and his eyes look a little foggy. I shake my head. "How much did you drink?"

He shrugs. "Lost count."

"Well, come on. I'll take you home."

He nods, but then hesitates when I motion for us to go around the dancers. A new song has come on. It has a catchy beat and I know it's Sam's kind of music.

"Um," he says, looking from me to the dance floor. "You wanna dance for a song before we go?"

I scan the mass of twenty-somethings practically dry-humping on the dance floor. I suddenly feel so freaking old. It doesn't seem that long ago when I was one of those guys letting loose on the dance floor. But all these guys look so *young*. My life has moved on from this.

Still, when Sam tugs my arm, I go with him. He finds a part of the dance floor with a few single girls rocking it together. I try and feel the music and sway a bit, but I'm not really feeling it, and seeing Sam dancing toward the girls is about ripping my chest apart.

I lean over to him. "I'm just gonna wait for you outside. Take your time."

Sam spins around and clutches my arms before I can pull away. "Nah, Luke, don't go." He puts his arms around my neck and continues rocking his hips.

I freeze, because this is new. Sam and I rarely touch each other. We've always been so good at keeping a bro-distance between us.

The hairs on my neck prickle and I inhale the honey scent of Sam's hair. "W-what are you doing?"

"If this is what it takes to keep you on the dance floor, consider yourself imprisoned." He slurs half his words and then laughs.

The song changes, and it's cheesy and slow. Sam draws his hands to my shoulders and I think he's about to let go of me, but then he bites on his lips and shrugs. He slides his arms back around me, and then goes further than that, bringing himself closer so we're cheek-to-cheek. He chuckles and his lips brush against my ear.

I shiver, and then my body switches to automatic and I wrap my arms around him. He sighs and leans into me. "Hmmm, interesting," he says.

And on the spot, I develop a love-hate relationship with that word. Interesting good? As in, yeah, I can get into this? Or interesting bad? As in, well at least now I've tried it and can say for sure it's not for me?

I pray it's the former.

I don't want to pull away, but I have to, because I'm getting hard and he'll notice. Sure, it'll tell him the truth about me, but I don't want to come out to him like that. Not while he's drunk.

And I think that sounds reasonable. Except, I also feel like I'm just making up another excuse.

As I start to untangle us, Sam tightens his grip and moves so he can look at me. "Where're you going?"

God, I just want to run my hands through his hair and kiss him so hard he'll gasp and so soft he'll moan.

"It's getting hot in here."

Sam gives me a disappointed frown and then shrugs before letting go of me. He follows quietly until we are outside and we've rounded a corner onto a barren street.

"Thanks for picking me up," he says and stops at the passenger side of my truck. I've beeped it open, but Sam doesn't open the door. He rests with his back against the car and looks at me.

I pause close to him, not sure if I should keep moving to the driver's side or not.

"You okay?" I ask.

Even though he's against the car, he sways and I reach out to steady him. My hand is at the sleeve of his T-shirt, half on the material and half on him.

Sam swallows audibly and I look up to find his eyes are latched onto me. Onto my lips.

"You meant it, right? That we can experiment?"

Before I can answer or move away, he leans in and kisses me. His lips are firm against mine and taste sweet from Coke.

"Sam," I say in a strangled voice as I fight all my desires to kiss him back. But then his body arches toward mine in a curve of curiosity and I can't help it. I smell his warm, honey scent and I'm shaking inside as I lower my head and kiss him back. I graze his lips and then tease them open with the tip of my tongue.

Sam grips the back of my head as if he's afraid I'm going to draw away again. And I want to laugh because he has nothing to worry about; that's the last thing on my mind, though it should be the first.

His tongue touches mine, tentative and uncertain. Then he pulls back, giving me a languid, glassy smile. His eyes drift away from mine to my lips again. It makes me nervous and excited, but annoyed. Nervous, because I know he's going to kiss me again, and excited because I'm looking forward to it, and annoyed because he's drunk and I wish he wasn't.

"This also interesting?" I murmur against his jaw as I kiss my way across it to his throat.

He nods. "I just want to get it, you know? I want to understand Jeremy."

And it's like ice water has been poured over my head—and other body parts—because suddenly I'm no longer drunk on a fantasy; real life is raising its ugly head and glaring at me.

Shit.

Yeah, of course. This is Sam coming to terms with his son's sexuality. Not his own.

Of course. I already knew that wouldn't have been the case.

And if it wasn't him trying to understand Jeremy, it would be something for him to cross off on his *20s Must-Do List*.

"Luke?" Sam asks. "You okay?" He sways again and I prop him up.

"I think I should be asking you that." I help load him into the car, which he finds hilarious for some reason.

"Alright," I say as I jump behind the wheel. "Let's get you home." I glance over at him, crumpled between the seat and door grinning, and shake my head. "You really did get wasted, didn't you?"

"Another thing I can tick off my list."

I turn the key in the ignition and the car rumbles to life. "How is that list of yours coming along then?"

He shrugs and shifts so he's leaning back on the headrest, messing up his mohawk. "I don't think I'll get it all done. Certainly not swimming with the sharks." He sighs. "Not enough time—or money. Why do we have to get old, Luke?"

I laugh. "I feel you there. I can't believe I'm in my mid-thirties. I look in the mirror and my image never seems to match the way I feel inside."

"You're fit. You don't look a day over"—he thinks about it —"29.12"

I reach over and lightly slap him on his arm. "So thirty."

He chuckles and closes his eyes. His next words are as slurred as all his others have been, but I hear it with more clarity than the others. Maybe because of the way it makes my heart freaking *flutter*. "But seriously, Luke, you look as good as you did when I first met you."

"I look good, eh?"

He smirks. "And you know it."

I can't help but smile. It hovers around my lips almost the entire way home. When Sam falls asleep, his head lolling around as I drive, I want to drive slower so I can commit everything about this moment to memory.

He's not going to remember nearly as much as I will, and I want to be able to give him all the wonderful and nasty details of his drunken state. Like the cute way he slurred his words, and the way drool runs down the corner of his mouth.

Looking at him takes me back to the countless times I got so drunk that I had no idea where I was anymore. Once I even ended up sleeping in a ditch somewhere in the Wairarapa.

Sometimes I cringe when I think of the crap I did, but it also makes me laugh. It's a story to tell. And it makes me feel I've lived, too.

I park the car in front of Sam's place and look over him at the house. I get why Sam needs to do this. More than that, *I* want his list to happen too.

He grew up far too quickly. I *want* that he cuts back a bit— that he gets to be the carefree guy he never got the chance to be.

"All right, love," I say quietly as I unbuckle my belt and lean over to do the same to his.

He stirs, opens and shuts his mouth, and then starts snoring. Chuckling, I climb out of the car and move to the passenger side. I duck my head in and lightly pat his cheek. "Wakey-wakey."

He rolls his head away from me, his mouth dropping open as he lets out another snore.

"If you don't wake up," I growl gently, "I'll have to carry you inside. I won't let you forget that detail for a long time, either."

He lets out a small sound, but his eyes are still closed.

"Fine. But you asked for it." I slip my arms under his knees and shoulders. It's awkward shuffling him out of the truck, but soon I have him securely against my chest, though his head is lolling back over my arm, exposing his neck.

I kick the door shut and carry him to the house. I'm thankful for all the weight training I do, because the guy isn't light. I grunt as I try to fish for my set of house keys, propping the backs of his knees on my thigh.

It's not working. "Sam. Help me for a sec, okay?" I brace his arms and gently lower his legs to the ground. He stirs and mumbles something, but he's holding most of his weight now.

I get the keys and unlock the door.

When I switch on the light, Sam groans and blinks. "Where . . .? Oh." He rests his forehead on my shoulder. "Ugh . . . I don't feel so good."

He gives a little burp and clutches his stomach. "Just hold on," I say, steering him quickly down the hall. He makes another sound—and it doesn't sound healthy. I fling open the bathroom door and yank up the toilet seat. "Chuck in there."

Sam doesn't waste a second. He collapses to his knees, clutches the toilet bowl and throws up.

I open a window, hoping the fresh air will help him, and then crouch next to the guy, rubbing circles over his back. There's a book at the side of the toilet—*Moby Dick* I find out as I push it against the wall, out of any potential splatter-radius.

Sam continues to throw up, swearing between each retch, and I lightly chuckle.

There's a movement in the hall and I turn my head toward the partially-open door. A bleary-eyed Jeremy comes into focus. He rubs his eyes when he sees me with his dad. "Huh?" he says, frowning.

"Nothing to worry about," I say. "Go back to bed."

"Need to piss," he says. "What's going on with Dad?"

Jeremy pushes the door open and his eyes ping wide. "No way." He laughs. "That's freaking epic."

"Leave your dad alone," I say. "He just ate something bad, that's all."

"Stop shitting me, Luke. I can smell the alcohol. Dad's totally wasted." He shakes his head, eyes holding a mischievous twinkle. "I'm never letting him live this down."

I let go of Sam to steer Jeremy out of the bathroom. "Go piss in the garden and get back to bed."

He laughs again, but does as I say. This time I shut the bathroom door. "How you doing?" I ask Sam.

He mumbles something and then flushes the toilet for the fourth time. Pushing himself up, he manages to stumble to the sink. "Oh, fuck. I look a wreck." He turns on the taps and washes his hands, face and mouth. After he does the second round of teeth brushing, he wipes his mouth dry and blinks up at me in the mirror. He looks exhausted. "I just wanna curl up and sleep now."

I make sure he gets to his bedroom, and while he sits on his bed and struggles to take off his shoes, I get him some water and a bucket. "In case you need to puke suddenly," I say, and rest it next to the bed.

He slides out of his jeans, but doesn't bother to remove anything else. He rests back against the pillows, throwing an arm over his face. "Have a funny feeling I'll regret this night in the morning."

I laugh, and leave the room. "See you tomorrow," I say as I shut the door to his house and make my way back to mine.

Chapter Twenty

SAM

Hangovers are nasty, nasty beasts. My head pounds as if it's trying to recreate last night's music. *Boom-boom-boom.*

After drinking **3** large glasses of water, I take a shower. When the cooking timer goes off, I clench my jaw. You've got to be kidding me. No way was that **5** minutes. I step out of the shower, dripping onto the mat, and turn the bloody thing off. Then, I hop back under the warm water and let myself indulge. Just this once.

Unfortunately, I only get another **2** minutes before Jeremy starts pounding on the door. "Dad, hurry up, you're taking forever."

I groan and tell him to go away.

"I gotta shower and go see Steven."

I rest my head on the plastic wall, hoping the pressure will make my headache disappear. "Can't you shower at your mum's and leave me alone?"

My boy laughs. "Okay, Dad. But you're so not getting away with this. Wonder what Mum'll think?"

I hear his retreating steps and open the shower door to call out, "Leave your mother out of this!"

I quickly turn off the taps, grab a towel, and wrap it around my waist. "Jeremy?" I say as I charge down the hall. I yank open the front door, hoping I'll still catch him, but I end up banging into Luke.

Peering over his shoulder, I say, "You didn't happen to see Jeremy, did you?"

Luke runs a quick glance down me, and smirks. "Saw him flying off down the road."

"Dammit. Carole's never going to let me hear the end of it."

An evil grin twitches at Luke's lips. "She's not the only one."

Looking at him—at his lips—flashes of the night before come back to me.

I blink away from him and step back inside, hands tightening on the towel around my hips. My skin prickles as a warm breeze floats over us. I think it might be remembering what I did to Luke last night, but I feel blood rushing to my face and I'm so aware of being only half-dressed.

"Er . . . get inside and make us coffee. I'm gonna get into some clothes."

Luke comes in, carrying a shopping bag I only just notice. "Right. You stop flaunting your nipple ring, and I'll make us brunch."

My hand flies to my piercing, and I can't stop from blushing further. I fiddle with the metal as I try to think of something to say. Luke is shifting his shopping to his other hand, but I do catch him looking at my nipple again. I pull my hand away from the ring. "This thing feels pretty damn awesome, you know."

Luke's face contorts and he bites his lip.

"Too much info?" I ask, laughing as I turn my back on him and move down the hall.

He mumbles something, but I don't hear him. I chuck on some shorts and a T-shirt. I spike my hair with some gel and, for the finishing touch, slide my sunglasses on. I look over the edges of them and wink at myself in the mirror. "You look pretty fucking ridiculous, Sam. Well done."

When I enter the kitchen, Luke is sliding a tray into the oven. He looks over at me and straightens. "And how do you feel this morning?"

"Stop laughing at me." I slump on a seat at the table and cross an ankle over my knee. "But to answer you, I could feel better."

Luke comes over with **2** mugs of coffee and hands me one. "Well you certainly looked like you had fun last night."

He looks down at my lips and I'm pretty sure he's remembering our little experiment. I'm not sure if I should bring it up—maybe make a light joke of it—or pretend I don't remember. What if he's hoping I was so out of it that I've forgotten?

"The dancing was fun, I suppose. But I'm not sure it's worth how I'm feeling now." I take a drink of coffee and hum at the goodness of it. Luke sits opposite me, relaxing back into his seat as he casually looks out the window. "Um," I say, "thank you."

"What for?"

I take another sip. "For picking me up. For cleaning the bathroom last night."

He shrugs. "No worries."

The table creaks as I rest my mug down. "Um . . . just to be a real pain in the ass, do you think you can drop me off in town to pick up my car?"

"It's on the plan I have for us for today."

I rest my arms on the table and lean in. "You have a plan? Tell me more."

"Okay, well . . . it's a bit different, but a friend of mine runs a carpentry class. I thought we should try it out."

I bite my lip. It sounds great, and I want to do it—especially since it's something else on my list I can cross off after—but I think of the measly **10** dollars I have left. "I'd love to, Luke, but, um, could we do it next weekend—or anytime after payday?"

He shakes his head and flashes me that double-dimpled grin of his. "Nope. And don't worry. First time's free."

A delicious scent is coming from the kitchen, and I hop off my chair to check it out. I peek into the oven and there are **4** mince pies baking. It's like Luke has read my mind.

I look over the kitchen bench at him. The sun is streaming over him and his profile is golden and warm. Hazel strands of his dark brown hair glow, and his lips . . .

I swallow at the same time he looks over at me, and then quickly crouch down out of view and take in the mince pies once more.

I hear his chair scrape back and then his footsteps as he comes into the kitchen. He looks down at me, folds his arms and frowns. "Watch-pies never bake, you know," he says. But he crouches down next to me nevertheless.

He's not looking at the oven though. He's looking at me. "You remember what happened with us last night."

It's not a question. It's a statement. Panic seizes me, and I don't understand it, but my immediate reaction is to shake my head.

Luke cocks his head and studies me for a moment. "I don't believe you," he says. "But okay." He looks at the pies. "We can leave it if that's what you want."

I don't know how to respond or what to say, and he's given me an out. It's easy and accessible, and I take it.

But the mince pies don't taste as good as they should after that. And I'm aware of Luke in a way I haven't ever been before, and it makes me nervous. He's not just my friend gazing out of the window; he's also a man whose lips I've felt against my own, whose tongue twisted with mine. It's unsettling to think I've kissed a *guy*, but even more unsettling is that it makes my cock stir.

It's the taboo in it, I think. The thrill of doing something a lot of people frown upon.

That, and kissing him last night made me feel free. Like I really am living my **20**s.

Yeah, that's what's making me stir. Not a *guy*. Just the freedom he represents.

Freedom you wouldn't mind a little more of. I swallow that desire down with my mince pie. But the way my body feels itchy and excited inside, I don't know how long it'll *stay* down.

I leave half of the piecrust on my plate and lean back in my chair, trying to get comfortable—or at least appear to be—but it's a lost cause. I'm too stiff and it doesn't help that my head is still pounding—with both the headache and my thoughts about Luke.

He glances at me, his eyes shadowed with his own thoughts, and I wonder if last night bothers him at all. Or if maybe, like me, he also found the kiss liberating and . . . exciting?

"Are you ready to go?" he asks, stacking our plates and taking them to the kitchen. "The class starts at one. It's in the city, so I can drop you off at your car after."

I get up slowly, readjusting my sunglasses. I'm glad I have them on for how much I've been staring at my friend. "Yeah." I clap my hands together in a show of enthusiasm I'm struggling to feel. "I'm ready to take an interest class. Bring it on."

Luke would usually laugh at something I said that was so lame, but this time, his lips don't even twitch. He's moved back to the table and is wiping it down.

He chucks the cloth into the sink, and then nods at the table. "Okay then. We're off."

And with that, he picks up the round table in an impressive display of strength and carries it on his back to his truck.

Chapter Twenty-One

JEREMY

Mum is fidgeting in the kitchen. She has that uncomfortable look about her that usually comes before she reminds me of the Golden Condom Rule and hands me a banana.

Now I wish I'd stayed out longer with Steven.

I stop texting and wait for it, briefly entertaining the idea of darting the hell out of there. I'd do it too, if it weren't for the fact I'm stuck at the table. By the time I would have untangled myself from the chair, Mum would have wedged herself between me and the door.

Fiddling with my phone, I wonder if I can make it ring somehow.

Anything to distract me.

I set to typing a quick message to Steven: *Ring me ASAP.*

Tucking her dark shoulder-length hair behind her ear, she

moves over to the table. When she passes the fruit bowl without pausing, I start to get a little nervous.

What does she want to say?

Does she know the truth about Steven? I gulp and eye her more carefully. She seems more nervous than angry, so I think I'm lucky on this count.

But I'm still getting uneasy. There's something in the back of my head trying to whisper something to me. *Come on, Jeremy, you know this is it. Mum is finally going to tell you that secret she's been holding back.*

I shake my head, because I'm not ready to hear that secret. "Uh,"—I stand abruptly—"I gotta piss."

She eyes me and tilts her head to the side, the way she does when she's trying to see through me. "You just went. Can you sit back down a second, there's just something I'd like to talk to you about." The chair she drags out makes a horrible squealing sound, and I hope it's not a bad omen.

I thump my ass back on the chair. "And . . . what's that?" I'm gripping my phone harder and now I *really* want Steven to ring and save me.

"Do you like this table?" Mum says, palming the thick polished wood.

I frown; somehow the way she says it feels like a trap. "It's sturdy. Much better than Dad's, anyway."

"Well," she says, "that's good."

"Okay?" I'm not really sure how I'm meant to answer that.

Mum breathes out slowly, wringing her hands together. "I know this time of your life, you're going through a lot of changes."

It's obvious she's referring to my supposed sexuality, and I swallow a lump of shame that comes with that lie. "Right. And?"

"I don't want to make any more changes to your life than necessary, do you understand?"

"Mum, you're being as clear as mud right now. But I think I'm sifting through it." Even if I don't want to be.

She rolls her eyes. "I didn't want to tell you this until I was sure how serious it was, but,"—she looks me in the eye, and her face is one big smile—"I've met someone, Jeremy."

I go blank. All I'm seeing is mud. That voice is back: *Ah, there it is. The secret. Don't act like you're so surprised.* I tell it to shut up, and sink further into the haze of shock. Or maybe it's denial. Something. "Huh?"

"Greg and I have been seeing each other for about a year now."

"A year," I repeat. And then I snap out of the haze. I hear what she's telling me and I'm pushing away from the table and jumping to my feet. "The T-shirt. Combs . . ." I don't want to hear anymore. Don't want to know what exactly Mum's telling me.

But she doesn't let me leave. She holds my sleeve as I try to pass her. "He's been here the weeks you've stayed at your Dad's."

That's just too much. *He stays here, as in sleeps and*—I shudder.

She bows her head. "Maybe I should have told you earlier. I just didn't want to mess around with your head."

"So why are you telling me now?"

"Because I want you to meet him. Get to know him."

I jerk out of her grasp. "Why would I want that?" I don't like where I think this might be going, and I hope if I'm loud and obnoxious enough, I won't have to hear it. Mum will change her mind and things will stay just as they are.

"Because he wants us to move in with him."

It's like when I get winded out on the field, except way worse. Some stupid guy I don't even know gets to upend my life. "Hell no."

"Watch your tongue. You haven't even met him yet. Give

him a chance. We're going to take it slowly, it's not like we're moving tomorrow, but someday in the near future. Just . . . meet him. I think you'll like him."

"You must be out of your mind. I don't want to have to change schools for this guy, and lose my friends, and my team. I don't want to like "Greg." I don't want another Dad, got it? I have one, and that's enough for me. Fuck."

"I know this is tough to take in all at once, but Jeremy, please. I want to live my life for me as well, you know?"

I have no answer to that. Even if I might understand her a little, I won't be able to get the words out around the anger and hurt balled in my throat.

Luckily, I'm saved by my phone ringing.

"It's Steven," I say, and stalk away from her. Before I pick up, I pause in the doorway and glare back at her. "Is that why you asked if I liked the table? You're already deciding what gets to move to the new house?"

Mum turns toward me. She crosses her arms and she looks stern, but there's something sad in her eyes that belies it. "I was rather thinking for you to use as a desk."

I shake my head and answer the phone, turning my back on Mum and facing a whole new set of problems.

Chapter Twenty-Two

LUKE

In Jack's carpentry workshop, we fix the table. Well, "we" is a stretch. I fix it, while Sam stares off into the distance. When I ask him for some nails, he hands me a hammer.

I pry the hammer gently from him and set it down on the workshop bench. Across from us is a couple assembling a clock. They argue and bitch with each other, but every second sentence is peppered with a kiss or three. I like and envy them at once.

Sam is staring at the hammer I set down, and blinking from it to my hands, and I want to know what he's thinking. I'm almost sure he's caught up about our kiss last night, because he's been acting strangely ever since I brought it up in his kitchen.

I wish he didn't want to leave it. Wish I'd never given him the option to pretend like it never happened.

I find some small nails and start hammering.

Maybe I need to give him another nudge.

Or maybe I just need to find my balls and tell him finally that I'm gay.

Jack chooses that moment to come around and check out our progress. He slaps our shoulders as he steps between us. "How's it going here?"

Sam jerks back to the here and now, and focuses on the table and then me. He has no idea how to answer the question, and I can't help but smile at him for it. To Jack, I say, "It's coming along. Might need to sand the edges here a bit, but then I'd say we're good. You managing to get anything done for your house? Or are we amateurs keeping you too busy?"

Jack gives a half-shrug, but he's hardly paying attention to me. He's turned most of his attention to Sam. "So *you're* him," he says.

Sam looks startled. "Huh?"

"Luke's neighbor. That's you."

"That's me."

"I've heard so many wonderful things about you."

I tense and Jack must feel it somehow, because he looks to me and gives me a reassuring wink, as if to say not to worry.

I worry anyway, and I'm gripping the hammer like a madman. I should probably put it down.

Sam has lit up at Jack's words though, and he throws me a smile. "Oh yeah? Is that right?" Then he turns to Jack. "But I have to confess, you're more of a mystery. He mentions your name when he talks about hanging out with the guys from work, but I only found out today you run a carpentry workshop."

For a second, a shadow of disappointment comes over Jack, but then he laughs and it's gone. "Well sometimes you do have to work hard to get this guy to . . . open up about things." Jack looks at me sharply.

Sam lets out a sweet-natured laugh and as he moves, his

earring glints from the lights above us. "Well that's true. But I have my ways. I could know all I ever want to know and more about you if I wanted to."

I shrug to Jack; the movement makes the hammer hit against the bench and I almost drop it. "Guess he just didn't *want* to know," I say, gripping it better.

Jack scowls, but his lips twitch. "Be careful, Luke. You don't want anyone to get hurt." He points to the hammer, but his gaze holds mine.

"Yeah," I say. With that, he leaves us.

But I'm distracted for the rest of the workshop.

When we're finished and the repaired table is fixed into the back of my truck, Sam slips his sunglasses on and snaps on his seatbelt. I turn the ignition and thread my way between the traffic to make a turn at the next intersection.

My hands tighten on the wheel as I look over at him. I have to tell him. I make the turn first and in the quieter street, I find a park. Once we've stopped, I clear my throat and begin. "There's something we need to talk about," I say, and Sam jerks his head toward me, swallowing hard.

Before I can continue, though, Sam says, "I know." He sighs.

"You know?" I say, frowning.

"I remember it, Luke." He blushes and looks out his window to the small park across the street.

Suddenly I understand what he's talking about. He's misunderstood me, and a part of me wants to correct him and get on with telling him the truth while I might have the courage, but a bigger part of me wants him to keep talking. I've been dying to know what's been going through his head, and now he's opening up to me.

So I nod. "Are you okay with it?"

He looks back at me and nods shyly as he pulls on his ear

with the ring in it. "Yeah, I mean . . . it . . . Wait. Are *you* okay with it?"

I want to laugh and cry out *Hell yeah!* but I temper myself and say, "Yeah, Sam, I am."

His smile comes with a breath of relief. "Good." He's wearing his sunglasses, but they're not dark enough for me not to see through them. I know he's looking at my lips right now, and when he blushes, my stomach dips, like it does driving around blind corners fringed by a deep gorge.

I want him to keep looking at me that way but, after a few seconds, he looks out the windshield. I run my hands over the bumpy rubber of the steering wheel. "So—"

My phone buzzes. Dammit. "Just a sec." I fish for the phone I placed on the dashboard. Sam finds it first and hands it to me.

It's Mum.

"Hey darling," she says. "Just ringing to let you know that I'll be down for that party end of next week. I'm very much looking forward to meeting your boyfriend."

My throat constricts and I glance at Sam. He's slipped his sunglasses to his head and is sifting through the crap in my glove box. I know he's looking for mints, and I open a small hatch in the console and pull one out for him. "Next week. You're here?"

"That's what I said, dear. I'm so excited about your sugges-tion. I can't wait to get out of this house for a bit."

Sam finally sees the mint I'm waving at him. He picks it from my hand, and even the gentle brush of his fingers echoes inside.

It takes me a second to focus on the call again.

". . . You have *no idea* how happy and relieved it makes me to know you have someone special in your life, Luke. Now," she pauses and there's the sound of the sliding door leading from the kitchen to the back veranda, "what should I bring? As a gift I mean. For the both of them. It's Sam and Jeremy, right?"

I can't tell her the truth about how things are. She worries too much. It stresses her, and she needs as little of that as possible right now. Also, Sam being in the car presents a little problem as well. "Mum, I trust you'll choose something nice. But I can't speak right now. Can I call you later?"

"Alright. You do that. Love you."

"You too."

Once I hang up, Sam grins at me, his cheek swollen with a mint. "Is your mum coming to the party?"

I nod and start the truck.

"Great. I can't wait to meet her."

And I really *can*.

~

I DROP SAM OFF AT HIS CAR AND THEN DRIVE BACK HOME. I GET there before he does and let myself into his place. I want to make us something to eat. It's a little early for dinner, but I'm already hungry.

I pull out some mince from the fridge. Maybe some Bolognese would be good. Or chili con carne—

The front door slams.

I jerk upright. Jeremy storms past the doorway and down the hall. A moment later his bedroom door shuts so hard the walls rattle.

I dump the mince on the bench and move to his room. Just before I get there, obnoxious metal grinds out from his stereo. I knock on his door and tentatively pop my head in.

Jeremy is quite dramatically flung out over his unmade bed, his head buried in sheets. He punches a fist against the mattress.

"Jeremy?" I ask, and step over a pile of discarded clothes

and a pillow to get to his stereo. I turn the volume down and Jeremy tenses, then slow rolls over. His eyes are rimmed with red.

"Hey," I say and sit at the foot of his bed. "What's up, Jeremy? Looks like you might be having a rough day."

"Nothing," he says, but his nose is blocked and the lie is obvious. "Just left my ball here." He shuffles to the edge of the bed. "I'll find it and be outta here."

He stands up and I reach out, grab his arm and gently coax him back to sitting down. "Sorry, boy, but I know something's up. And I want to make sure you're okay."

Jeremy sniffs, and nods, and then shakes his head. "I'm fine."

I wait for it, and then it happens. He sobs, his mouth pouting. For a moment I see the young Jeremy, the one I know so well. But before I can latch on to the familiar, the teenager is back. "It's just screwed up!"

"What is?"

"My mum," he mutters back, staring at his hand in his lap. "I mean, Dad's going bonkers, but *Mum* . . ."

"Okay," I say slowly, "what happened? If you talk about it, maybe I can help."

"You *can't*, Luke."

"Well, okay. But if . . . if . . . I mean," I scramble for the right words, but I feel lost. "You know you can come to me about anything, right? Anything. I'll be there and I'll do my best."

He shrugs. And then, after a pause, "So what do you do when your mum says she's got a fucking boyfriend? And that she wants you to meet him *and* be nice because he wants us to move in with him sometime."

I try to think of a suitable answer. I wish I had a right answer for Jeremy, but I don't. "This is a big change for you," I say. "It'll take some adjusting, sure . . . but maybe the guy is great. If he makes your mum happy, is that such a bad thing?"

Jeremy stares at his hands as I talk. Then he sniffs and shrugs. "I don't want another dad in my life."

I sigh. "What's bad about having more than two parents wanting to take care of you? You don't even know what this guy—"

"Greg," Jeremy supplies.

"You don't even know what Greg's like. What if he's awesome? Maybe he takes you out for trips and comes to your soccer games to cheer you on? Maybe he helps you with your homework when you're stuck, or helps get your mum to warm up to something you really want. I mean, it could be great."

"I don't want him telling me what to do and being more fucking important to my mum than I am."

I move so I can gently rest my hand on top of his head. "I know your mum and your dad. One thing I can tell you with absolute certainty is that you mean more to them than anyone else ever could. And rightly so."

Jeremy gives a half-laugh that makes his shoulder jerk, but his head remains bowed. "Yeah, but . . . I still don't want him in my life."

He pushes to his feet and shuffles to his desk. Keys rattle, and then he shoves them into his pocket. He grabs his ball and hugs it close. "I gotta go meet Steven again," he says, barely glancing at me before moving to the door.

"Want a ride?"

He shakes his head. "Nah. I'll walk. Maybe it'll help me think or something."

I want him to talk with me some more. Open up a little. Let me convince him that more than one dad wouldn't be so bad. But he's not going to listen. Standing stiffly, I nod. "Right. Well." I move to leave his room. "You know where you can find me."

I hear a muttered, "Yeah, glued to Dad's hip." I pause for a second, unsure quite how to respond, and decide on laughing it off and ignoring him.

When he's left, I sauté onions on the stove. I go over the conversation with him again and again, trying to figure out why it's making me feel so damn hollow.

I'm mulling over it, the mince browning nicely in the pan, when Sam is suddenly standing next to me.

I start. "Ah. There you are. You must have driven like a granny."

Sam drops a bag onto the bench and grins at me. "Nah, stopped somewhere first."

I want to pry some more, but first I have to tell him what happened with Jeremy. When I've finished, he lets out a slow breath. "So Carole told him." He sighs. "It's a tough change. I haven't wholly adjusted to it myself."

Sam leans back against the counter and looks into the distance.

"How do you mean?" I ask, my voice quiet and barely audible over the sizzling of the mince in the pan.

He shrugs. "It's nice having Jeremy just around the corner. What Carole and I have had the last ten years has worked. I'm going to miss being so close, having things this easy. I like the idea he can just come and go between us if he feels he needs to, you know? But if he moves up to the Heights . . ."

I lay a hand on his upper arm and rub lightly. I don't care if it's not the bro-gap we're meant to have. "We'll teach him to drive and get him a car, okay? Then he'll be able to do the same thing."

He smiles brightly for a moment, but then it fades. "Am I going to be stuck in the same crappy house forever? Maybe I need to move on too. Make a change . . ."

Then move in with me. It doesn't have to be this place. In fact, better it wasn't. But just stay with me.

He shakes his head suddenly. "Nah. So long as you're my neighbor, I'm not going anywhere."

I stir the mince harder.

Motioning toward the bag he'd dropped on his way in, I ask, "What's in there?"

Sam grins, but there's something sly about it too, and for whatever reason, he's blushing lightly. "Are you up for an all nighter?"

I look at him and raise a brow. "That depends. Does it involve dancing again?"

He barks out a laugh and slaps a hand on my shoulder. Then he inhales the scent rising from our dinner. "That smells great. Thanks for cooking."

He shuffles behind me to my other side and pulls out two glasses from the cupboard. Over his stretched arm, he winks at me, and it goes straight to my groin. "Promise there's no dancing involved." He takes the glasses and fills them with orange juice. "It does, however, involve my bed and a darkened room."

I almost drop the orange juice he hands me. It jerks and splashes over the rim onto my hand. I suck it up and pretend like I'm not thinking of us all over each other, fucking till dawn.

I quickly drain the juice and go back to stirring dinner. "What'll we be doing then?"

He moves back to his bag and draws out a few DVDs. "A *Star Wars* movie marathon."

"In your bed?" This is coming from Sam? When he isn't drunk?

He glances at me, blushing for a moment, and then tries to cover it with a shrug. "More comfy to watch for so long in bed than in the lounge." He looks at my lips and quickly away. "So, you up for it?"

I am a little too up for it, if anything. "Sure."

"Then it's settled. We eat, and then jump into bed."

I'm slumped against the headboard in Sam's bed, all my clothes still on and becoming more and more wrinkled. My jeans are cutting into me at the backs of my knees and at the hips after sitting here for the last three hours.

I look over at Sam, whose gaze is fixed on the TV. We'd both started out sitting on the furthest edges of the bed, but after the first movie, Sam had wriggled in closer to the center.

I'm doing all I can to love the feel of the bed's edge eating my ass cheek. I'm not about to fall off the bed, but I'm as close as I can get to it.

I'm trying to pay attention to the film, but who am I kidding? I'm too hyperaware of Sam and the fact we're in his bed, and that—oh God—he's just shrugged out of his jumper.

He's wearing a T-shirt under it, but still. We're in bed. He's stripping. My mind is wandering . . .

I force my gaze back to the screen. I don't know if I can handle a whole night of this.

When my ass cheek starts to go numb, I shift slightly.

Sam looks over at me, his profile washed in the greens and blues that come from the screen. He bites his lip and says hesitantly, softly, "Come closer, Luke. You're about to fall off the bed over there."

"Nah, I'm good," I say. But it's the wrong—or right?—thing to say because Sam reaches over and snags my arm, tugging me closer.

He looks bemused and draws a deep breath. "I'm not going to bite."

Oh, but I wish you would!

A glance over Sam, and the alarm clock on his side table

tells me it's close to midnight. "Maybe I should call it a night," I say. "I don't want to crash in your bed."

Sam's fingers trail off my arm, leaving behind a shiver. He turns back toward the TV. "Oh. Yeah, that's cool."

But I hear the disappointment in his voice. And I hate that. "I want to do the movie all-nighter with you," I say, trying to make it better. "It's just . . . you don't want me drooling on your pillow when I conk out . . ."

He laughs and looks back at me, more relaxed. With a shrug he says, "I don't mind. The movies are just . . . it's better doing it together, you know?"

"Yeah, yeah, you're right. It's just . . ."

He looks at me, biting his lip, and my fingers itch to grab him into an embrace and kiss him. "I'm not the most comfortable in my jeans," I say.

"So, um," Sam says, "take them off and hop under the covers."

There's something in the way his eyes light up when he suggests it that has me swallowing. Something is happening here, I'm just not entirely sure what it is, and what my role is supposed to be.

Uncertainly, I swivel my legs off the side of the bed and shimmy out of my jeans.

It's much more comfortable as I slide between Sam's sheets in only my boxers and T-shirt. When I glance over at Sam, he has his gaze toward the TV, but his fingers are clenched tightly on top of the duvet.

"I think I, um," he says, "maybe I'll do the same?" His voice rises at the end in a question, and I can't help but laugh at that.

"It's your bed. You're the boss."

He nods and shifts to the edge of the bed where I hear him undo his zip. The mattress moves as Sam lies back on the bed and raises his hips to slide out of his jeans. The move is so beautiful and erotic that I'm hard in three seconds flat. Shit.

I rearrange myself and the sheets so nothing is noticeable and glue my gaze to his wardrobe door like it's the most interesting thing I've ever freaking seen.

Every one of my senses is screaming to look back at him. To get closer. But somewhere in the back of my mind is a calm, collected voice that's telling me to be careful. That if I'm not, I'm going to end up hurting really bad.

I want to listen to that voice. I do listen to that voice. But . . . I'm not sure how long I'll be able to do it.

Chapter Twenty-Three

SAM

T his is why I'm still single.

I have no idea how to seduce anyone. I can't even seem to flirt with my best friend. I've been trying to all evening. A whole **5** hours of lingering looks and casual brushes—*and watching films together in my bed!* But it seems everything I say or do falls flat.

Okay, maybe I'm being a little unreasonable. It's not exactly going to be Luke's **1**st response to pick up on flirting from a *guy*. But I expected something, at least.

The thing is, I can't stop thinking about our kiss last night and wondering what it would be like . . . with a man.

I want to tell him I want to experiment.

But I can't seem to say the words. They're trapped behind this lump in my throat. The lump partly made up of excitement and nerves, and partly—*mostly*—made up of freaking out. Shit. I wanted to try having sex with a guy!

For something to cross off my list, I quickly add to that last thought.

But still.

I look over at Luke, who's puffing a pillow and stuffing it between his back and the headboard. I look at his lips and remember what he'd said. *We can definitely try it together.*

Not just we can try it.

We can *definitely* try it.

That has to mean he's as curious as me, right?

The question is: how do I take him up on his offer?

I'M NOT BOLD ENOUGH TO PHYSICALLY SHOW HIM WHAT I WANT until the sleepy haze of the next morning.

I don't remember falling asleep—or watching the last movie. I must have drifted off. I shift slightly as I open my eyes, and I feel the warm weight of an arm draped over my waist. Part of my T-shirt has ridden up, and Luke's arm is resting on my skin. I move closer into his embrace, feeling the slide of his skin against mine as I press my back and ass into Luke as subtly and sleepily as I can.

When nothing happens, I wiggle again.

Luke stirs, then I feel the sheets move as he lifts his head up.

Fear takes over, and I quickly shut my eyes.

"Are you . . . awake?" Luke says.

I squeeze my eyes shut tighter, and then I feel Luke's hand on my shoulder, pressing me down until my back is against the mattress.

"You *are* awake," he says, sounding surprised, and . . . awed.

I give myself away with a tight swallow. "No, I'm not," I say. "I'm really, really asleep."

His laugh rumbles through me, and he shoves one of my legs to the side. Before I know it, he's crawled on top of me. When his weight rests on me, I open my eyes.

Now it's my turn to be surprised. This is definitely crossing the bro lines in a major way.

He's staring down at me with a soft, amused, happy—and, er, sort of hot—look on his face. "You were rubbing against me," he says, and I feel my body burn with embarrassment, and I want to sink into the mattress. "Are you . . . are you curious?"

I bite my lip. "I just want to do something a little . . . taboo. If . . . I mean . . . we could experiment . . . you don't have to . . ." The words sound pathetic now that I'm saying them, and my head is telling me that maybe this whole idea is a bad one.

Unfortunately, I'd just gotten harder when Luke pressed his weight against me, and my cock is whispering to me that it is still very keen to, you know, *just try it out.*

I count to **3** seconds before Luke responds.

He has a guarded expression on his face, one I've seen **1000** times before when he's unsure of something. But then he closes his eyes, and there's a trace of a dimple shadowing his cheek. "Tell me what you want."

What I want. Vivid pictures of us flash through my mind and I feel a hot blush rise to my face. "I don't know what I want."

He nods and slowly pushes off me. I miss the warm weight of him once he's gone.

"But I do want to try it," I admit.

He throws an arm over his face and then makes a noise in between a laugh and a groan. "Shit. I can't. Can't."

I twist on my side. "Okay. That's cool. I know it's a bit out there. You don't have to be the one to try that taboo with me," I say.

He stills. Then after a long moment, "Are you saying you might try it with another guy?"

I shrug, but I know he can't see me, so I try to put it in words. "It's not like I'm any good when it comes to seducing people, so I don't know if I can even get another guy."

"Believe me," he says, pulling down his arm and staring at the ceiling, "you'll be able to."

"*You* barely picked up on my flirting and you know me, so I wager not, but anyway . . ."

He turns on his side and locks his gaze with mine. He opens his mouth to say something, and then closes it again. "I don't want anyone else to be the one to . . . taboo with you."

"You don't?"

He blinks and looks over me at the windows. "Some random guy," he says through his teeth, "might not treat you right. If . . . if you're gonna fool around. You should do it with someone you trust." He drops his gaze to my face. "We'll take it slow. You can decide any time if you don't want to go through with anything."

"Well," I say, blushing just talking about this. "I was thinking it might be better to just do it all and get it done with. I mean, it's gonna hurt and all that, so I don't want to draw it out too long."

This time Luke shifts onto his back and throws both his arms over his face. It's definitely a groan coming from him this time and he's shaking his head. "No," he finally says. "Absolutely not. If we . . . if I'm involved with this, then we're doing it right. And that means slowly."

I sit up on my elbows. "How slow are we talking here?" I want to get this done before I'm **30**. Which is in **2** weeks now.

He lowers his arms and stares at me. "As slow as I say." He leans toward me and his next words brush over the crook of my neck, and it goes right to my crotch. "And experimenting or not, we'll make sure we enjoy it too."

I blink hard for a couple of seconds. "That sounds . . ." I gulp. "Sounds good."

Chapter Twenty-Four

LUKE

Holy shit. What am I doing? What did I just agree to?

I swing myself off the bed, reaching for my jeans that are pooled on the floor. Sam shifts behind me, and I pause for a moment before glancing at him over my shoulder.

He's sitting there, his black hair mussed and T-shirt crinkled, half-smiling, half-frowning at the duvet on his lap. Almost thirty or not, he still looks so young to be a dad. Sometimes I wish for him that things had been different, that he'd had a chance to live more of his own life and figure out who he is.

If he had, maybe he'd have done all this experimenting already, and I wouldn't be sitting here chastising myself for agreeing to be his taboo thing. And I wouldn't be so excited about it either.

It's better to have and lose than never have at all, right?

At least this way, I'll know he's safe and he'll be taken care of. Because I will be careful, and considerate, and even though he won't know it, I'll be giving him more than sex—every time I touch him it will be with love.

What about afterwards? What about when he's finished and he doesn't love you back? I suppress my fears.

Sam looks up at me and I go back to putting my jeans on.

"We've got Jeremy's game today," I say, trying to distract myself from the impulse to spin around, leap on him, and drag my lips over every sweet inch of his body. "You'd better get your butt out of bed."

He looks a little disappointed, but he gets out of bed.

Things are a little tense between us as we prepare ourselves for Jeremy's game, like both our nerves are strung tight in anticipation of what's going to happen next.

I can hardly focus on driving and twice Sam's asked me to either speed up or slow down. I try rolling my shoulders to make myself relax, but nothing seems to be working.

At least Sam seems to be just as wound up. He keeps fidgeting with his seatbelt and humming under his breath.

When we get caught in a spot of traffic, I look over to find him watching me. He blinks quickly and then looks toward the radio. "Music?"

I nod and drum my thumbs on the steering wheel. "Sure."

Neither of us speak until we arrive at Kresley Intermediate. We get out of the car, and I come around the front, asking Sam to grab the balls.

Sam freezes. "I know I want to be wild," he says in hushed tones. "But not *that* wild. We're at a school."

What the . . .? And then I get it. I crack up so loud and so hard, it has Sam frowning. When I jerk my finger to the soccer balls and gear in the bed of the truck, he swears and reddens.

"Well," he says, chuckling at himself. "Guess it's clear where my mind's at."

And that's the moment it happens.

The moment I don't think.

I lean over and kiss him gently on the mouth. Just a short, soft kiss, before I reach into the truck and yank out the soccer balls.

It's only when I turn and take a few steps that it dawns on me what I've just done.

Yes, we agreed to experiment, but I'm pretty sure that didn't include chaste kisses during the in-between times.

I swallow the sudden nausea rising up my throat as I turn back to him.

Sam has a cute frown cutting his brow and two of his fingers are touching his lips. He looks so lost and confused, I want to gather him up and keep him tight in my arms until he feels sure of things again.

"Uh," he says, "is that part of the deal?"

"Well . . ." I drift off and shrug. I'm thankful we're here before anyone else and I've not made an even bigger fool of myself. "Do you want it to be?"

"I don't . . . know. Maybe it's better if it's only us that know we're fooling around? It might, you know, bring up too many questions. Though . . . maybe it might help Jeremy feel comfortable about coming out?" He answers himself by shaking his head. "But I think he'll just think it's too weird, Luke. Because it's *you*."

I'm nodding. Nodding way more than I should be, but I can't seem to stop. I know if I do, I won't be able to keep my eyes from tearing up. "Yeah, sure. I get it."

A van comes into the parking lot; one glance at it, and I know Carole is here with half of Jeremy's team.

Sam follows my gaze, turns around, and waves. I want to go up and say hello to everyone. I know I should. But I need some space for a few moments.

I hitch the bag of soccer balls and gear over my shoulder and make for the field to set up.

Shit. Shit. Shit.

I'm stupid for doing this. So Goddamn, out-of-my-mind stupid!

I try thinking of a way to pull out of this whole experiment thing, but then I remember that Sam will find someone else if I don't. And I can't stand the thought of him with any other guy but me.

I yank out a knot in the soccer nets. No effing way, *ever*. I'll just man the hell up and not let my feelings get the better of me.

"Oy, Luke!"

Jack strides across the field in his striped black-and-white ref's T-shirt. Mine is lying somewhere under the balls with my whistle.

"Jack." I incline my head and get back to setting up the goals.

He comes over and helps me. He must read my mood, because he doesn't say anything. At least, he doesn't until we've finished preparing the field and the two soccer teams are gathering at the sidelines.

"Should I even ask?" he says, his gaze lingering on Sam pacing the side of the field with his thumbs hitched in his pockets.

I let out a rough laugh. "Perhaps not. I'm a fool though, that much is true."

"Yeah," he agrees, coming over to me and clapping his hand on my back, "but you're a fool in love. It's forgivable."

I turn to Jack and his caring, soft gaze, and I wish I could love him back the way he once wanted me to. It would be so much easier having my feelings reciprocated. I clear the small lump in my throat. "Thanks, man."

He pulls a whistle from his pocket and loops the cord over his head. "No probs."

"And cheers for reffing."

"You owe me lunch sometime."

I grin as I dig for my ref shirt. "Sure thing."

"Now get your gear on, and let's get this game rolling."

THE GAME IS A CLOSE MATCH. BOTH TEAMS HAVE TALENT AND enough cockiness to power a stadium. Jeremy and Steven really show off their skills in the first half, but after a nasty tackle, Steven is thrown off his game.

At the break, I go over and draw him aside. "You're hurt, aren't you?"

He tries to hide it, but the pain echoes in his face as he walks.

"Is it a pull? Or did you twist something?"

Jeremy is looking over at us, frowning, and I think he knows as well as I do his friend is hurt. I don't care if it costs them the game, though, I have to take him off the field.

When I tell him so, he protests, but not for long.

"Crap, Mr. Luke. He pushed me, you saw it."

"Yeah, and he was yellow carded. But you can be sure Jack and I will be watching you all for any other offenses. You know I don't tolerate nastiness on the field. With that in mind, you make sure you tell Darryl to watch his mouth."

Simon from defense comes up to us. He's looking down at Steven's ankle. "Man, are you okay? Jeremy's mum has some ice packs, maybe you should put one on."

I notice the way Steven freezes at Simon's approach. "Um, yeah," Steven mumbles. "Okay."

Steven hobbles away toward Carole, who's smiling and beckoning him over. It strikes me as odd that Simon is the one offering to take some of his weight and get him over there, and Jeremy . . . doesn't.

Is it because Jeremy doesn't want to be too close in case he gives himself away? Or is there something else going on?

Jack calling me breaks my train of thought. "Shall we get back out there and get this game done?"

I check the time and nod. Pulling the whistle to my lips, I blow it to get the second half started. Then I grin at Jack. "Let's."

Chapter Twenty-Five

SAM

The 2nd half of the game is more intense. With Steven out of the game, Jeremy falters a few times. He lines something up, perfect to cut to his wingman, and then there's no one there. Or at least no one that can read his thoughts like his friend seems to be able to.

I'm excited and nervous as I watch the game, and it's not all to do with the game itself. For the 1st half, I kept getting distracted by Luke running. I've seen the guy run thousands of times before, but it's like I'm seeing him through a sex-filter or something, because now every move he makes is making me a little hot inside.

Doing the taboo—or just *thinking* about it—really seems to do it for me. I watch his corded leg muscles as they flex with each step, the way his T-shirt clings to his tight chest and stomach, the way the sweat glistens as it runs down his neck . . .

I wonder what he'll look like when we get naked together.

I wonder if he'll be turned on enough by *me*.

I wonder why the hell I can't think about much else but sex. *With another man.* Christ, I really must be having a mid-life crisis.

And then I think about that kiss back in the parking lot and I shiver. Those **2** seconds had been unexpected, and not something we should do again.

But . . . Luke's lips softly grazing over mine . . . well, yeah. It'd also made me warm inside. There was something sweet and touching about it that curled and purred nicely in my belly. It wasn't sexual at all, it was just . . . comforting. Like giving me a hug with his lips. And how many times before have I wanted to be close enough to give him a hug? To show him I'm happy he's around?

I bite my bottom lip as I watch Luke give **1** long blow to the whistle and serve a free kick to the Oriental Lions.

Why not have the kisses part of the taboo package for a couple of weeks? What harm could it do, really? I mean, if we kept it from Jeremy. Because I meant what I said about not wanting him to know. The boy is already going through big changes in his own life, and with his mum. He doesn't need to worry about whatever it is that I'm up to. Especially when it's only going to last **2** weeks and that's it.

Not to mention, Jeremy would probably freak out if he thought it wasn't just him that was gay but his dad too—

Not gay! Just . . . curious.

A female voice catches me off guard and I spin sharply to face Carole.

She raises her eyebrow and shakes her head. "Where were you off to in that head of yours?"

You don't want to know.

"You're blushing. My-my mohawk-head, this has to be good." She comes closer and touches my pierced ear. "He wasn't having me on then."

I shrug her off. "How's Jeremy feeling since you told him? Does he seem to be coming around?"

Carole sighs, and a breeze whips a wisp of her hair over her face. She pulls it back and tucks it behind her ear. "Let's just say I'm not his favorite at the moment." Her voice is tight, but she laughs anyway. "Between your . . . whatever you're going through, and my sudden news—I think we might be in the running for best parental fuckups of the year."

She folds her arms and watches as the Oriental Lions kick toward the open goal. The goalie pounces on it before it touches the line, though. We both let go of the breath we were holding. The game was at **0-0** and I hoped it'd stay that way until we scored.

When the ball is firmly safe, I look over at Carole. "How well did you take turning **30**? And just how well are you taking our son turning **15**?"

She gives a snort of laughter. "Oh God. I had a pajama party. All my girlfriends came around and we drank Mojitos till dawn. It was something I always wanted to do . . ." *as a teenager* goes unsaid, but I hear it anyway.

I slip an arm around her and hold her close to my side for a moment. Despite all that we've been through, she is still one of my closest friends. We could never have been lovers though; there was too much emotion and grief between us for that. But we were each other's best supporters. Especially in the beginning, when we wouldn't let our parents help.

"As for Jeremy turning fifteen . . ." Carole presses her lips together in thought for a moment. "I'm just so glad he won't follow in our footsteps."

I press a small kiss on her temple. "We have an awesome kid. I guess **2** wrongs *do* make a right."

We stay close to each other the rest of the game, cheering our side on until the time ends, and the extra time ends, and then it's down to penalty kicks. We're extra quiet, all of us, with our breath held.

Finally, the whistle goes off, declaring the winner.

3-2 to the Hutt Penguins.

It's madness on the field. Half the boys are sulking, but the other half are cheering wildly. Luke and Jack make the two teams line up and shake hands, but as soon as they're done, Jeremy and Darryl are high-fiving each other, and two other guys are piggybacking around the field, whooping. Simon rushes over to Steven, who's hobbling over to them, and yanks him into a hug that has them both toppling to the ground laughing. And the goalie is being hoisted up into the air and paraded.

I seek Luke out, and am startled to find he's looking over at me. I say goodbye to Carole, who slaps my ass in return, and thread my way through the chaos. "Hey ref, good game."

Jack chimes in over Luke's shoulder. "Thanks."

Luke rolls his eyes, and rubs the back of his arm over the sweat beaded at his brow.

A fresh breeze washes over us, bringing the smell of Luke's body closer, and suddenly I'm imagining the tanginess of it. Heat rushes up my neck, and it's getting worse with the curious way Luke is eyeing me. His lips turn up at the edges to make his dimples show—and God, but now I'm wondering what they'd feel like against the tip of my tongue.

Luke moves forward as if to pass me, then stops at my side, leaning in so his mouth is close to my ear. "Is your head still where I think it is?"

I blush some more. "Yeah. I can't seem to, ah, help it."

"Then don't." His voice tickles its way to my groin and makes it pay attention. I dig my hands in my pockets and answer the only way I can, with a nod.

He leaves me with a chuckle to pack up.

I wonder how he can be so confident, how he doesn't seem

bothered by what we're doing—*about* to do—in the slightest. I wish I were more like Luke, able to be so self-assured . . .

"Hey, Mum," Jeremy says in the distance. "We're going to Pizza Hut now, and then maybe to a movie or something."

Carole answers, "You'll be careful? And home by nine."

Jeremy nods before running off with barely a 'see ya.'

I shake my head. "God I hope he's smarter than I was at his age." My gaze finds and latches on to Luke again. *And smarter than I am right now.*

Chapter Twenty-Six

JEREMY

Pizza Hut is a riot. The Oriental Lions throw insults at us most of the time, but we give as good as we get.

Steven pinches all of the olives off my pizza and I take his jalapeños. On the outside, I think I'm doing a good job playing cool. But on the inside, I can't stop thinking about Mum and *moving*. I hate the thought of all this—everything I have here—being snatched away from me.

I stop eating and pick at my food. I told Steven all about it yesterday, so I know he knows what's really on my mind.

"I thought winning would help you get it off your mind," he says to me while chewing a fried mozzarella stick.

I shrug.

My phone buzzes, and I fish it out of my pocket and stare at a message from Suzy: *Nice win. Wanna come over and celebrate?*

Well now *that* could be a distraction that works.

I lean over to Steven and show him the text. "I know it's bros before hos, but give me the okay on this one."

He shakes his head. "You and your tiny dick can go and have fun. I'll be fine."

He doesn't need to tell me twice. I've barely left my chair and Simon is slipping into the free space. I wonder what's going on with those two as I head for Suzy's.

I forget about it when I'm knocking at her door.

I forget about it even more when Suzy drags me into her bedroom.

"I'm so glad we've got some more time to ourselves," she says, getting right to business. She presses herself against me, and I'm so glad Luke opened up the locker rooms for us to shower after the game.

"Yeah." My breath is coming out rough, and gets rougher still when she moves my hand to the skin below her skirt. "You have no idea the lengths I went through to secure us some more time together these holidays."

She laughs. "Oh really?"

I skate up her thigh slowly, because while I'm crazy horny right now, I'm also fucking nervous. I don't want to hurt her, and I need to give her time in case she wants to change her mind.

"Yeah, really. Steven let me pretend to be gay with him so we could get my parents off my back."

"He wasn't grossed out by that?"

I almost slip up. I almost say *Ah, no.* But some slither of good sense is still in me, because I rein it back in and nod. "Yeah, but, he's my best friend. He was just helping me out."

She shudders, but I'm not making much of it. I'm oblivious to anything other than the edge of her undies on the pads of my fingers and my aching major that is screaming for me to do more naughty things.

Suzy nudges my hand and lifts the side of her undies for me to wiggle my fingers in.

She's soft and wet and I can't move my fingers in any further because of the way her undies restrain my hand—but it doesn't matter, because the feel of her over my fingertips has just sent me over the edge.

I come in my pants. For a second it feels brilliant, and then I'm left spluttering and embarrassed.

Suzy doesn't seem to care. She looks proud she could get me to make such a mess in my pants. She giggles and kisses me again. "Maybe next time we can get a little further. I'll show you the bathroom."

When she shuts the bathroom door behind me, I look into the mirror and curse. But I'm also smiling, because wow. Not only have I had head, I've just touched a girl down there. And it was awesome.

And she was going to let me do that—and more—again! It's almost enough to make me not care about Mum and *Greg*.

Almost.

Chapter Twenty-Seven

LUKE

It starts out well in theory. Jeremy is at his mum's and we'll have both our places to ourselves. We also have the whole evening and night ahead of us—all the time in the world to settle in and take things nice and slowly.

Except, it all turns to custard when my truck gets a flat close to the Petone Foreshore. I have a spare and I can change it, but it's started raining outside and I'm pretty sure I lent my car jack to Sam, which means it's sitting in his Honda, a twenty minute drive from here.

"Least you got a parking spot," Sam says, finding something about all of this hilarious, while I think we've been cockblocked by God.

"The way I see it," I say, scanning the street, "is that it's a sign."

Sam stops laughing and shifts uncomfortably, biting the bottom lip I want to taste again. "Sign?"

"Yeah. Maybe we aren't just meant to jump in the sack cold turkey. Maybe we actually need to have the turkey first."

He blinks at me like I've gone crazy, and I love how thick and fast tenderness unfurls for him. I click open my seat belt and reach over to do his.

"Yeah," I add, "I remember you telling me something about never having been on a date before."

Sam drags his gaze from me to the restaurants lining the street. "I never went on a date as a teenager. I have been on a few—albeit, unsuccessful—ones as an adult."

"I know," I say, unable to stop a grin. "But since you're reenacting those lost years now, it fits that you get that lost date as well."

"We're two dudes."

"Semantics."

His hand moves to his crotch, and I don't fail to notice that he's aroused. "Actually, I think it's a little more than *semantics*."

"So what if we are two guys? Why not go on a date if we feel like it?" I lean over and rest a hand on his knee, I move it up as I speak, making him gasp as I press his straining cock through his jeans and rub. "Just as much as I can feel this, I want to take you on a date."

"Luke!" Sam's gaze flashes to mine and, along with confusion and apprehension, there's hunger in there. He blushes and it makes my cock throb. "You must *really* want to take me on a date."

I chuckle, lick my lips, and bring them close to his ear. "I want to make that list of yours as memorable as possible." So memorable, he'll want to go back there again and again. With me.

Gods, I'm the most stupid man alive.

This can only come back and bite me in the ass—and not in the good way.

But it's too late. It's happening now. So I tuck the concern in a dark, lonely corner of my mind, and focus on the fact that Sam wants to do this. That if I don't do it, some other guy might.

Never going to happen.

"Memorable, yes." Sam shifts, pushing against my hand, and I give him what he's asking for, stroking him through the taut material. I'm happy to go as far as he wants—needs—to with this, but after a minute, he clasps my hand still. "I'll come like this, you know. It's been that long." He lets out a shaky breath. "I wouldn't want to go on a date feeling like a dried prune, all shriveled and sticky."

As I laugh, he peels my hand off him and lowers it on my own hard-on with a wink. I like how open and playful Sam seems to be around all of this. It gives me a warm buzzy feeling, like I could smile without it ever fading.

"Okay then, let's have dinner and a glass of wine, and taxi home."

Sam looks out the window and hesitates. "I, um, I don't get paid until—"

I cut him off. "I was the one who suggested this date, so I'll pay. If you decide you like going on dates with me, you can pay for the next one. All right?"

He pauses. "The next one?" After a second, he cracks open his door and nods slightly. "Um, all right, then."

Chapter Twenty-Eight

SAM

Dinner was good. The two glasses of wine, better.
The kiss in the back of the taxi?

That's the best.

Luke starts it with a slow swipe of his wet lips over mine. I swallow once, then let him deepen his kiss. He plunges his tongue into my mouth, carefully twisting and twirling, teasing and tasting mine. Thrills shoot through me, equal measures of nervousness and neediness. I can't help but be aware of the taxi driver, though, and it makes me respond a little stiffly.

Luke holds my face, slowly moving one hand to thread it through my hair. With the tips of his fingers he brushes against the nape of my neck, and my skin prickles.

I forget the driver.

All I can see, smell, hear, taste, feel is this kiss, and the promise of something more liberating than I've felt yet.

Finally we arrive home. Luke tosses a few notes to the

driver, grips my hand firmly and slides me out of the car on his side.

We've barely spoken since jumping into the taxi, and we don't talk now either. I follow his lead into his place.

As he juggles the keys in one hand to open, I swallow harder and faster. What is our next move supposed to be?

I'm glad Luke seems to be taking charge of things. I like the comfort of not having to worry—he always has the ability to make me feel like that. Sometimes it's as if he can read my mind; he knows what I want, and he makes sure I get it.

Still, this is new for the both of us, and I want to help us fumble around with it too.

I look around the darkened front yard as if it would give me a clue how I should do that, but there's nothing.

I don't know what I should do exactly, but I'm just buzzed enough not to overthink things, and when Luke sits on the couch, I sink on his lap.

The hiss he gives tells me he's surprised at my legs coming around on either side of him, but the definite bulge in his pants says he's up for it as much as I am.

"Does this feel good?" I ask, bracing my hands on his shoulders and shifting my crotch against his, up and down.

He lets out an expletive and then grabs the back of my neck, hauling me in for a deep kiss. I love how easy it is to get him excited about this, and I chuckle in between his tiramisu-flavored kisses.

"What could possibly be funny right now?"

"You," I say. "I thought it'd be harder for us to get into the zone for this, but . . . maybe it's been as long for you as it has for me?"

I know he's been on dates and scored before. It's easy for me to tell, because he takes his truck and doesn't come back until the next day. "You know what I just realized?" I say, fumbling at the edge of his T-shirt and skimming my hands over his hard stomach. "You've never brought any of your dates home. Don't you like getting lucky in your own place?"

He rests his head on the back of the couch and looks at me, and it strikes me as a shy look, which makes my stomach flip. "I like it plenty enough."

I study my fingers rubbing the edge of his T-shirt. When my skin touches his stomach, it jerks slightly. "Then why—?"

"Just"—I look up. His eyes are tightly shut, crinkling the skin at the sides. His chest heaves as he takes a deep breath —"Just hadn't met anyone I want to bring back here."

I drop my grip on his T-shirt. I can see I've hit a sensitive spot. "You'll find someone," I say. Even as I hate the thought of having to give him up someday, I really do want him to be happy. "Just promise me I get to be best man."

He lifts his head and the tone of his voice makes me shiver. "You're always my best man, Sam."

His hands gently grip my sides and skate down until they're resting on my hips. He leans forward and tentatively touches his lips with mine. Pulling back a brief moment, he studies me and his face is unreadable. He nods as if answering a silent question.

Feather light he brings his mouth to mine again, catching the corner, and then his lips move across my light stubble to the back of my jaw, under my ear where I'm most sensitive.

I've never had anyone kiss me there before and it makes me gasp and shift closer against him. I feel tingly and light, as if I could float off him, and I can't handle it—

Luke reads my mind again. He firmly smoothes his hands over my hips to my ass and pushes me into him, bracing me there, keeping me grounded. My straining cock grates over Luke's, and even with the clothes between us, the touch is so intense I hum.

His lips continue to whisper down my neck, and I thread

my hands in Luke's hair, teasing it like he had when he put the dye in my hair.

Feeling has taken me over, and there's not much room for thinking about why this feels as good and as easy as it does, or why it's much more gentle and tender than I imagined it would be.

I'd thought we'd fail at this. I'd thought we'd laugh our way through all our "experiments," but it doesn't feel like there is a place for laughter here.

Luke nibbles his way to the neck of my T-shirt, leaving a wet trail that chills in the air. I shiver and draw myself as close as I can against him, slipping my hands up under his shirt to his chest.

When I find his nipple and tease it between my thumb and fingers, Luke moans, and his warm breath tunnels down my front. I like that this is as good for him as it is for me, and I do the same thing to his other nipple. This time he arches against me and murmurs something.

I want to keep playing and testing his responses, but the wine buzz is wearing off, and I'm becoming more . . . aware. I must have frozen, because Luke draws back to look me in the eye. "Are you okay? Do you want to stop?"

I shake my head. "I . . . not unless you do . . . it's just . . ."

"What?"

I look down at our laps, and then hurriedly away from our hard-ons. I know I'm blushing like a freaking virgin, and I'm self-deprecating enough to laugh. "I have no idea what I'm doing. I'm . . . starting to get a little nervous about what comes next."

Luke grasps my chin and turns my head to face him. He smiles warmly. "Nothing has to happen next. We can just make out like this. Two guys on the couch . . . that's pretty wild. Maybe that's enough?"

I nod, but it's not what I want. And I wonder why it isn't

enough. With no answers forthcoming, I shake off the thought. "This isn't freaking you out, right?"

"Actually, yeah, it is. A little bit."

I shift to move off him and give him the required bro-space again, but his hands move to my shoulders and hold me there.

"If it's freaking you out being with another guy," I say, "how is it you seem so sure of yourself?"

He sighs, lifting one of his hands off my shoulder to grind the heel of his palm against his forehead. "Trust me, I'm not. Sure of myself, that is."

"I don't want you to feel like you *have* to do this with me, Luke. It's my stupid list, not yours. You don't have to take part."

He runs his hands up and down my arms as he speaks. "If anyone, it should be me helping you with that list."

I sigh and slowly peel myself off him and flop next to him on the couch. My cock is still aching for release, but now I'm completely lost as how to continue. Even though I really want to. I glance at Luke's lap and at least it looks as if he's having a similar problem.

"Well, you certainly can't *hate* this."

I don't quite know how it happens, but one moment I'm sitting there, and the next, Luke is on top of me so that we're horizontal, my back to the sofa and our chests and crotches pressing together.

My breath comes sharply as I look at him. He touches my nose with his as he studies me a moment. "You want more, Sam," he says softly. "Yeah, I can see that. If you want me to take care of you, I will."

All I can do is nod.

Which is plenty answer enough. Luke kisses me hard and raw and I'm left breathless and arching against him.

"I'll make it memorable for you," he says, and pushes my T-shirt up, the backs of his fingers sliding up over my stomach to my chest. He looks up and smiles at me, and then he and his dimples disappear from view as he lowers his mouth to my nipple with the piercing, and swirls his hot tongue around it.

I clutch his back and wish I could angle myself to bury my face and smother my groans in his soft hair as he sucks and lightly tugs at the metal.

I'm thinking maybe I'll keep the nipple ring after all.

He nips at the skin around it, and sucks, and breathes. I rock my hips against his stomach. Then he trails kisses over my hairless chest to my other nipple, and I don't know which feels better, the flicking of his tongue as it hardens, or the cool air swirling around the nipple he left behind.

"I—I *like* it." I sound surprised, and I am.

Luke purrs deep in his chest. "Just *like* it?" he says against my skin as he peppers kisses slowly down my stomach.

"More like a **6** if we're scoring it," I say. More like a ***10***, actually, but I don't think I can say that to him.

He bites lightly around my bellybutton before sinking his tongue in there. "Fine, fine, a **7**," I say, and throw my head back as I strain simultaneously to get my stomach closer to him and to pull away.

Luke chuckles, and it's deep and masculine and it vibrates warmly over my treasure trail.

He hooks his thumbs into the waistband of my jeans and skims around the skin there, making me arch toward him. And somewhere I'm aware I should be embarrassed by this, but it's not enough to make me stop. Whatever's about to happen, I think—no, I damn well *know*—I want it.

Because I can then cross it off my list, I think to myself. *It's all about the list!*

"You know I'm a competitive guy," Luke says, running his tongue along the top edge of my boxers. "I expect at least a nine and a half by the end of this."

A **9.5**. God, what will that feel like? Can I even handle it?

Luke snaps the button of my jeans and unzips my fly. My cock springs free, hitting his nose, and before I can tense and worry, Luke breathes out deeply through the material against my shaft.

I shiver. No way I can handle an **8**, let alone a **9.5**.

His mouth closes around me and the material, and he hums. My cock throbs in response. He sucks through the material. The friction has me grabbing at the nearest cushion and clutching it tightly. I bring it to my face to cry into, and it smells of Luke, hearty like roasted chestnuts and a dash of sweat.

I breathe it in and hold my breath, letting it out in small increments in time to each of Luke's pulls on my cock.

Soon it's too warm with the cushion and I toss it off me.

"Raise your hips," Luke says, leaning forward to skim my nipple with his tongue again. I arch on reflex, and he uses it to draw my pants and boxers over the curve of my ass and then shimmies them to my knees.

I'm mumbling something, and I don't know what it is until Luke glances up at me and his dimples light up his face. "A nine, eh?"

More like a **19**, but whatever. I don't care about anything anymore, the least of all that it's a man that's giving me the best foreplay I've had in my life—

Luke's wet lips touch the naked head of my cock. He licks once around the top, lingering a moment on the slit, and I shudder out a breath as I push forward. His hands massage my ass as he slowly sinks his mouth around me.

I buck forward, unable to restrain myself. "Sorry," I manage, but Luke doesn't seem to hear it. That or he doesn't care. He sucks me, his cheeks hollowing, and he moves his mouth up and down so I'm dipping in and out of him—

I swear then. Loud and long. But *fuck!* I'm being reduced to a bundle of nerves and I don't think I can handle it much longer. I feel like I'm spiraling out of control like water from a garden sprinkler. I want to be reined back in, collected—

Again Luke reads me, somehow knowing I need him holding me tighter, gripping my ass with just enough bite to his fingers that I feel more together.

"I'm gonna come," I say, trying to withdraw from his lips, but Luke digs his fingernails into my skin, keeping me right where I am.

"Nine and a half! Nine and a half!" My head snaps back as I thrust into him one more time, my hands pulling Luke's hair as I come in **3, 4, 5** thick ropes into his mouth. He drinks it, milking my orgasm in a way I've never felt before.

He pulls away before I get too sensitive. I'm pushing myself into a sitting position. Luke meets my gaze and my eyes fall to his red, swollen lips. "You okay?" I ask.

His body shakes with a chuckle, and then he leans in so his face is barely an inch from mine. "Yes, I'm very okay. Can I kiss you?"

There's something about the request that niggles at me, but I nod. Our kiss is soft and careful, mostly because I'm afraid of bruising his lips any more than they might be already.

Out the corner of my eye, I see his hand fly to his hard cock. I pull out of the kiss, and stammer. "I guess, I have to . . . you know . . . return the favor."

I shift off the couch, pulling up my pants as I do. I drop to my knees between Luke's legs, but he stops me, resting a hand on my forehead before I can lean in to undo his pants.

"You don't have to do it just because you think you should. I don't care. I'm good."

I sit back on my haunches. I can't say I have any idea how to give anyone head, and his offer makes a part of me sigh with relief.

But there's this other, bigger, part of me that wants to see my friend get his release too. I want him to know just how amazing it feels to have someone bathing your cock with their tongue and sucking it deep into their mouth. Even if it is coming from a guy.

I just want to give him some pleasure.

He's always so generous with me and Jeremy, always keen to give, give, give to us, but when it comes to taking, he's way too reserved. He doesn't expect anything, and I wish he would sometimes. I wish he knew how much I want to be able to give *back*.

And I know it's only fooling around, and he deserves so much more from me than I can ever possibly give him, but at least I can give him *this*.

"I want you to take it," I say, lifting nervous hands to his zipper and pulling it down. "Please."

I hook my thumbs into the waistband of his pants and gently tug.

"Are you—"

"Yes, I'm sure. Lift up."

He arches enough for me to slide his pants and underwear down to his ankles.

I gulp as I stare at him. He's about the same size as I am, but his cock is thicker and has a dark, prominent vein running down the length of it. I have no idea how his **8** inches will fit in my mouth.

I rest my trembling hands on his thighs as I try to figure out the math. Slowly I inch my way up closer and closer. This is definitely wild of me. The tight knot of nerves and excitement inside tightens.

"If you—"

Luke is giving me another chance to back out, and I silence him with a stern scowl. It's my "dad" scowl, and it works wonders. He shuts up with a smile.

I wipe the smile off his face when, in a rush of confidence, I lean in and suck him into my mouth.

Luke hisses, but by the way his hips jerk, I know it's the good kind of hiss. He tastes warm and slightly salty with pre-come, and the skin of his shaft is silky under my lips. It's . . . different, but not bad. More eerie than anything.

I slide my mouth up and down him, tasting and swirling my tongue like Luke had. His hands come up to rest on the back of my head, but he drops them again and squeezes them into fists at his sides.

Twice he hits my gag reflex and I have to pull away, but soon I find a rhythm that works, and I use my hand at his base to add to the feeling.

He says my name and hearing it fall so wantonly off his lips makes me want to give him more somehow. With my free hand, I fish under his T-shirt for his nipple and roll it between my fingers, sucking as I do.

He moans, and stiffens. "Sam, I—"

I know what he's about to say, and I think of drawing off him, but I'm also curious to know what a man tastes like. I give him one last suck, and he shudders and comes thick into my mouth. I swallow on reflex, and like he did with me, I stay with him until he's done before pulling off.

"Bitter," I say. And not as bad as I maybe had expected. "Did it feel good for you?"

His eyes are hazy from lust and I sense something softer in there too. Fondness maybe. Instead of answering, he leans over and kisses me. It's soft and sweet, and now I get what niggled at me before. I've said I didn't want this. Said we shouldn't do these kisses.

But . . .

I think I might have been lying, because I do want them. The kisses just go with everything. They make it more intense somehow, and I like it. A lot.

Too much, maybe.

I like how they make my stomach flutter and my heart race.

I like how they make me feel like I am able to give Luke the same physical pleasure he's given me. But more than that, I like how comforted it makes me feel. Like I've done something right.

Luke pulls back and rests his forehead against mine. "It felt amazing, Sam."

"Hmm, yeah, after helping Jeremy with that math assignment, I never thought I'd like the word *sin* again." I laugh. "But it seems to have worked really, deliciously hard to redeem itself tonight."

Luke pulls back. "You don't really think two guys together is a sin, do you?"

I curse myself for my poor choice of words. How could I say such thoughtless things? How would Jeremy ever trust me enough to come out if he thinks I think like this? "I don't think it's wrong," I say hurriedly to Luke. "But it is . . . taboo, you know? No one really talks about it—it's sort of an off-limits subject. You can never know what someone's reaction is going to be, and that makes it hard for people to talk about and for guys to come out, you know?"

Luke nods and rests his forehead back against mine. Our breaths mingle a few moments longer, and then I have to move before my leg starts cramping. I straighten and stretch, and head for the bathroom, which somehow ends up a race between us to see who gets there first.

I win, but I suspect Luke let me win at the last moment.

Chapter Twenty-Nine

LUKE

I let him win.

How could I not? Sam doesn't know it, but he's just gifted me something precious—an intimate moment where I could give him such pleasure. Where I could see him open up in ways I've never seen before, completely coming undone under my touch.

I let out a shaky breath as I lean back against the wall outside the bathroom. It was the most erotic moment of my life.

Oh God, and then watching him, *feeling* him giving me that back—it was all my dreams at once, and for a few moments, my world was just the way it should be. We were living together and had just come home from a day at work, and we were taking the opportunity to get busy while Jeremy wasn't in the house.

My hand flies to my lips. They're tender, and when I brush the pad of my finger over them, I'm taken back to our kisses.

Sam said he didn't want in-between kisses, and while these weren't that, technically, since we were caught up in the "experimenting" moment of it all, they felt . . . different. They spoke of more than sex—of our friendship, of how much we care for one another.

They were loving, and not just from my side. Sam meant them too. I know it.

I'm smiling when he comes out of the bathroom. He reddens as he looks up at me, and then shrugs as if to get rid of the slight awkwardness. "It's free now," he says, his gaze dipping quickly over me before darting to some fleck on the wall beside me.

I push off the wall and move to the bathroom, pausing at his side on the way. "I hope it was memorable for you."

His gaze snaps to mine, and after a moment, his lips twitch into a grin. "Well, you know, it wasn't a ten, but—"

I hit his arm and he feigns being hurt. But he's doing a terrible job because he's laughing.

"It was interesting," he amends.

And I hate that word with a passion now.

"What about for you?" he asks. "Still feeling freaked out?"

I don't want to lie about this, don't want to reduce it to a joke. I meet his gaze squarely. "In some ways, yeah, I'm still freaked out."—*Because it's you. Because this is what I want for us for real, and you don't even know it*—"But it felt amazing being with you, Sam. I enjoyed it a lot." *More than you could possibly imagine.*

His grin falters and a small frown cuts into his brow. He nods once and shifts his weight to his other foot. Suddenly that fleck or whatever it is on my wall is extremely fascinating again.

I can't stand waiting for a reaction. I'm too afraid I won't like it, so I sweep past him and into the bathroom. Once the door is shut, I rest my forehead against the middle panel. How is it possible to feel such elation and such misery at once?

I give myself a hard laugh and clean up.

I expect Sam to have left when I'm done, so it surprises me to find him sitting on my couch, pressing the creases out of one of my cushions he has on his lap.

When he sees me, he lifts the cushion and tosses it over. I catch it and spin it between my hands.

"I think I'm gonna head home and crash," he says, pushing himself to his feet, but I know he has more to say than that, else he would have left already.

I wait for it, and then he crosses the room to me, stopping just over the border of the bro-gap. "Thank you, Luke. Not just for the fun on your couch. But the date too. And just . . . you said if anyone, it should be you to help me with my list . . ."

His lashes, cast low as he talks, lift and Sam's brown gaze is meshing with mine. "I like that. It fits."

He looks at me longer than he usually would, and I want to read into it, but then he glances away and steps back. "Right. Well I'm off to bed. I'll see you in the morning." He smirks at me. "Maybe you can help me design a tattoo."

He runs out of the house with me chasing him, telling him he'd better not do any such thing, and if he so much as even *thinks* about scarring his body again, I'll lock him up and throw away the key.

I know he's teasing me, though. And I'm glad for the way it breaks the leftover awkwardness between us.

When I go back inside, I get ready for bed. I take my laptop to bed with me, and put my thinking cap on for things Sam and I can do for this next week without Jeremy.

It doesn't take me long to figure out what—though it takes a few hours more to organize it.

When I'm done, I shut my laptop, slip it onto my bedside table, and pick up my phone.

It rings three times before he picks up.

"Luke?" he says, surprised to hear from me, by the sound of it.

"You in bed?"

"Yeah. Reading. Just about finished this last book."

"Good. Then catch some shuteye after."

"Shuteye?"

My grin widens, and I wonder if he hears the excitement in my voice. "Yeah, because you'll need your sleep. Tomorrow we have to get up early."

"To get your car fixed?"

Oh shit, I'd forgotten about that. But the truck could wait. "No, not that. Something a little more . . . spontaneous."

Chapter Thirty

JEREMY

I'm sitting in the kitchen, watching Mum struggle to whip pancake batter. It's quite the amusing sight. I offered to help, but she just waved me off, making it clear this is her fight.

I'm not complaining. I love pancakes, and as long as I get to help eat them, then everything's cool.

I lunge for the phone on the counter when it rings. I'm expecting it to be Steven.

I'm surprised when I hear Dad's voice coming down the line. And he sounds . . . well, *animated* is a kind way to put it. Not like a rabid squirrel on steroids, at all . . .

Mum swears at the electric beater when more batter spits at her.

I shake my head. Between my mum and my dad right now . . . it's like I'm being raised by animals.

I snigger. "What've you been taking, Dad?"

He pauses, and I never should've gone for the cheek,

because now his Dad-tone is back. "Is Carole there? I want to talk to her. I'm not going to be around for the week."

There's the distant sound of an intercom, and it sounds suspiciously like—"Where are you, exactly?" I walk over and peer into the bowl Mum's huffing over. I avoid the batter splotches and pat the flour off her arm as the rabid squirrel comes back.

"Airport. Luke's spontaneously organized a trip down south."

"He did what? Without me?"

Luke must be listening in to our conversation, because his voice suddenly tunnels down the line. "Do well at school next year, and you can come on our next trip."

Mum's looking up at me, mouthing *Who is it?*

Dad laughs down the line as I mouth back to mum. *Dad.* "Pass me on to your mum now."

"She's busy," I say.

"No she isn't," Mum says, wiping a splash of pancake batter off her cheek and snatching the phone out of my grip with remarkable speed and precision.

I slump to the table. I should probably set it, but I can't be bothered.

Mum murmurs and laughs, and after a word to Luke about making sure Dad gets back in one piece, hangs up. "Swimming with the sharks. Jesus. Your dad's finally gone bananas."

Not the phrase I'd use.

"He's gone batshit crazy, all right," I say, and stifle a grin as I remember how drunk Dad had been last week. I've kept that tidbit to myself, though. I can be the spawn of the devil sometimes, but I'm not all evil.

"So what's got you making pancakes, and on a Monday, no less?"

"I have the day off."

"Oh. Why?"

Mum fishes for something in the kitchen drawers, and finally comes up holding a ladle. "Here it is." She glances at me. "Set the table please?"

I peel myself of the chair and grab the spreads. Jam, peanut butter, and maple syrup.

"I wanted to spend at least one of your holiday days with you. And anyway, I worked overtime last Friday, so this isn't even using a holiday day."

When I grab the plates from the cupboard, Mum hums and says. "Three plates, Jeremy."

That's when I feel the prickle of my hairs at the back of my neck. "Three?" I say tightly. "Why's that?"

She looks at me firmly, and I know what's coming, I just don't want to hear it. "Greg's visiting. He'd like to meet you. He'll be here any—"

I shove the plates back in the cupboard. "Actually, I'm not hungry."

"Jeremy." Mum has that listen-to-me tone. It's one that usually makes me sit up and pay attention. But it's not working on me right now.

"You two have a nice morning together. I'm heading out."

"You'll stay here, Jeremy, and you'll mind your manners."

"I've told you, I don't want another Dad in my life. So Greg can just go screw himself."

"Watch your tongue—"

"You know what I don't understand? Why can't you just keep him for the weeks I'm not here? If the most important person in your life can take seeing you every other week, surely he can too."

My mum's voice breaks. "Oh, Jeremy, love . . ."

But I ignore whatever she's about to say. I blink back tears and run up to my room, snag my keys to Dad's along with my cell phone and charger, and then ignoring my mum's pleas, I leave, not even bothering to shut the door behind me.

Chapter Thirty-One

SAM

I n the late afternoon, Luke and I arrive at our destination in Stewart Island. It's a cute little bed-and-breakfast that this family owns. The entire trip here, including the flight, the drive, and the ferry ride, has left me speechless.

I mean, we've talked, grumbled, and laughed, but we've both avoided acknowledging what this trip means to me. I'll actually have a chance to cross everything off my *20s Must-Do List* before I turn **30**.

The owner of the bed-and-breakfast shows us to our room on the top floor. It has a homey cottagey feel to it with the exposed wood on the slanted ceiling, non-functional wooden shutters at the sides of the large windows, Kauri furniture, and patchwork quilts covering the two queen-sized beds.

"It's lovely," Luke says to her, flashing his winning smile. "And thank you for being able to put us up on such short notice."

The owner nods, flushed and happy, and leaves us to it, shutting the door behind her.

I drop my hurriedly-packed suitcase on the bed closest to the door and move to check out the en-suite bathroom. It's small, with only a shower, but it's clean and the décor fits the main room, with solid wooden cabinets and framed cross-stich pictures on the wall.

I feel Luke come up close behind me and peer over my shoulder into the room.

"This is really great," I say, watching Luke in the reflection of the mirror. He smiles, and it's large and soft, and I don't think he knows I can see it. I look away before he catches me staring.

When I turn around, he's stepped back a few steps. He's wearing shorts and a *Stay Calm and Suck It Up* T-shirt, and he looks like summer has kissed him.

"Yeah," he says, sliding his hands in his pockets and rocking back on his heels. "It's pretty damn neat."

I try and fail not to notice the way his T-shirt has ridden up on one side and a wedge of skin is showing at his side. I've been noticing a lot of small details about him all day. Like the small scar on the side of his neck that is slightly silvery in the light. Or the fact Luke has a few freckles on his ears. And the bluish-black bruise under one of his knees.

I want to ask about it, but I don't want to draw attention to the fact I've really been *looking* at him.

All of a sudden, I'm back to last night, to us on his couch. The memory of Luke's mouth around me has me choking on a breath. I'm not sure how many times I've choked like that today. **5**? **6**? **20**? A lot, anyway. But I just can't stop thinking about what we did together.

Each time the moment comes back to me, I repeat the mantra: *It was just experimenting. Fooling around.*

That's it.

Really.

He lifts his eyebrows questioningly, and I shake myself back into the moment. I exhale slowly, moving over to the windows. Sand and ocean views wink back at me.

"This must cost a fair bit," I say as I tilt the window open.

Luke is lifting his suitcase onto the bed and unzipping it. "Nothing for you to worry about."

I turn sharply, shaking my head. "Yes, Luke, it is. You can't expect me to take all this and not contribute."

Luke drops the flap of his suitcase and skirts around his bed and over to me. He's keeping a bro-distance between us, and I can't say why, but that bugs me. After what we got up to yesterday, I don't see why we can't at least be casual about the odd, friendly touches here and there.

Surely we're both secure enough in our sexuality to know hugging or leaning on each other doesn't mean anything.

"It's not what I want, and it's really not much. So don't worry," Luke says, his voice is firm and he's looking at me the same way he always does when he's putting his foot down. He won't take no for an answer.

"Okay," I say, going for a different tact, "then I'll pay for both of our dives tomorrow."

Luke shakes his head. "No, you won't, Sam. This trip is my birthday gift to you. Please just enjoy it."

"That's very"—I swallow, and for some reason my palms are getting sweaty. I rub them over my shorts—"very generous. Too generous, I think."

Luke shrugs that off. "Nah. You only turn thirty once. Next year it'll be back to basics."

"Shouting me dinner and a movie? That's not basics. I love that."

Luke's breath hitches and then he nods stiffly before quickly turning to his suitcase again.

I move to mine to unpack as well. The Bed and Breakfast is

such a contrast to my shabby house, and as I set my clothes into the dresser next to Luke's, I think one day I'd like to have a place as nice as this. Maybe **3** or even **4** bedrooms, **2** bathrooms, a garage . . . It doesn't have to have the knickknacks or quilts . . . but just . . . it'd be nice to graduate to something a little more mature.

"I'm out of battery," Luke murmurs, tossing his cell phone on the bed. "Crap. Didn't bring a charger, either."

He shakes his head and continues unpacking.

I can't help my gaze—and thoughts—wandering to Luke again. I chew on my bottom lip for a moment, and then I just brave up and ask what's been on my mind for a while now.

"Why do you do this for me?" I say it to Luke's back as he rummages to empty the rest of his suitcase. He stops, his back muscles tensing. He doesn't look around. I continue, "I don't just mean bringing me here to swim with the great whites." I fiddle with my zips, and slide my suitcase off and under the bed. "I mean, why are you so cool with me acting this crazy and, well, let's face it, *stupid?*"

I wince just thinking about how drunk I got last Friday. I slump on the bed, sitting, and facing the door.

"Because you need it," Luke says quietly and I feel the mattress bow as he sits on the other side of my bed. "Because you deserve some time-off."

"It won't be forever," I say, glancing back to the quilt between us. "I just need to get it out of my system."

Then I hope . . . I hope that maybe then I'll be a better Dad for Jeremy. One who can relate to him, and who doesn't feel those little inklings of jealousy.

The warm hand on my shoulder startles me and I jerk. Luke drops his hand and goes back to bro-distance. "So long as you don't get a tattoo, you have my support to just go with it."

I kick off my shoes, twist on the bed, and face him. "I want to clear something up. And this is nothing to do with us . . .

you know, fooling around. This is something over and above that."

Luke stiffens. "What's that?"

I reach over and punch him lightly on the arm. "This bro-distance thing we have—*had* going. It's shit. Sometimes I just want to bump arms, or give you a hug."

I'm blushing as I say it, but it needs to be said. And I'm glad it's finally out there in the open.

Luke breathes out with a small, relieved laugh, and suddenly, I'm being pulled into a hug. "You've never said a truer word."

I relax against him, and when I move away, my toes come against Luke's side. I wiggle them until he laughs and captures my feet. "Let me go!" I say.

"Nope. I think not." He squeezes harder, fingers biting into my skin in the same way he had last night. And suddenly my body is waking up in interest, and my cock is getting hard.

Because you're still curious. You haven't finished all the experimenting you want to do.

Yes. Experimenting.

Being wild.

Getting it out of my system.

That's all it is.

I hurriedly snap my foot from his grasp and roll off the bed. I fluster. "I, uh, how about we go for a swim?"

Luke frowns, but stands up and moves to the drawer. "Sure," he says, pulling out his wetsuit. "It's going to be cold though."

Good thing, too.

Chapter Thirty-Two

LUKE

Abolishing our unspoken bro-gap rule is the best and worst idea Sam's had.

The best because I've hated that rule with a passion for years now and it feels so good to not have to worry about freaking him out when I touch him.

The worst because all these little swipes and pinches he's been giving me while we're lying on towels, soaking up the sun is arousing me like no one's business.

It's a good thing I lay face down after our swim.

I'm really going to have to learn how to get a grip on myself, and fast.

"It feels strange being so far away from home," Sam says, rolling from his back to his side and propping his head up. "I can almost imagine that everything there, Jeremy being gay, Carole finding a man she wants to move in with, my dead-end café job and rundown house, that they are someone's else's issues. Not mine."

I fold my arms under my head to use as a pillow. "Sometimes a bit of distance is good. It can help make more sense of things. What would you tell that guy with all those issues?"

Sam hums. "I'd tell him . . ." He thinks for a moment, pinching sand between his fingers and letting it go. Breezes pick up the sand and scatter it over my back. "I'd tell him to seriously think about the future he wants and do something about getting it."

"What type of future does that guy want, do you think?"

"I don't know. I think . . . I think, secretly, he wants to go back and finish school too. I think he might want to go to Polytech and do a course in journalism or something."

My lips twitch into a smile. "Journalism, eh?"

He blushes and pinches my arm, his sandy fingers prickling against my skin. "Yeah, something like that, okay?"

I'm still half-hard, but I twist onto my side anyway. My swimming shorts are loose and they'll keep me covered enough. "If I could give that guy some advice? I'd say he should go for it. Take out loans if he has to and apply for government aid, but he should go for it."

Sam sits up suddenly, staring out toward the rolling ocean. "But can he do it while raising a teenager and making sure they have enough to live on?"

I sit up too, mirroring him. "Yeah, he can. Because he has his son's mother who'll help as much as she can, and because he has this amazing next-door neighbor, who'll do about anything for the two guys."

Sam's gaze pans to mine, and it's soft and . . . tender. He doesn't speak, just gives me a grateful smile, scoots closer, and wraps his arms around me.

We stay that way for just over a minute before Sam pulls away. "I, ah, I think I'm ready to go back, take a shower—I'm covered in sand in places you don't even want to know about."

He laughs as he stands and picks up his towel.

I do the same, slinging my towel around my neck.

We walk along the empty beach, planning all the things we can do on the island in the week that we're here. ". . . maybe even do part of the three day round hike in the bush——" I stop talking suddenly.

We've just walked past a large rock, and what I thought were seagulls squawking turns out to be two naked figures, fucking like there's no tomorrow. I can't see who's underneath, but the guy on top is bucking and grunting, his ass flexing.

Sam has stopped next to me and is gaping at them too. I swallow roughly as I feel Sam's hand clasp around mine. My cock certainly likes the idea of what it sees, and in combination with Sam's touch, it's quickly hardening.

Hurriedly, I move again, charging toward our bed-and-breakfast. Sam is right at my side, and when I glance at him, I can't fail to notice that he's gone especially quiet. There might be more of a bulge in his swim shorts too, but I could be imagining that.

Neither of us says anything about it. We continue talking through our plans for the upcoming days. My voice sounds a little husky though, and Sam seems to be chatting much faster than usual.

Back in our room, we grab our stuff for a shower. Sam goes first, and I stretch myself out over my bed as I wait, trying hard to concentrate my thoughts on, well, anything other than sex.

I'm not even remotely successful.

In a record two minutes, Sam is out of the bathroom with a towel around his waist and rivulets of water dripping from his hair to his torso. I move quickly when he walks out to hide any hint of my arousal, but the way Sam is staring at my middle, I don't think I was fast enough. "Free," he says and swallows.

I pick up my fresh towel. "We're on holiday, you know. You didn't have to have such a quick shower."

Sam blinks and moves to his bedside. "I, ah, yeah, I guess. But . . . I wanted to make sure you had some hot water left."

"Thanks, but next time I want you in that shower for at least fifteen minutes. *Indulge* in it."

Sam smirks at me as I move into the bathroom. "Indulge, eh? Yeah, yeah, I think I can do that."

There's a twinkle in his eye that I can't stop thinking about as I soap my body. My right hand is itching to take my hard-on and pump it until I come, but every time I touch myself, Sam's last look comes back to me.

It's only a sense I have, but I think . . . I think Sam wants to fool around some more.

After I'm finished and have dried myself, I step out into the main room. I halt at the sight before me.

My senses are right.

Sam is sprawled over his bed, his back to the ceiling. His towel is nowhere to be seen, and his head is angled toward me, watching me with that twinkle in his eyes.

"Do you want to know what it's like to be naked against a guy?" he says in a low, rough voice.

My cock is aching just looking at him stretched out, legs slightly spread, arms thrown onto either side on the bed. His fingers just curl at the edges of the mattress, and—

I need to be closer.

I loosen the knot of my towel and let it fall. His breath hitches and his fingers seem to squeeze against the bed.

"Do *you* want a guy against *you*?"

He swallows, and nods. "Yes," he says, and clears his throat. "I mean, you know, because I'm curious. Experimenting. Being wild. Getting it out of my system. *That's all.*"

I wish he'd left out the list of excuses. I know this is just curiosity for him, but I want to forget that for a moment. I want to imagine I'm moving over to him because he wants, *needs*, me to touch him and bring him slowly to release.

At the side of the bed, I pause, sweeping my gaze over him and drinking in his long, gently muscled body. He's still slightly damp from his shower and it glistens in the dim afternoon light streaming in from the window.

My cock throbs to be nearer and Sam's audible swallow suggests he wants that too. I touch the back of his ankle and draw a line up to the back of his knee. Sam breathes out heavily. "That feels good."

I trace back to his foot and lift it, this time rubbing it. "When was the last time you had a massage?"

"Never."

I stop. Never? "Then that should be on that list of yours too." I lower his foot. "Wait there a second."

A murmur follows me as I move into the bathroom. I rummage through my toiletry bag for the small bottle of coconut oil that's been in there since my birthday—a gift from my sister who makes soaps and massage oils.

I come back to Sam, whose eyes are laughing.

"What?" I ask.

"Um, nothing."

I press the cold bottle against his thigh. "Nothing?"

He chuckles, deep and throaty. "Okay, it's just, you walking around naked and hard like that. It's sort of bizarre and amusing. I mean, in all the years, Luke, I'd never imagined seeing you like this."

"And I never thought I'd be seeing *you* like *this*, either." Though it's true that I've *imagined* it.

"Touché. God I want your body."

His words make my cock jump and I shift to the base of the bed where he can't see me as I give myself a quick stroke.

"How is the weight training going?" I fumble to undo the

bottle and when it pops open, a splash of oil jumps out and lands on Sam's calf.

He twitches. "I don't seem to be as dedicated as you are to sport. But I'll keep at it. What have you got there? It smells like coconut."

I pour a little more liquid in the palm of my hand and place the bottle on the dresser behind me. Picking up Sam's foot, I begin to massage. He immediately moans and buries his face into the pillow. "It's massage oil," I say. "Trust me, after I'm done with you, you'll wonder what you've been missing out on for so long." I thread my fingers between each of his toes, making sure to touch every inch of his foot.

When I'm done with the first one, Sam let's out a forlorn whimper. "Nowhere near done yet," I reassure him, picking up his other foot and giving it the same treatment.

From there I move up, massaging his calves.

I've gone through a quarter of the massage oil when I slide myself between his legs and start on his thighs. His ass clenches every time I dig deep into the muscle and my cock responds with a twitch of its own. With the occasional tugs I give myself to keep from exploding as I work over him, my cock and balls are shiny and slippery with oil.

I massage his other thigh, all the way to the slight crease before Sam's ass curves. "You just tell me if I'm pressing too hard," I say, kneading and stroking his skin.

"No, I . . ." Sam's swallow is audible. "I like it when you're firm. It's . . . better."

I slide my hands, one on each of his thighs now, up and over his ass. He sucks in a breath, and I continue up his back. I'm leaning over him now, only inches separating our bodies.

"I'm going to straddle you," I tell him as I shift my legs to either side of his hips. "I can do your back better this way."

I rest most of my weight on my knees on either side of him. The patchwork quilt is rough in places where it's seamed together. The slight scratching feels good, though not anywhere near as good as Sam's warm, smooth hips under me. My balls rest on the top curve of his ass and a small bead of pre-cum is leaking from the tip of my straining cock.

I grab the bottle of oil I now have next to Sam on the bed, and tip a generous amount on his back.

The oily liquid rolls down his spine and he shivers under me. The feeling must be light and tickly, and I sense Sam wants me to swirl my hands in the liquid and put more pressure on him.

I lean my weight into it. He groans and his backside is arching slightly under me. "You're so good at this."

"I took a course back in the day."

I rub and squeeze his neck, holding him there. I dip down so my mouth is at his ear. My words skate over his cheek. "Has this been firm enough for you?"

He tries to nod, and then he clears he throat. His voice comes out a little parched. "Yes . . . I think so."

I close my eyes and breathe in the sweet coconut scent mixing with Sam, and his hair tickles the tip of my nose. I give in to my own needs then, burying my mouth into the crook at the base of his hairline, behind his ear. I kiss him there and then pull back, sitting up and scooting down his body until I'm sitting with my legs on either side of his thighs.

Using the remains of the oil from his back, I smooth my hands over his ass and massage. When the side of my hand dips into his crease, Sam hums and pushes back.

I'm hesitant to lift my hands off him as he writhes so openly under me, but I want more oil.

This time, I pour a trail of oil between Sam's ass cheeks. Tossing the bottle to the side, I slip one finger down his middle as I chase after the oil. Sam lifts his ass slightly. "Ten, ten, ten," he hums as I brush over his opening and to the base of his balls.

The tip of my cock brushes his ass cheek as Sam moves again. "Lie on me now, Luke. I want to feel all of your weight . . ."

I pepper kisses from the base of his spine to the top of his neck as I come down to rest on him. He's so warm and slick under my chest and I fight back a sigh to be feeling him like this at last. Arranging my cock gently so it rests between Sam's cheeks, I slide my hands firmly up his side and down each of his arms, slowly and firmly.

Sam's breathing comes heavier under my weight. I lace my fingers through the backs of his and squeeze. A soft, needy moan escapes him and Sam tightens his ass. It grips my cock, begging me to move, and I do, slow and languid. I rub my cock, sliding it over Sam's hole to tease but not penetrate.

It feels so good and *right* having Sam pressed so close to me, having him respond so passionately to my touch. I lightly bite his shoulder to stop myself from blurting out how much I love him.

I can't say the words, they're going to remain trapped on the tip of my tongue—but my body has no such restraint. Every thrust is careful and loving as it spells out how much Sam means to me.

I groan into his hair as Sam arches back trying to capture and suck my cock into his ass. And it's so tempting. The way he juts, the way his muscles try to grip my cock's head and pull it down where it needs to go.

I resist, but when Sam curves his ass again and the tip of my oiled cock meets his ring, I moan long and hard against his neck and push, just slightly, feeling the give and resistance.

Sam's head twists to mine as he tries to kiss me. His right hand slips out from under mine and fishes for himself, even as he thrusts his ass more toward me.

The ring of his hole pulses against my tip and oh God, I want inside of him. I want to give him what he's begging for, I want to sink myself into him and fill him up, and make love to him.

"No condom," I manage, still not strong enough to pull away. He grunts, and pushes back anyway, too lost in his lust to care.

But I care. I'm clean, I know it, and I trust Sam is too. That's not the issue. The issue is that I've never done it without a condom before, and I only ever want to when I'm in a steady, long-term relationship with someone. Someone who loves me back, and isn't just *curious*.

I stifle a sigh as I force my cock back from him. I crawl back. "Turn over, Sam."

He lets out a disappointed sound, but rolls over. His gaze is almost blackened with lust. *He likes this. He likes what you're doing to him.* And my heart pumps faster, more erratically.

Sam blinks up at me, sucking his bottom lip into his mouth. I rest my hands on either side of his shoulders and lower myself slowly on top of him again. Our cocks press together for a moment before sliding next to each other, and Sam's metal ring presses hard against my nipple.

I link my fingers with his again, arms outstretched, and look down at Sam. His eyes drift to my mouth, and I take it as a request and lock us together at the lips. I tighten my grip on his hands, bracing him so I can lightly thrust. "You're so . . ." *beautiful*—I want to finish. Instead I let it drift off, bucking a little harder.

He pants under me when I take one of my hands and wrap it around both of our cocks. Unoiled, his cock has the perfect friction against my slickened one. Each stroke of us together brings us closer and closer to the edge. But I'm holding off on falling over until Sam is there with me. I need us to do this together.

Sam moans softly, "Luke, I'm——"

My name so sensually falling off his lips adds to the sensations pounding through me. Everything in me tightens. I stroke us harder and faster and Sam trembles under me.

He stiffens and holds his breath, and I feel the first hit of his come against my lower stomach.

I gasp, balls drawing up harder as I pump once, twice more—

I dip my mouth and kiss him so I don't cry out his name as I slam into an orgasm. It rolls on and on and it's not until it ends I feel Sam's hands at my back, pressing me down against him.

I dip my head down to his neck and breathe out. Sam's lips brush against my ear. It's a small kiss, and my heart swells and I feel like crying. *Why can't this be more than fooling around for him?*

Oh please let it have been more. Even if only a little. Maybe, just maybe, he felt something more than physical pleasure.

Slowly, I pull myself off him, turning my back quickly in case he catches any hint of that hope in my eyes. I sit on the edge of his bed, staring at the bathroom door, waiting for . . . waiting for him to tell me this moment touched him too.

A hand brushes over my back, and the mattress dips as Sam sits too. Without looking back, I rest a hand on his knee. Suddenly I'm too nervous to hear what he'll say. "How about I get us something to clean up?"

Sam chuckles. "Yeah, it might be better if I take another shower. A longer one this time, I promise."

Suddenly arms are around my neck and Sam's front is pressed against my back. "That was . . . was . . ." He gently laughs and presses his face against my hair. His breath tunnels down my nape. I'm tightly strung, hanging on to his every word. "I don't even know."

Could that mean . . . could he possibly think—

My thoughts are interrupted as Sam continues, "I guess I could cross this one off my list over and over."

List.

List. List. List.

A tear slips from the corner of my eye and I discreetly swipe it away.

I can't do this anymore.

I gently shake Sam off and stand up, then reach for the towel I'd dropped earlier.

"Are you okay?" Sam asks, and I hear his feet hit the floor.

I shrug, keeping my back to him. "I, ah, yeah. I just . . ." I take a breath and let it rush out, "I don't think we should experiment anymore. I think we've done enough."

Sam stops shuffling toward me, and a thick silence stretches between us. I hear him swallow, and I wish I could trust myself to turn around and talk to him without falling apart.

When Sam speaks, he's hesitant and uncertain. "Was it not so good for you then?"

I drop my head back, staring up at the beams in the ceiling, and sigh. "It's not that." *God, no, far-far from it.* "I just . . . suddenly realized how much of a bad idea this is."

"Bad idea?"

"Yeah, bad idea."

There's a note of irritation in Sam's voice now. "I don't get you, Luke. If I recall, you're the one that first suggested we could try this together. Then you're, pun intended, lukewarm about it. I told you that you didn't have to fool around with me, but suddenly you're all there and willing again. And now it's a bad idea?" He sighs and it sounds like he's dropped back to the bed. "You could have just said no from the beginning. Now I feel like I've forced you to do something you never really wanted to do—"

I cut him off right there. "No! No, you didn't force me to do anything I didn't want to do. Believe me, I wanted both these times with you, and I—God—I *really* liked doing this with you. I just don't think we should do it again. That's all. I think we should go back to being friends." After a space I add, "Without the bro-gap, of course."

I risk glancing at him. He's sitting on the bed, head lowered, staring at my feet. His back heaves with a large breath, and then he nods. "Sure. I mean, of course. I hope this doesn't get weird between us." He looks up at me then, and his thick lashes seem a little wet. "We'll look back on this in a couple of years and laugh at ourselves. Promise me we will."

I look away again. I hope one day I will be able to see past the pain of this and laugh. But right now, that's hard for me to imagine. I head to the bathroom.

"When you get to my age," I say carefully, "I'm sure we'll have quite the laugh looking back at this *list* of yours." And with a wobbly smile I hope passes as sincere, I just shut the door.

Chapter Thirty-Three

SAM

I toss and turn all night, unable to catch more than a few lousy winks of sleep.

It was just experimenting. Just fooling around. Being wild. So who cares Luke doesn't want to keep doing it? That's fine. Just . . . fine. I get it.

I do.

It doesn't even matter.

It doesn't.

I twist on my other side, facing the door. But it doesn't help to take away the memory of Luke pressing his warm weight on mine, gently thrusting, the lingering kiss behind my ear—

Argggh. I need to sleep. Sleep it all off. Maybe when I wake up in the morning, I can forget about how much I . . .

I can just forget.

When the bathroom light comes on sometime around the

crack of dawn, I shove a pillow over my face and groan into it. Surely it can't be time to get up already?

Slowly pushing myself into a sitting position, I seek out my cell phone I placed next to my bed. **5:30** in the morning.

Why on earth was Luke up and showering already? I lie back down and listen to the sounds of him through the wall as he showers and clunks about once it's done.

When I hear him start to murmur, curiosity gets the better of me. I sneak out of bed and hover near the door. It's shut, but it's thin enough for me to hear him.

"Just take a deep breath," he says, rising bravado in his tone. "You can get through it. Nothing bad will happen."

I frown and press myself further up against the door. What is he talking about?

I find out soon enough, and when I do, my lips pull at the edges and my belly does a little flip.

"They're just *animals*. With sharp teeth. With killer sharp teeth—Jesus, Luke, just calm the fuck down, and suck it up. This is for Sam."

So . . . Luke is afraid of sharks . . .

I swallow a chuckle.

What in the world possessed him to take me shark-cage diving if he is so freaked out by them? I shake my head, close my eyes and breathe gently against the door. *Luke, Luke, Luke. What are you doing to me?*

I hear a shuffle, and leap back into my bed just before the door swings open. I close my eyes and pretend I'm sleeping.

Luke moves around in the semi-darkness, getting dressed as quietly as he can. I hear the sound of a pen scratching over a piece of paper. Then the air stirs around me when he comes closer.

It takes me everything not to open my eyes when I feel him lean over me to drop the note.

10 seconds later, the door to our room opens and shuts. As soon as I hear it, I spring forward and flick the light switch beside my bed.

I let out a shout, heart punching my chest. Luke is leaning against the door with his arms crossed. "What the . . ." I yelp. "You just scared the shit out of me!"

"So what was that about?" he says, pushing off from the door, shaking his head.

"What was *what* about?"

He stops at the side of my bed, a small smile twitching his lips. "I heard you, and just as I opened the door, I caught you leaping into your bed, and then *pretending* to sleep."

"So you trick me into thinking you've left the room?" I grasp the piece of paper he dropped next to me and scan it. *Yes, I'm scared of sharks. Yes, I know you overheard me. Yes, we are still going cage diving.*

"I pretended to leave the room yes. Just as you pretended to sleep."

I flop back onto the bed and laugh. "I don't even know why I did that." I look at him looking down at me, and I suddenly want to reach out and pull him down on top of me. I want his weight on mine, keeping me together as I figure out what this fluttering feeling in my gut is all about.

But he doesn't want to be close like that anymore.

I drag my eyes away from him. "We don't have to swim with the sharks, Luke. Just having this holiday is enough. I don't have to get everything on my list done."

Luke snorts. "Yes, you do. I know how much you want it, and it's okay." I try to interrupt, try to deny it, but Luke sees through me better than anyone else. And his next sentence wraps it up perfectly.

"I'm going to face my fear of sharks, just as, in time, you'll have to face your fear of turning thirty."

~

On board the *Taniwha 6* cage-diving vessel, our guide prepares the cages for us. There are four others hopping about in excitement, dressed in thick wetsuits, and I wonder if I have the same goofy grin on my face.

I move over to Luke, leaning against the side of the boat, frowning at the light swells of water. "It's freaking me out not seeing them, and knowing they're down there."

A fish splashes near the surface, and Luke skedaddles away from the railing to the center of the deck. After a quick glance to the startled passengers, he flushes and folds his arms as casually as possible. But there's a slight tremor in his cheek, and he shakes his head as he mutters. "Obviously no one else on this boat has ever seen Jaws."

There's a bench bolted onto the deck, and I grip Luke's elbow and draw him to it. Sitting, I press our sides together and nudge his upper arm with my shoulder. "We don't have to go down there. We can watch from here." Then more quietly, I add, "I don't want you to hate this."

I want to wrap my arms around Luke and offer him the comfort he's always offering me. But things are still somewhat awkward after last night. Nothing that has affected our day too much, but there's still a whisper of embarrassment hovering between us. Noticeable on my part, at least. I want to get over it quickly, but I'm not sure how.

Luke lets out a nervous laugh. "Oh, I'm certain I will quite loathe this. But I'm doing it anyway."

"I'll stay by your side the whole time we're under."

"You do that." He stands up and lets out a shriek, plunking himself back on the bench. I glance out in the direction he looked in. There are 2 sets of fins slicing through the water's surface. I swallow back a laugh.

And as simple as that, I cut through any lingering discomfort from last night and wrap an arm around him. "I think I'd better start now," I say.

He looks from my eyes, to my nose, to my lips. Something briefly warms his expression. I wish that look would stay, but not even a smile brings it back.

The guide beckons us over to him and the others.

"Ready?" I ask.

Luke shakes his head as he stands with me. "Nope." But he's already picking his way toward the cages. I follow him, and as the guide goes through the instructions once more, I let my gloved knuckles rest against Luke's at my side.

When we're finally submerged in the cool water, Luke finds my hand and grips it. He's not staring between the metal bars of the cage like everyone else, but looking at me. His goggles make his eyes appear larger, and there's no mistaking his fear. I squeeze his hand as I take a testing breath through the regulator connected to an air hose on deck.

I'm unsure which is greater: the anticipation of seeing a great white—or that growing sense there's something deeper and more unknown lurking inside me.

I think it's the latter, but like the water around us, it's murky. I settle on squeezing him once more, and then turn to look out of the cage.

The water has a greenish tinge to it, and clouds of fish swim past us. Then breaking though the murkiness, coming closer with its toothy smile, is a great white. I lose my breath. The massive twenty-foot shark moves with such power and beauty—it's simultaneously the most thrilling and terrifying experience of my life.

Luke's clutch on my hand tightens and I tear my gaze away from the shark to my friend, who's still not looking anywhere but at me.

I signal to him that I'm okay, that this whole thing is just . . . incredible, that I'm so unbelievably thankful for this moment, and for him sharing it with me. And I think he understands, too, as his grip lessens a fraction.

I tug him closer to my corner of the cage and he follows. With our gear, there's no smiling possible, but that's what I'm doing inside. Slowly, I take Luke's hand and curl it around a metal rod, then do the same with his other hand. Once he's holding on, I move, bracing him from behind, my arms wrapped around his chest.

When the next great shark appears to our right, Luke jerks. I press my body against his and I swear I can feel the pounding of his heart against my palm.

And it's this. Not the sharks—*this* that makes my pulse jump wildly, and exhilaration coil in my gut.

LUKE IS STILL SHUDDERING AS WE MAKE OUR WAY BACK TO THE bed-and-breakfast. "Never again, never again," he keeps muttering under his breath. "Those fuckers are even scarier up close."

"We're still alive," I say, winking at him as we trudge up the incline to our accommodation.

"Yeah, I dunno about that," Luke says. "I think a part of my manhood died back there. Fear mauled it half to death. With its very sharp, killer teeth."

"I loved it when you shrieked on the boat after seeing their fins. Wish I'd caught that on camera."

Luke growls at me and readjusts the shoulder strap of his bag with all our crap in it. "You just wait till I'm close to forty and see what shit I can put you through—"

My phone starts singing from Luke's bag. He unzips the side pocket where I have it stashed, and hands it to me. The screen flashes Carole's name. "It's Carole," I say to Luke, glancing up at him as I grip the phone harder.

Luke beckons me to pick it up. His expression is passive now and he grips the strap of the bag harder.

"Hey Carole," I answer the phone, "Is something up?"

A frustrated sigh tunnels down the line. "God, Sam, I don't know what to do with him right now."

"Okay, tell me what's happened."

Luke inches closer, leaning in to hear as much as possible. I angle the phone so we both can listen. Luke quickly meets my gaze in thanks.

"He refused to meet Greg yesterday morning, and he just left."

I tense. "He ran away?"

"Yes and no. He ran away from me, but he went to your place. I've tried ringing him and banging on the door, but he won't let me in. He's being stubborn about this, and he refuses to come out. I—I had to leave him there in the end. I thought if I gave him the day and night to cool down, he'd come back today." Carole speaks faster and faster toward the end, and I hear the distinctive sound of a sniff. "But he's still not listening to me. I sent him a text asking for us to talk about it, and he doesn't even reply."

I don't know when it happened, but my hand is gripping Luke's arm and I'm bracing myself against him. "All right Carole, it's okay. It's going to be fine." I sound calmer and more in control than I feel. My expression must give me away, because Luke nudges even closer, drawing his other arm around me into a loose hug. "I'll give Jeremy a ring and talk to him. We'll sort this out, okay?"

"Maybe he's right," Carole says. "Maybe another man in my life is too much for him—"

Luke cut her off, speaking into the phone. "Listen to me, Carole, if you find someone that makes you happy, you embrace that. If Jeremy can't see past himself, can't see that Greg makes you happy, then he's still got a lot of growing up to do. Don't let him win this one. This is a fight you'll have to stand up for."

I tilt the phone toward my mouth. "Exactly what he said. I'm going to hang up now, but I'll call you back once we've talked to Jeremy."

Luke steps back. "Let's get to the bed-and-breakfast and you can call him from there."

I think about what I'm going to say, but I'm still unsure when I sit on my bed and dial home.

Jeremy doesn't pick up the landline—to be expected, I guess. I try his cell. After a few rings, Jeremy's groggy voice hits my ear. "Yeah, what's up?"

"Pretty sure you know exactly what's up, boy."

He sighs. "Mum's talked to you, huh?"

The bed dips next to me as Luke sits down. "Come on, Jeremy, what's this all about? Your mum is worried about you."

"Actually," Jeremy says with a snort, "she's more worried about me meeting *Greg.*"

I shake my head. This is exactly the sort of behavior I don't know how to handle. I find it impossible to tread the delicate line between sympathy for Jeremy going through a tough change, and firmness against his poor attitude. I take a breath. "Jeremy, that's not true—"

"Sorry, Dad. I just can't talk about it, okay?"

"You're going to have to face things sooner or later—"

"Then I opt for later. Much, much later. Like when I'm eighteen and have left for uni."

I grit my teeth in irritation. Dammit, he can't be reasoned with. Especially not over the phone. "Look, I care about you, son. I don't want you upset and alone in the house."

"I'm almost fifteen. I can take care of myself. I know how to open a can of baked beans. Anyway, Steven came over yesterday and we played video games. Trust me, I'm finding ways to distract myself."

I try to block out the sudden mental images that have come to mind. I just hope they're being safe. I bow my head in a moment of panic—because jeez, just yesterday I was reminded how hard it sometimes was to keep a clear head in these situations. My hand grows slippery against the phone, and I swap hands and hold it against my other ear. "Distracting yourself is not dealing with the issue, son."

"I don't freaking want to deal with it, okay! Jesus."

Jeremy disconnects.

"Fuck," I say, tossing the phone on the bed between Luke and I. "I don't think I got through to him."

Luke lets out a long breath, then shifts off the bed and pulls out my suitcase from under the bed. "I'd give him a ring myself if I had any battery, but I don't know how much that'd help." He settles my case on the bed next to me and unzips. "There's only one thing we can do then."

I push off the bed and move to the dresser to start packing. "I'm sorry this cuts our trip short," I say, stuffing my clothes and shoes into my suitcase, glancing at Luke who's doing the same. "But, thank you. For getting it. For doing this for me. . . . You can stay here if you want. I can go on my own . . ."

Luke's glare has me swallowing the rest of my offer.

"I'm coming."

Thank God. "Okay."

Chapter Thirty-Four

JEREMY

It's the second night I'm staying at Dad's. Mum seems to have given up trying to get me to come home, which is fine. It's good for me.

Yeah. While she's cuddling up to *Greg*, I can enjoy having Suzy over.

I look at her sitting on my bed, laughing at the shit strewn about my room. "And I thought my room was a sty."

I can't joke back though—my belly feels like it's being juiced. Tonight, well . . . maybe tonight's *the night*.

I want it.

I really do.

And not just because I want a distraction.

Not just because I know my mum will hate me doing this . . .

"Come here, you," Suzy says provocatively, licking her finger before curling it at me to come closer.

I stumble over the comics I'd been reading earlier, catching myself just before toppling onto the bed.

I'd better click into suave gear. "Suzy, Suzy, Suzy," I say shaking my head as I climb onto her, knees on either side of her lap. "You look beautiful tonight."

She grins, cups my cheeks and kisses me. "I know," she says. "You're not half-bad yourself." Her fingers find the edge of my T-shirt. "Maybe you should take this off."

Off goes my T-shirt, then my jeans. But I'm not stripping my boxers until things have evened up. Also, I'm still too nervous to get a stiffy. I need some more inspiration.

My phone buzzes on my desk; I glance at it, and seeing "Mum" on the screen, I swallow and ignore it.

When I turn back to Suzy, she's just in her skirt and purple bra.

Normally, I'd have been lost at such a sight, but I can't seem to throw this uneasy feeling in my gut. Maybe touching will be more distracting . . .

We start by kissing, and soon she's pinning me to the bed as she makes out with me, her length rubbing against mine. Yep, touching works wonders. I've practically left all thoughts in my head, and am focusing on the thoughts of another *head* entirely.

I'm glad I stashed the condoms under my pillow, within easy reach.

My hands wander up the backs of Suzy's thighs and I push her skirt up as they do. "Are you even a little bit scared?" I ask her.

She blinks and shrugs. "A little."

I drop my hands and reach for her face to pull her in for a kiss. "Me too. A little. We, ah, I mean, we don't have to—"

The feeling of cool air suddenly swoops over me and I tense. I can't see, but I have a feeling my door was just shoved open. The way Suzy is draped over me doesn't look salvageable.

"Shit," she says, wincing. "Guess now we *can't*."

That's all the brace I get before Luke's voice booms, sending a shudder of guilt through me that makes me hurry to push Suzy away. Not that she needed much help. She was flying off me.

"*Gay, eh?*"

Fuck.

Chapter Thirty-Five

LUKE

In a single moment, everything clicks. I understand why the Steven-Jeremy thing felt off to me and why I could never get a feel for Jeremy being gay. Hell, it even makes disturbing sense why the kid was glowing after the movie night with his "friend" last Friday.

"This whole thing. The whole thing was a ruse."

My voice is loud, and Sam must have heard the edge of anger in it charging down the hall. I'd suggested for him to let me try and speak with Jeremy first, thinking that maybe he'd open up to the friend-neighbor. But somehow, I'm thinking the "Greg" conversation is going to be put on hold.

Sam's presence slides next to mine. I still have my gaze glued to Jeremy. Suzy is shoving on her top, and it's enough of a picture for Sam to guess what's going on.

"Jeremy?" Sam says, in that hard, fatherly tone of his.

"Tell him, Jeremy," I say, folding my arms and stepping to

the side when Suzy makes a hasty retreat. "Tell us both about how you pulled the wool over our eyes."

Jeremy is ducking into a T-shirt he'd snagged from the floor. "I don't know what the hell you're talking about."

"Of course you do! Don't try to deny it. I wasn't born yesterday. You wanted us to think you were gay. I'm guessing you hoped you could get away with more time alone with the girls?"

Sam breathes out a "shit" under his breath. And I know he's beating himself up inside for not seeing through all this. "Is that true?"

"I never said I was gay," Jeremy mumbled, but his cheeks are red and he can't look at us. He's lying.

I shake my head slowly. "You didn't, did you. But you *implied* it. You let us believe it."

"You can't prove that!" Jeremy snaps.

I take two steps into his room. The bed separates us, and I stare him down. "Your mum caught you kissing Steven, I hardly think you two bumped lips accidentally. You played us all, kid. Just admit it."

Jeremy stutters, and Sam sighs. "Jesus, Jeremy. Why?"

The kid looks to his Dad and then to the floor.

"Answer us," I say firmly.

Jeremy snaps his head up and glares at me, his hands balled at his sides. "I don't have to answer anything to *you*."

Sam charges around the bed to his son and grabs his arm, twisting the boy to face him. "You don't speak to Luke like that. Ever. You hear me, boy?"

"Why should I tell him anything?" To me he mutters, "You're not my fucking dad."

The force of his words reaches inside me, squeezing, tearing, pulling. I don't even realize it as I lean forward and yell at him. "We don't share the same blood. So what? You're my son, too, Jeremy. You're *my* son, too. Don't say you don't understand that."

Suddenly the words catch up with me, along with realization of what I've admitted. Jeremy glances to the foot of his bed, Adam's apple jutting as he swallows.

I stumble back a step, my anger at Jeremy for deceiving us drowning into something else. My gaze flies to Sam's, and he's staring at me like he's been suddenly winded. He blinks from me to Jeremy, his hand sliding from his son's arm.

That's the last thing I see before turning and leaving the room.

I walk out of their house, over the yard and up my driveway. Opening the truck, I pull out my suitcase, and move it inside. I dump it in my bedroom, and go into the kitchen. A glass in hand, I fill it with water, and drink.

When it's empty, I lean back against the kitchen counter and stare at the rim.

My grip tightens on the base of the glass. A deep breath shudders out of me.

I slam the glass into the sink and brace a hand against the cupboard above. Soon, I'm banging my palm against it over and over until I can't feel my hand anymore.

Chapter Thirty-Six

SAM

I'm torn between needing to deal with Jeremy and wanting to chase after Luke. I rock back on my heels, and sit on the end of my son's bed. I clasp my hands together, resting my elbows against my knees.

"Okay, Jeremy, unless you want to be grounded for the rest of your teenage life, I'd suggest you tell me the truth."

Jeremy backs up to his windowsill and perches on it and the closed curtains. "Does that mean I won't get grounded if I spill?"

I shake my head. "You're smarter than that. But dragging this out longer than necessary will make things worse for you." I look over at him, fidgeting with the edge of the curtains at his sides. "Why lie about your sexuality?"

It takes a moment, and then he speaks. "I like Suzy and I wanted to spend more time with her over the summer."

"So why didn't you just tell us that?"

"Come on, Dad. You and Mum are so worried I'm going to repeat the same mistake you guys made and ruin my life— you'd never let me have a girlfriend."

"There would be some rules, yes—"

"*Some* rules? Have you met Mum? If I'd said I had a girl-friend, I'm pretty sure she would have had me under a lock-down. I wouldn't be allowed out without a chaperone."

"Look, your mum and I know what it's like. We've been in the same situation. Our parents didn't want us to date anyone. We were too young and so on. What happened? Your mum and I snuck out together one night, and long story short, nine months later you were born."

I unclasp my hands and rub them over my knees. "We are not naive enough not to know if you want to go out there and have sex, you will. So you can be sure both your Mum and I see no point in telling you not to date Suzy. We'd rather know who you are with so we can be supportive and make sure you're being safe. That's why we go crazy on the sex talks and the . . . Golden Condom Rule."

I shift on the bed, wishing I could pull Jeremy over and tuck him against my side as I used to when he was young and innocent. "Just give us a chance," I continue. "We only want the best for you. We worry about you. Constantly. That's our job. None of us—and this includes Luke—none of us want to see you get stuck in life because of a stupid decision." I close my eyes and sigh. "We need you to be honest with us, okay? We need you to trust us. And we need to be able to trust you, as well."

Jeremy's head is bowed and his shoulders are slumped. "What's going to happen now?"

"I think the first step is you going back to your mum's and telling her the truth."

He stiffens and mutters. "I don't want to go back there."

I rub my palm over my forehead and thread my fingers through my hair. "Because of Greg?"

He shrugs.

I push off the bed and move over to him, resting a hand on his shoulder. "I'm sorry this is hard for you, Jeremy, but you're going to have to suck it up and learn to live with it. Your mum has met someone that makes her happy. You want her to be happy, don't you?"

He turns his head away, but not before I catch his glistening eyes. I sigh and rub his hair fondly. "We love you, Jeremy. You come **1**st, you always will. But let your mum have a close **2**nd, okay? Please?"

His voice croaks. "I already do with you and Luke. Can't that be enough?"

I suck in a surprised breath. "What?"

"You heard me, Dad. I come first for you, but Luke is your very close second—sometimes I wonder if he's second at all."

"What are you on about—?"

"You were so sad when he left. I heard you crying the night he flew out."

I swallow. He'd heard that?

"I see things too."

I'm unable to move, my hand frozen in place on Jeremy's shoulder. "See *what*, exactly?"

Jeremy swings his gaze to me, and his bottom lip is trembling. He blinks and says quietly, with a dismissive shrug, "How happy you are when you're with him."

"Sure I'm happy," I say carefully. "He's my friend."

"Let me put it differently. *You light up like a freaking lighthouse when he comes into the room.*" Silence cradles us for a few beats. Then he adds, "Luke does too."

Jeremy shifts slightly, so my hand skates off him. "You know he pays for heaps of stuff for you and pretends it doesn't cost him anything—or little? Last year that soccer camp I went to? It wasn't free, but I knew neither you nor Mum could afford to let me go. I was so upset about it. Luke found out what was wrong and the next day at school my coach tells me my spot has been secured and is all paid for."

"H-he did that?"

"Tip of the iceberg, Dad. Every week when he rang from Auckland, he always asked me how you were holding up. He always sounded so sad he wasn't here with you."

"Us." I croak. "He missed being here with *us*."

Jeremy shrugs. "Yeah, but you're his number one."

"He just called you his son," I say through the tightness in my throat.

He sniffs and wipes his nose on the shoulder of his T-shirt. "I know. So if I'm like a son to him, what does that make you?"

"I—I . . ." I stammer, lost for words, until Jeremy's lip quivers again. "Hey, come here." I wrap him into a hug. He's rigid at first, but soon his arms come around me and he molds against my chest. Hot tears leak into my shirt. I kiss the top of his head. "You're my number **1**, Jeremy, and Luke knows that. He wouldn't want it any differently. That goes for your mum too."

"I don't want to move. I don't want to change schools. I don't want to lose my friends or my team."

"See? *That's* the discussion you need to have with your mum. She's not trying to take everything away from you, okay? She just wants you to give her this."

He pulls back, snatching the tears rolling down his cheeks and flinging them away. "I . . . guess I should head back to her place, huh."

"Yeah." He slides off the windowsill and skirts around me, picking up his stuff.

"Jeremy?" I say as he zips up a backpack.

"Yeah?"

"Your phone, please."

Reluctantly he pulls the phone from the front pocket and hands it to me. "Being grounded is going to suck, isn't it?"

~

"IF I'M LIKE A SON TO HIM, WHAT DOES THAT MAKE YOU?"

I know I have to speak with Luke, but I'm not sure I can form any coherent sentence.

I pace my dining room area, running my fingers over the repaired table at each pass. I glance out the window toward his place. I can't see much in the dark save for his lit front windows.

"Just get over there," I say to myself and push myself to the shelf where I have a set of his keys.

What am I nervous about anyway? So what Jeremy sees that we're close? We've been friends for over seven years. It's nothing new.

My stomach flips and a fizzy feeling rushes through my veins. I try tamping it down with a hard swallow, but it won't let up.

I don't bother with shoes, and the cool ground on the soles of my feet helps to keep me steady as I walk over to Luke's.

I knock lightly on his door before inserting the house key and letting myself in like I've done a thousand-and-one times before. Except . . . except this time it feels different. This time all I can think of is the trust Luke has to let me come into his place whenever Jeremy or I feel like it.

We've always had our houses open to each other, though. Friends do that.

Before I turn right to go into the lounge, where I know Luke will be lying on his couch, staring up at the ceiling, I glance into the kitchen. As I do, I see the hundreds of meals we've made in there together, and the hundreds of laughs and hours of drama we've shared.

So you know his kitchen as intimately as your own, and vice versa—it always made sense to eat together.

I inch toward the lounge and pause in the doorway. I can see the back of the couch from here. I know Luke is on it because his feet are sticking off the edge.

I also know because he's murmuring on the phone. His voice sounds heavy and tired. "No, Mum, I didn't get your messages. My phone didn't have any battery, and I was down South."

Down South, taking me to see the sharks.

Suddenly, I need to find out what he actually paid for us to do this. I know it can't have been cheap. The flights alone . . .

I tiptoe out into the hall and go into the bathroom. Pulling out my phone, I type in the name of the diving company.

When I see the cost, I blanch. **600** dollars per person?

I keep staring at the number, trying to make sense of it and come up with an explanation.

Friends can be that generous—

But I'm shaking my head, and my throat is so raw.

I shove the phone back in my pocket and walk back to the lounge. Luke still hasn't heard me, lost in conversation with his mum.

"I screwed up this time."

I stiffen in the doorway. There's so much hurt leaking from Luke's voice.

He sighs, and then continues, "I should have just told you the truth, and I should have told Sam about me right from the beginning. From the first moment we met."

About him?

My pulse beats faster, and the wooden floorboard under me betrays my presence with a groan.

Luke springs off the couch and twists toward me. He licks his lips and swallows. Then his eyes close as he says into the phone. "Sorry Mum, I've got to go."

The phone hits the couch. "Sam," he says, holding my gaze, searching it.

"What should you have told me right from the beginning?"

I hold my breath, not sure if I'm hoping he'll say what I'm guessing he's about to say, or if I'm hoping—begging the universe to be wrong.

He skirts around the couch, coming over to me. "Sam, I—"

I stop him with a raised hand. "What should you have told me?"

He breathes out, looks down at the floor between us, and then back up to me. "That I'm gay."

I'm nodding. Nodding because it's making sense, but not making sense at all.

I don't realize I've forgotten to breathe until I'm suddenly sucking in a fresh gulp of air. "All this time? Why didn't you"—I close my eyes and try to keep my voice level—"why didn't you tell me?"

Luke opens his mouth and shuts it again, shaking his head.

"How many things have you paid for, for me and Jeremy? How many things don't I know about?"

"I don't know."

"The carpentry workshop you took me to. You said the first time is free. Was that true?"

He doesn't answer, and it's answer enough. Everything in my head is spinning as I try to calculate that math. How much has Luke been giving us?

Dad's words come back to me: *Numbers that can tell you about life.*

But now I don't think that's all true.

I calculate **300** dollars for Jeremy's soccer trip. The bi-weekly takeouts: **22** dollars. The flights down south: **200** dollars. The bed-and-breakfast: **100** dollars. The shark dive: **600** dollars. The carpentry workshop: **50** dollars?

And those numbers are only the beginning. What about the

other ways he's added to our lives? The number of times he's taken Jeremy to the emergency room: **3**. The distance he travels to drop or pick Jeremy up from school: **25** km one way. The times he's watched Jeremy and fed him dinner when I had to work late: **20**? **30**? More? The times he's taken us camping: **12**. The times he's changed my tires: **4**. The times he picked me up from a bar, drunk, and cleaned my bathroom the next morning: **1**. The times he's held me over the last week: **23**. The times he's hurt me: **0**. The times he's let me down? Just this once.

Numbers. They can tell a lot. But they can never be enough. They can't calculate how much Luke means to us. *Me.*

Can't calculate how much I want to mean to him—

This is all too much. I can't absorb all the math without crying it back out again. Shaking, I brace one hand against the doorframe for support.

Luke takes a step closer, but I wave my other hand in front of him again. "I just"—I lose my voice and have to clear my throat—"Luke, I—I can't think right now. I have to . . ." I glance toward the door.

"Sam, don't. Please. I'm so sorry. I wanted to, but I just couldn't bring myself to tell you. I couldn't bear the thought of you saying no."

The edge of the doorframe where I grip is digging into my palm. My head wants me to escape with my thoughts so I can gather them into something that resembles sense, but my body doesn't want to leave at all. It wants me to stay right here.

I focus on Luke. His eyes are tearing up, something I've never seen before, and I feel it echo in my own eyes. "Saying no? No to what?"

"No to loving me back."

"I—I've always loved you, Luke. You're my very close second. And Jeremy is right," I bow my head as the numbers finally push their way out the corners of my eyes to dampen my lashes. "Sometimes you're even my first."

I sense Luke wants to come forward but is holding himself back, as I wished. "I mean," he says softly, "I can't bear the thought of you not being *in* love with me."

I shatter in a **1000** pieces in all directions until I have no idea where I am anymore. I don't know what to say or do and my instinct is to curl up into a tight ball until I'm all back together again.

"Hold me," I gasp. And Luke's moving—in **1** second, he's pressing me against him, firm hands rubbing my back, outlining me, reassuring me I'm still all there.

I breathe shakily through the shoulder of his shirt. "I'm angry," I say, even as I clutch him tighter to me. "God, I'm so angry." And I'm digging my fingers into him as if to prove the point.

"You're allowed to be angry. I should have told you."

I close my eyes and rest my forehead against the side of his neck. "I never . . . I never would have fooled around with you . . . You should have told me. This is the reason you were so hot and cold about doing the taboo with me, isn't it? I've hurt you. I didn't even know it, but I was hurting you."

"It's not your fault, Sam. I had all the opportunities to tell you the truth. I didn't."

"Because you *couldn't*."

We stand there together, Luke never lessening the pressure of his hands, but soon I feel him shaking, and when I pull back enough to look at his face, his eyes are wet and slightly reddened at the edges. He can't look at me either, concentrating on something at our sides.

"If nothing else," he says with a taut voice that's on the edge of breaking. "I still need to love you as a friend."

"I'd do anything to go back and say no. I never . . . you were never meant to get hurt," I say and slowly pull away from him. It's not fair of me to make this harder on him, and he needs some space. "And I need your friendship too."

His body crumples, shoulders dropping, head sinking toward his chest. He struggles to speak, and I apologize again. "Just give me a little while," he says, not daring to look at me. And I'm thankful he doesn't see my tears, because I know that would make it worse for him.

"Yes, Luke. Anything you need."

Chapter Thirty-Seven

LUKE

I haven't seen Sam for two days. Three times a day I go for a run and stretch afterwards, which makes up most of my day. Run. Stretch. Talk to myself. Run. Talk to myself. Stretch.

I need the physical exertion to get rid of the tight, painful ball in the pit of my gut.

But it's not working.

So I run harder, stretch longer.

The ball just compresses and lets out waves of ache that make my insides heave.

It's like the hope I lived on has been surgically removed, and a tumor of something bloody painful has taken its place.

It doesn't help that wherever I look I'm reminded of the reasons I love him.

At the dining table, Sam is sitting across from me, a confused frown etching his brow as he attempts to understand Jeremy's assignment.

On the couch, I see the first time he came over: Sam looks a little too lean and tired as hell, and there is something about him that just makes me want to help. *"You're real friendly, Luke."* He rests his head back against linked fingers, and closes his eyes. *"I think I'll like having you as a neighbor."*

Outside, I see the way he bounces in his step as he traverses his garden and rests his elbows on the fence separating our places.

Everywhere I look makes me love him more. I wish I could reach into my memories and kiss him or hold him or make love to him—

But this isn't good for me. I need a way to hold back the "in" part of my love for him.

On Friday, three days of no contact with Sam, I take out Sam's *20s Must-Do List* from my pocket. I can't throw it away just yet. I'm not ready. But I will spend the day without it. . .

It's not on me when I eat my breakfast.

It's not on me when I take my truck and drive into town.

It's not on me when I buy Jeremy's birthday gift.

It's not on me when I meet up with Jack for lunch.

It's not on me as I tell him what happened.

It's not on me as I ask how he got over me.

It's not on me when he doesn't answer.

I rest my ginger beer on the coaster in front of me and carefully look at him. His shit-eating grin is in place, just like it always is, but this time I can see behind it to the pain it's hiding.

"Fuck. I'm so sorry, Jack."

Jack's grin just widens. "Hey no, no need to be sorry. The years have made it easier. Sometimes, like admittedly, right now, I'm reminded of . . . the hurt, but most of the time it's good. I'm fine. Besides, I have a lot to keep me occupied, what with refurbishing my Rory Street cottage and all."

"How's that going?"

"Slow. Torturous. Expensive." He laughs and takes a sip of Coke. "But I've employed some help that should be starting at the end of the week, so I'm hoping to get it done by the end of summer."

I sigh. "Maybe I should help. I've got a lot of energy I need to vent."

"Don't want any fists through the new walls, thanks."

I take another swig of my ginger beer. "Right." I let out a slow breath that hovers toward a laugh. "Want to know something so utterly ridiculous?"

"Always."

I shake my head. That tightness inside is pulsing painfully. "The last few days when I was fooling around with him, I kept telling myself that's all it was, fooling around, right?"

"Sure."

"Yeah, but at the same time, I was planning the rest of our lives together."

"Of course." When I glare at him, he shrugs. "Been there, done that."

I'm about to apologize again, but he stops me. "Get back to the utterly ridiculous. It was keeping me amused."

I grunt out a laugh. "Yeah, well, as I said. I was dreaming of our future. I thought I'd buy that house you're working on and move us into it. I already planned how I could drive out and drop Jeremy off close enough to school he can walk, but not so close that I'd be an embarrassment. I had images of Sam coming home from Polytech and studying at the end of the table, snipping at us to be quiet as we make dinner around him."

And other images of me claiming Sam in every room of the house, letting his moans and shouts soak into the wooden floors and walls.

"I even imagined him sick and pale in bed, just so I could bring him soup, and rub his feet, and make him feel better."

I take another sip of ginger beer, but it's empty. It's a good sign of how long I've poured myself out to Jack. In a few years, I know I'm going to cringe remembering this.

Shit.

But Jack is cool. He orders me another drink, and tells me to just get the shit out. "What the hell else are friends for?"

So I do. I get it all out.

It doesn't make the aching go away, but it makes me tired enough to think I might sleep tonight.

BACK AT HOME I FIND JEREMY SITTING AT MY DINING ROOM table in a baggy T-shirt and shorts, with rings around his eyes. He looks like he's having a rough day himself.

Jeremy smoothes his hands over a piece of worn paper —*familiar* paper—and looks at me, shrugging. "I'm so frigging bored being grounded. I figured misery likes company, so I came here. 'Course, I could have hung out with Dad, but the constant frown he's wearing is giving me a headache. That, and his taste in music is terrible."

I want to ask more about how Sam's doing, but I bite down on the impulse. Instead, I pull out a chair and slump down on it. "Other than the grounding, are you doing all right?"

He nods. Shrugs. Shakes his head. "I talked to mum, but I —I still don't want to see Greg. I know I'll have to suck it up and whatever, but I hate him already."

I brace both elbows on the table and fold my arms. "Tell you what, Jeremy. Every week you're at your Dad's, you can come over here and we can man-bitch about all the things you don't like. This can be your free space to vent and let it all out. No judgments, just a venting-hour."

"Man-bitch, eh? I think that's the gayest thing you've ever said, Luke."

I reach out and slap the back of head. He laughs, and

slides over the paper he had in front of him. "That's Dad's writing."

I level my gaze at him. "Yes, it is. It's the list of things he wants to do before he turns thirty."

"The list has been folded many times," he says, holding my gaze, and I know what he's trying to ask. But I think he might already know the answer.

"Why do you think that is, Jeremy?"

"You've been taking care of it. Making sure Dad gets everything on it." He blushes suddenly. "I don't wanna know if he *got* everything on that list, but I'm right about you wanting to give Dad whatever he needs, aren't I?"

"You know the answer to that already."

He nods. "How long have you been in love with him, Luke?"

I let the words settle and the ache pass before I can answer. "A long time, I think. But it was only once I got to Auckland, when I didn't have both of you there, that I realized it."

"Does that mean I knew you loved him before you did?" He shakes his head. "Because I knew before then. It was the day you made pancakes, and Dad was frustrated because someone got sick at his work and he was called in for the shift. You took a pancake from the stack, cut a smiley face into it, and put it on his plate." Jeremy shifts and drums his fingers on the table. "It was some sappy shit. But it made you guys laugh . . . anyway, there was something in the way you looked at Dad, and I sort of just knew."

"I guess you saw it first, then."

Jeremy leans back in his chair, and starts tapping the table's edge. His foot must be jiggling, because I can feel the tremors through the table. "So . . ." There's a slight twitch to one corner of his mouth. "Gay, eh?"

And it's the first genuine laugh I've had since the moment I said those exact same words to Jeremy. "Yeah."

He looks at me and nods, that slow, cool-guy nod. "Right. It's good to have that out in the open. Now I can actually get proper advice."

I raise both eyebrows, and Jeremy quickly corrects himself. "It's not actually for me. Just someone I might know."

"Gonna go out on a limb here and guess you mean Steven. I got a feeling. You can tell him from me that if he wants anyone to talk to about stuff, I'll try to be the coolest Mr. Luke ever about it."

Jeremy pushes away from the table and stands up. He has the same habit of shifting from foot to foot that his dad does when he's got something more to say, but isn't quite sure how.

"What is it, Jeremy?"

It comes blurting out, and Jeremy's cheeks flare with color. "I did get what you meant . . . about what you said the other day . . . I don't want to go calling you"—he swallows—"Dad or anything. But I want you to know, like, I got it."

My throat is so tight. Tighter than it's ever been before. Nothing more than a gurgle comes out. I blink, and then I'm out of my chair and yanking the boy into a fierce hug. He hugs me back, a little awkwardly, but I don't care. I scrub my knuckles over his hair and step back.

"Thanks," I manage.

He shrugs like it's no big deal, but I know better than that. "Maybe we can kick the ball around some time? I'll kick your ass this time."

"Don't count on it. These old bones have life in them yet."

I walk him to the door. Just after he steps over the threshold and onto the porch, he turns around again. He's biting his bottom lip and his hands are shoved in the pockets of his shorts. "Just one more thing."

"What's that?"

"He may not know it yet, but Dad's totally in love with you too."

I clench my jaw and cast my gaze toward the fence that separates our houses. "Don't say things like that. It doesn't help me to get over it."

"Get over it? What the fuck?"

"Language, boy."

"Language . . .? You've got some messed up priorities. Get over it? What type of attitude is that? You have to fight for it. *Make* him see it."

"That's not how it works."

"Why the hell—*heck* not? Better than waiting years for him to see it on his own."

"There's nothing there for him to see, or he'd have seen it already."

"That's why it only took you seven years to figure it out yourself? And is that why he's not sleeping? Why he doesn't eat? Yeah, that makes all the sense in the world."

And with a snort, Jeremy turns on his heel and leaves.

Chapter Thirty-Eight

SAM

Wednesday. **1** week now.

One week since Luke told me he loves me. Is *in* love with me.

Every time I replay the moment, it's like I'm being picked up and thrown in the air: the rush of falling rippling through me, ending with the fear of slamming into the ground.

I love the feeling, and it scares me.

I can't seem to stop replaying the moment though. There's something nagging at me about it. Something that pulls and stretches at my muscles, and robs me of sleep.

I'm trying to put my finger on it.

I know I'm not gay. I double-checked that. None of the guys I looked at online did anything much for me. I mean, some of them were attractive, but they didn't turn me on.

The girls didn't turn you on either.

I groan and rest my forehead against the dining table. I

breathe in the smell of wood and all I can think of is Luke hefting the table onto his back, taking it to the carpentry workshop, and fixing it for me.

Thoughts like these make those giddy, uneven, ground-falling-beneath-you sensations come. I'm having so many of them that I'm actually afraid one of these times, the ground will fall away for good, and I'll just be falling. And there'll be nothing to stop me, to hold me together.

I rub my forehead over the wood, the pressure helping to pull me out of the feeling.

I turn my head, facing the window as I hug the table and stare at the fence separating our places.

It's hard knowing he's right there, and I can't go over and see him. It's like Auckland all over again, but worse. Because this time it isn't sickness holding us apart, it's us. Me.

And I know Luke says he'll be fine, that we'll still be friends, but . . .

But . . .

It'll never be the same.

God, everything is messed up, and all because of my stupid list. All because I can't face the fact I'm turning **30**.

Why did I have to be so foolish? Why did I need the thrill of being wild?

Why did I have to do the taboo with Luke?

It's the list that's at fault. The list that made me crazy.

And is it the list that made you like it?

The dropping sensation comes again. I grip the smoothly sanded edges of the table until it's hurting my palms.

Yes, I liked being with Luke—really liked it. But it was the taboo of it.

It was.

Guys just don't do it for me. My Internet experimentation proves as much.

The phone rings a sharp tone that momentarily pushes that

nagging feeling away. I retrieve the phone. It's my boss. "Do you know what I'm holding in my hand?"

I'm pretty certain I do. "You received my resignation letter."

"You couldn't have handed this in yourself? Couldn't have come talk to me about it?"

With the mess that I am this week, I couldn't have gone in to work. I'm sure I'd have frightened off half the patrons. "Sorry, no."

A sigh comes down the line. "It was too good to be true to believe you'd stay forever. What do you have lined up?"

"School. Got to think about the future." About what I really want for myself. How I want to be living at **40**. What type of role model I want to be for Jeremy. I need to make this change. It's been simmering for a while now, made clear that day on the beach with Luke.

"This is why you should have spoken to me, mate. We can scratch each other's backs here. I can give you work to fit around your schedule. Just something to keep you on your feet while you're studying. Think about it, and come in when you're ready to arrange something."

After the call, I lean back against the kitchen counter, staring at the sunlight slanting across the dining table. I stare at it until I start blinking in blobs of light.

I need to get out of the house. Away from seeing Luke everywhere I turn.

I scrub my face. My earring grates along the tip of my thumb, and without thinking, I yank it out and throw it on the bench. I fumble under my T-shirt for my nipple piercing and take that off too.

Grabbing my keys and wallet, I take my Honda and head for the hairdresser's. I get my hair re-dyed and cut the way I used to wear it, short and messy. I hope it will be relaxing, but it just reminds me of my home dye job. With Luke.

This time it doesn't feel anywhere near as good.

Back in the car, I angle the rearview mirror and take a look at myself. Staring back at me is no longer the wild, wannabe punk, but a dad who turns **30** in three days.

"Good thing you didn't get a tattoo," I murmur. "Maybe now things can go back to the way they were. The way they should be."

When I get home, I'm going to find that list of mine, tear it up and burn it.

Except, I don't drive home. Something's pulling me to Carole's.

I park outside her place. What am I doing here?

Why do I so badly want to go in and talk?

I squeeze the steering wheel hard, and stare out onto the street. The sun's setting and the streetlights have just flickered on.

Jeremy.

That's why I'm here. I want to show him I'm no longer bonkers. That I'm going to be the dad he needs.

Yeah, that's it.

I knock on Carole's door. She answers it while talking on the phone. Her eyes light up with surprise, but she quickly steps back and motions me in.

"Hey, Greg, I've just gotten a visitor. Can I call you back later? . . . Love you, too. Bye." She hangs up and looks over at me, running a calculating gaze over me. "Never thought I'd say I missed the mohawk. But there you have it."

Carole motions me into the kitchen but instead of taking a seat I stand at the kitchen island, digging my thumbs into my pockets.

"So what brings you here?" Carole says, automatically putting on the jug and grabbing out the instant coffee. She pauses before setting the jar down and looks at me. "Or do we need something stronger?"

I shake my head. "Coffee will be fine. I'm just here because I was in the area. Where's Jeremy?"

"He's out with Steven." She glances at the cow clock on the wall behind me. "He should be back in half an hour or so for dinner."

"And how are things with you and him?"

"Strained, but . . . maybe getting better."

"Has he met Greg yet?"

Carole unscrews the coffee jar with what looks like more force than necessary.

"I'll take that as a no."

Her hand stills on the lid and she stares at it. "Greg's been so understanding. He's such a good man, Sam. If Jeremy just gives him the chance . . ."

I move around the kitchen island and bump my side against hers. "He will. He's processing a lot at the moment, but he's a good kid. He'll suck it up and get over it."

She nods, and tucks a short lock of hair behind her ear. "You're right. Grab me the milk, would you?"

I pull out a bottle from the fridge and hand it over.

"So why are you really here?" she says, scooping two large teaspoons of coffee into each mug.

"Jeremy, of course."

She sizes me up once again, and shakes her head. "There's something else. Your hair looks neat, but the rest of you looks like it hasn't seen sleep in days. So, are you going to tell me? Or do I have to make your coffee Irish, and milk you for your answer?"

I shrug and sit down at the table. I pick up a discarded pen and click the top.

She's right, of course. It's the real reason I'm here. Because I need a friend, need someone to listen—maybe throw some perspective on things. Maybe she'll get what's been nagging at me.

"Luke's gay. I may have fooled around with him a bit."

Carole snaps her gaze at me. The reaction I expect. What I don't expect is the sudden grin she's giving me. She throws her head back and laughs. "Finally. Thank the lord for that. You guys have danced around this forever."

Huh? "Huh?"

"You've no idea how long I've been waiting to hear that. I was beginning to think your head was so far up your ass, you'd never see the light."

"I shouldn't have fooled around with him, Carole."

Her humming laughter stops abruptly. "Okay, now my turn...huh?"

"I had this list of stuff to do before my birthday. Doing something sexually taboo was on that list. It wasn't supposed to be anything more than experimenting. Last week, though, I find out that Luke . . . that he . . ."

"Loves you?"

I blush and click the pen faster. "Yeah."

"Oh Sam, love, you look so confused."

I use the pen to rub away my frown. "I am."

She brings over our coffees and sits across from me. "Tell me about it."

I drop the pen and pick up the coffee. The liquid smells so rich and the mug is warm in my hands. "I'm not gay. I'm pretty sure. I tried looking at other men . . . I got nothing. But I —I can't stop thinking about what it was like with him. I—I liked it."

Carole leans back in her chair, taking her coffee with her. After a sip, she says, "So maybe it's not men you're attracted to. Maybe it's just Luke."

I slosh coffee over my front as I take another sip. "N-no," I say, getting up to grab a handy towel, and soak up the mess. "I liked it because it was taboo. It's wild. Forbidden, somehow.

The thrill of it seduced me. That and wanting to do everything on my list."

Or had the list become an excuse in the end?

"Because it's forbidden, eh?" Carole's eyes narrow in thought. She rests her mug on the table and stands up. There's a sparkle in her eye as she moves toward me. "Is that what makes you all hot and bothered?" Her voice is all breathy, and she bites her bottom lip.

I drop my hand with the soppy handy towel and take a step back. "What are you doing?"

She keeps coming closer, and I back up until I've banged into the cutlery drawers. "Greg would never have to know," she says, sliding closer and closer—

I try to sidle off to the side, but Carole's hand reaches out and snags my arm. Her fingers dance their way down to my hand.

I jerk her off. "Carole, get a grip on yourself." I'll never, not ever, seduce a woman involved with someone.

She backs up, batting her eyelashes, and her lips are quirking into a grin. "But it's so *wild*. Forbidden. Don't you feel the thrill of it?"

No. No, I don't. Not in the least.

And that's the point, isn't it?

Carole slinks back to the table, and once she's cradling her coffee again, she says, "The idea of experimenting is to find out a truth of some sort. The experiment I just did with you points to a conclusion of sorts, does it not? But the real question here is: what do you draw from *your* experimenting with Luke?"

The floor gives way under my feet.

And this time, I just keep falling.

AT HOME, IN BED, PHONE IN HAND.

I dial his number. The number I know by heart, inside out, and backwards.

It rings **2** times. It's late. He'll be in bed. I know he'll know it's me.

It rings **1** time more.

He picks up. "Sam?"

"I just . . . I needed"—*to hear you*—"to make sure you're still there."

"I am."

It hurts as I swallow. "I miss you. I—I've been thinking a lot over the week. I"—The rest of what I need to say seizes up inside me—"I did it, Luke. I quit my job and applied for special consideration for admission to Polytech."

"That's great, Sam. We'll have to celebrate that. Soon."

I grip the receiver and press it more firmly against my ear. "And . . ."

"And?"

I close my eyes as I breathe out slowly. The words don't come with it. "And, um, I hope you have a good night, Luke."

Chapter Thirty-Nine

JEREMY

Being grounded sucks major balls.

I hate not being able to stay over at friends' houses, not being allowed to play video games or watch TV. I hate the fact I have to be home for dinner every night.

The worst of it though, by far the worst, is not having my own phone.

I tried convincing Dad to give it back to me when I got to his place this evening, but he laughed me off.

It means my nightly calls to Suzy have to take place over the landline. And boy if that doesn't hinder all the phone sex we could have been having!

Not that we've ever actually done that before. But if I hadn't got caught with my pants down, that might have been a possibility. Now we've barely seen each other. I think she's freaked out about meeting my parents, and I can't say I blame her. I worry my mum might start up the whole Golden Condom Rule with her too.

I wouldn't put it past Mum to bring out the bananas the first time I invite Suzy over.

I check my clock radio. It's eleven at night, and Dad's already in bed. Now's the perfect time to sneak into the dining room and grab the phone.

I snatch it and haul ass back to bed. Once I'm in, I press the phone's *on* button—

I'm surprised to hear Dad's voice coming down the line.

"I like these calls."

"Me too."

"But I want to see you again."

There's a short silence, and then Luke's choked response. "I do too."

"When?"

"I don't know."

I roll my eyes. These two really need a good kick up the butt. Why can't they just get it together finally?

I hang up and wait ten minutes before checking if the line is clear. It is.

But it's not Suzy's number I end up dialing. It's Steven's.

He sounds sleepy. But he wakes up pretty quickly when I tell him Dad and Mr. Luke are in love.

"Really?"

"Yes. Really. They're just acting like teenagers about it."

"What does that mean."

"They're overthinking things. Look I've got this idea. A ruse of sorts. And I need your help with something."

Steven grumbles. "The last time you said that, I had to kiss you in front of your mum."

"Don't sound like it was a chore. You know you loved it."

"Just tell me, does this ruse of yours involve kissing."

"Hopefully. But not us, so don't get your hopes up."

He laughs. "Damn."

"No, that's a good thing. I think Simon would beat me up at practice if he ever found out I made you kiss me."

Steven goes strangely quiet, and I twist onto my other side, the sheets tangling around my legs. "What has Simon got to do with it?"

"Jesus. Are all of you blind or something? I'm not everyone's Matchmaker Mary."

"Just your Dad and Luke's?"

"Shut up. Look, Luke's been good to me. And I was a bit of a shit to him recently. I figure I owe him one." And also, maybe I want Dad to get everything done from his list too. "Now, forget that, and let me tell you my plan . . ."

DAD'S STARING BLINDLY AT THE WEIGHTS LYING NEXT TO THE writing desk in the dining room. Just standing there. Staring.

I'm holding back a bark of laughter—'cause there never was any way in hell Dad could have gotten "crazy, nasty" fit.

I pour myself some chocolate milk, and debate how I should go about the first step of my evil, genius plan. I've spent all morning and early afternoon sussing out the finer details. Now to get the ball rolling . . .

I glance at Dad over my shoulder. "So did he tell you then?"

Dad startles, and shifts over to the table. "What's that? Who tell me what?"

"Luke, of course." I shake my head, and aim for a bitter tone. "I can't believe he'd move again so soon after coming back."

"Move?" Dad looks quickly out the window. "What are you talking about?"

"Just something he said in passing. Thought he'd have told

you already." Now to the next step of the plan. . . . "Dad, I need your help with something. Something important."

He turns his pained gaze on me. Excellent. "What's that?"

"I need you to help me convince him to stay. I really don't want Luke to move."

He swallows hard.

I don't give him time to think, I plow on. "You need to put on some sneakers, and drive me down to the local park . . ."

Chapter Forty

LUKE

I'm surprised when Steven shows up at my door on a
Saturday afternoon. "Mr. Luke," he says, crossing his arms,
and dropping them again.

"Mr. Steven. Sorry, if you're looking for Jeremy, he's not
here."

"No, I was looking for you."

I notice the way he's twisting uncomfortably, and suddenly
I wonder if he's here to *talk* about certain things. I open the
door wider. "Want to come in?"

He shakes his head, and maybe he gets what I thought he is
here for, because he blushes. "No, it's . . . it's Jeremy. He asked
me to come and get you. Quickly."

I grip the edge of the door harder. "What's happened?"

"Nothing bad or anything," Steven hurriedly says. "He just
sent me to bring you to the local park."

"Next time start with 'nothing's wrong.'" I move down the hall to grab my keys.

"You have to bring a soccer ball," Steven calls after me. "And your game."

I pause at that, and then for the first time in a week, I'm really grinning. "Oh I'll bring that, all right."

I'M JUST GOING TO HAVE TO FACE IT: THERE'S NO WAY I'LL EVER get over Sam.

That becomes evident the moment I step foot out of my truck and see his Honda parked at the other end of the parking lot. Already, my pulse has quickened, and I'm scouring the fields next to the lot for any sign of him.

Well, crap.

Steven is mumbling something as he comes around the truck with the soccer ball in tow, but it's background noise next to the voice in my head, telling me that seeing Sam so soon is a very bad idea and to hurry up and find him already.

I spot Jeremy first. He's chatting to Simon, who's unzipping his parker. There's a girl there too with hair tied back off her face, wearing short shorts, a singlet, and socks pulled to her knees. Three guesses who that is.

I jog across to them, a breeze picking up snippets of their conversation and sending it my way.

"Put out the cones and we can get started."

I slow to a walk. "Hey, Jeremy—"

And then I see him.

He's a good fifty meters away, the late afternoon sun is picking out the golden streaks in his once-again brown hair, and a sudden wind molds the back of his T-shirt against him.

He's gesturing toward the field as he chats with . . . is that Carole?

What is going on here?

I snap my gaze back to Jeremy, who's deliberately not looking at me. I'm about to bring out my teacher tone and demand an explanation, when from the corner of my eye, I see Sam turn.

He's seen me. I know it. His body tenses, and he's no longer paying any attention to Carole chirping next to him.

I look back over, and this time I can't take my gaze off him.

Neither can he take his off me.

I glance down, blinking at the T-shirt he's wearing. I recognize it immediately. *Stay Calm and Suck It Up.*

I swallow the soccer-ball-sized lump in my throat. Seeing Sam again . . . Seeing him in something of mine . . . It relieves the ache inside at the same time as making it worse—like the pangs are more constant but less intense.

"Get your butts over here!" Jeremy shouts to his dad, effectively breaking our connection.

Steven rocks up beside me and throws the ball to Jeremy. "Damn I wish I could play."

Jeremy rolls his eyes. "You are sideline ref."

Simon sidles between Steven and me, and casually punches his shoulder. "No playing around with balls until your foot's better." A tight silence follows that, and I have to swallow back the urge to laugh. Simon is shaking his head. "Uh, I mean—that came out wrong."

"I sure hope so!" Steven whispers—but it carries, and the way Jeremy snorts, I know he heard it too.

Simon just stares at Steven, who's gone a shade of red that could almost be called burgundy. Simon reaches out, takes him by the hand and pulls him away as he says in a shaky voice, "I think we need to talk for a moment."

Carole and Sam stand on either side of Jeremy. The kid tosses the ball up in the air and catches it. There's a wicked glint in his eyes, and I'm going to find out what his angle is.

Except not right this second, since Suzy's clearing her throat and giving Jeremy a look as she inclines her head toward Carole.

Jeremy hooks the ball under one arm. "Oh yeah, Mum, Dad, Luke, this is Suzy."

Suzy reaches for a wide, warm smile and extends her hand for each of us to shake.

Carole is stiff but cordial, and I wonder if that'll be the exact reaction Jeremy will have when he finally meets Greg. Sam has a friendlier smile and a nod for her. I tell her it's nice to meet her again—formally this time, and make a mental note to make sure Jeremy has access to all the protection he needs.

"Let's get this game going then," Jeremy says, and yells to Simon over my shoulder, "Set up the perimeters when you're done."

"Okay," I say, snatching the ball from Jeremy as he knees it high into the air. "Tell us what you're up to."

Jeremy shrugs all too innocently. "Boredom is the father of creativity."

"The *mother* of creativity," I correct.

He thinks about it, and shakes his head. "Not in this case."

"Sounds like we ought to ground you more often," Sam says.

Jeremy chooses not to hear it, but I grin at the thought. "We're going to play a small game of soccer," Jeremy says. "Three on three with twenty-minute halves." He throws me a look. "Losing team makes dinner for the winners. I hope you brought it, Luke."

I level my stare on him. "Oh, I brought it and then some."

He takes a few seconds before he inclines his head. "Good. You, Carole, and Dad are one team against me, Suzy, and Simon. Age versus beauty." He jerks a thumb toward his dad. "He can't play for squat." He winks at Suzy. "And neither can she."

Suzy barks out a laugh. "Right there."

Jeremy smirks. "Just remember not to use your hands."

"Like Irish dancing. Got it."

"No, not—" He shakes his head and looks at me. "So as you can see, it looks like we'll be about even on ability. Mum's pretty decent, but Dad . . ."

"Give me some credit," Sam murmurs, looking like he wants to snag the soccer ball and bounce it off his son's head. "At least I know the rules."

"Well you'll have Luke, so you'll be fine." Jeremy lets the words linger a moment before continuing, and I wonder if he's trying to master the art of subtext. If he is, I have to give him a solid B for effort. "So, are we all clear on the rules?"

I look over to Sam and catch him staring at me. He quickly pulls his gaze back to Jeremy and shifts his weight from foot to foot, mumbling, "Yes, very clear."

"Excellent. Steven! Simon!"

The two come jogging back to us, both flushed and grinning. A quick look at the field shows me they were at least productive as they "talked." There are cones along every side of our soccer pitch.

Jeremy scores a coin from his mum, and tosses it. "Heads," I call out.

He peeks at it and his face scrunches up. "Your call."

"The ball. And Jeremy, age will always win over beauty."

A cheeky smirk is thrown back at me. "Two minutes to discuss strategy, then we're starting." Jeremy snags Suzy and jerks his head for Simon to follow.

There's so much I want to say to Sam, but Carole is there and it's not the moment. Instead I say, "Right then, let's show these guys us over-thirty-year-olds can give them a run for their money."

Sam's quick to throw back: "I'm not thirty *yet*. Still have a few hours left."

Carole hangs back and protects our goal.

Jeremy—his usual cocky self on the field—is using his fancy footwork whenever anyone gets close to him.

Luckily, I have the ball. I touch it and pass it to Sam. He immediately kicks it back to me, and I swallow a laugh, and tap it to him once more. "Nice and easy does it, just dribble it up field."

He says, with a small kick of the ball, "Every time I have it, Jeremy's on me. That boy's got crazy spider legs."

"Don't worry about him," I say, unable to suppress a chuckle, "just keep moving that ball. You can get it past Suzy, and when you do, you can pass to me."

He gets past Suzy, but before he can pass, Jeremy is there, grinning in much the same way as those great whites.

"Well crap," Sam says. "I should just give you the ball, right?"

"Nope, that'll take too long." And Jeremy kicks the ball through Sam's legs and chases after it.

The nerve!

I cut over the field and close in on him and mark him close. This is one shark I'm not afraid of. "You're going to pay for that one."

"Look who's come to the rescue. Gonna get the ball back for him?"

"You bet I am."

And, guessing the fake he pulls, I get the ball and pass it back to Carole with my heel. She kicks it to Sam but, unfortunately, Suzy gets to it first.

Jeremy says quietly. "Nice to see you fight for him somewhere . . ." He leaves the sentence hanging, and looks up at me for a moment before jogging back to Suzy.

"Wrong way, wrong way," he calls suddenly as she makes a sprint with the ball to our goal.

Simon, attention drawn to the sideline, almost manages to let the ball slip past him.

"Eyes on the ball," Jeremy yells. "The soccer ball!"

Sam and I jerk to a halt and I'm sure he can see the laughter in my eyes as much as I can in his, and then he skims me down and blushes.

I don't know what to make of that. Was Jeremy right about what he said? Could it be Sam just hasn't seen it yet? That maybe he . . . maybe . . .

Or is thinking like this setting myself up for another fall?

Steven blows the whistle for halftime. We take five minutes to gather at the sideline, and Carole surprises us with a cooler full of water and some snacks.

I take a long, cool drink, and while it clears my throat, it does nothing to clear my thoughts.

Sam pulls Jeremy aside and, curious at exactly what the boy thinks he's up to, I stroll nearer, straining to listen.

"I don't get how this is supposed to make him st—"

Jeremy cuts his dad off. "You'll figure it out. I have to save Suzy from Mum."

"But—"

Jeremy is already hurrying to Suzy's side, calling over his shoulder. "Just enjoy the game, Dad. You wanted to play a sport before thirty, didn't you?"

"What? How did you—?"

But Steven blows the whistle for the second half. Sam stalks toward the field. When he sees me, he growls. "That boy's up to something. And after this game, you and I need to talk!"

Back on the field, Jeremy coaches Suzy through scoring a goal, cheering and lifting her up after she kicks it through the cones.

When I snag the ball from the kid, late in the second half, I take it and run, carrying the ball quickly to our goal and slipping it home. Sam jumps up, looking like he's about to swing his arms around my neck and pull me into a hug, but he turns it into a high-five instead. "We over thirties really still have it!"

I send him a wink. "Not quite thirty yet, remember?"

He flushes. "Yeah, but soon enough."

We take our starting positions once more. Jeremy begins with the ball. A bad pass has it back in our possession in no time. Sam sends the ball to Carole. She takes it, mutters something along the lines of "I'll give you kids *age*," and dribbles the ball down the middle of the field, fakes a pass to Sam on her flank, and scores.

It all happens so swiftly and suddenly, the goal is followed by a moment of quiet shock.

And then, "Damn, Mum. Think I know who I got my talent from."

"Hey!" Sam says, but his scowl fast disappears into a grin. "Nice one, Carole."

Then we're in the last five minutes of the game. Jeremy keeps looking at his watch, and the lack of concentration makes it easy to swipe the ball from him. "Think next time I'll be asking *you* to 'bring it,'" I say to him.

That stirs him up. Next thing I know, he's on the ground, his foot sliding forward to take possession of the ball.

Simon catches the rough pass, and dribbles, cutting back to Jeremy just before the goal.

I can see what's going to happen. Jeremy will simply tap the ball home, and we'd be tied 2-2. I wait for it.

But it doesn't happen.

Jeremy misses the goal. A goal he should have made—a goal even Suzy or Sam would've managed.

The whistle sounds, marking the end of the game.

And we've won.

This time Sam does throw his arms around me into a

cheering hug, and I'm not going to tell him I think the game might've been rigged. When Carole trots over, we include her in the team hug, and I notice how quickly the warmth of his touch becomes impersonal and distanced.

"Oh gosh-darn it!" Jeremy says, swinging his arm and clicking his fingers. "We lost." His disappointment is so fake it looks Photoshopped by an amateur. "Guess that means Simon, Suzy and I have to cook." He turns his gaze to me. "Dinner will be ready in an hour. Stay out of your house until then." To his dad he says, "Hang with Luke and make sure he doesn't go anywhere too far." He pauses a second. "Wouldn't want your Shepherd's Pie to get cold."

Sam nods, and untangling himself from me and Carole, asks her, "You hanging with us too?" There's a slight edge to his voice, and if I'm not mistaken, it sounds like he doesn't particularly want her there.

"No, no," she says, grinning. "I, ah, promised I'd call Greg. Yeah, Greg. I'll just meet you at your place in an hour, that right, Jeremy?"

Jeremy looks from me to his dad. "Yeah. One hour. That should be plenty enough time to sort things out."

"He couldn't have been more obvious," Sam says, hopping into the passenger side of my car. "Pushing us together like this." He sighs. "He hates that things are weird between us. That we haven't hung out in over a week."

I draw my seatbelt and click it in.

I lean back and stare at the field, picturing us playing soccer, as he adds softly, "So do I."

I take in Sam's frown and clenched fists in his lap. There's a quiver at the edge of his lip, like he wants to say something more.

Dammit, but I want to reach out, lift his chin, kiss his lips.

Fight. I want to fight for us.

And in the same breath, I can't bear to hear him say no again.

"Nice T-shirt," I murmur as I grip the steering wheel hard with my left hand and turn the key in the ignition. "How about a drive?"

"I accidently packed it in my suitcase after Stewart Island. I like it." His head dips to the side, and in my imagination—it has to be—he smells it. "A drive sounds good. The bays?"

It's quiet between us as I steer around the bays. Sam is rubbing his palms over his thighs. "Remember the last time we drove out here?"

"Yeah." I clear my throat. "You said you want me to teach Jeremy how to drive."

Sam stops his hands on his thighs and shifts in his seat. "How can you so casually mention that, while at the same time you're planning to move?"

"*What?*"

"When were you going to tell me?"

"Again. What? Where'd you hear that I'm moving?"

"Jeremy. He told me this afternoon, and said I have to help him keep you from going. Somehow playing soccer with you was meant to help. Don't ask me how, exactly."

I frown. The meddling boy! Why would he—

I pull the truck into a turning bay much the same as the last time, and stop the car. I laugh and shake my head. The laughter edges on something rawer, though.

You didn't fight, so he's trying for you.

I don't know whether I want to hug him or kick his ass.

"It's good to hear you laughing, Luke," Sam says, flinging open the glove box out of habit and the need to fidget more than a search for a mint. "But I wouldn't mind joining in . . ."

"He's got some cunning, all right." I swivel in the seat

toward him, opening the small nook in the console where I keep the mints. I unwrap one. "I'm *not* moving anywhere." I let that process a moment, and hand the mint over. He takes it, but he doesn't seem to see it.

I continue, "He knows how I feel about you, Sam. Seems he knew even before I did. He came to visit me the other day, and I told him it wasn't until I was away in Auckland that it suddenly . . . clicked for me."

I wait a moment, and Sam lets out a slow, unsteady breath. "So you're not moving?"

"No."

"You're not moving," he repeats to himself. "You're *not* moving." He drops the mint on the dashboard. With trembling fingers he clicks open his belt, and gets out of the car.

"Sam?"

Out the windows, I see him move around to the back of my truck.

I call again, unbuckling my belt and leaping out of the drivers' side. "Sam?"

I find him doubled over at the back of the truck, gripping onto the metal railing at the back. He's shaking, and something like a sob or the need to throw up wracks his body.

"Shit, Sam, are you all right?" I bundle him up in my arms and draw him tight against me. He grips me like I'm the only thing to stop him from flying away.

"It feels like . . . falling. Can't stop it."

He's not making any sense. I smooth down his hair, and hate that all I have to offer him are the usual words of comfort. "Hey, it's going to be fine."

"It's just you," he says over and over. "I knew it the moment she said it. It's just *you*."

I slide one of his legs between mine to bring him even closer, to let him know I've got him. All of him. His breathing slows, but his grip doesn't give up. I twist us so his back is against the truck and the cool breeze from the sea isn't hitting him so much.

He draws his head back just enough to look at me. "I get it."

"What's that, Sam?"

"I get what Jeremy's doing." He glances to his side, out toward the sea. "He's trying to give me my own Auckland." He shakes his head, and I tense, balancing on this aching, suddenly rising cliff of hope. "But—but—" He swallows, and his hands slide off my back.

I close my eyes, waiting for the rest of it. For him to say Jeremy tried, but there is no Auckland for him. There never will be.

His breath hitches, close against my chin.

"He didn't have to, Luke."

Fingers touch the sides of my face, and I open my eyes. What is he talking about? What did he just say—?

He leans in and presses his lips against mine. One soft kiss, his top lip lingering on my bottom one. "He really *didn't have to*—"

My hand slides firmly between his shoulder blades to his neck, where I squeeze as I crush him into me. I steal those words from his mouth with a deep kiss that I don't want to stop, and that Sam is not stopping either.

No, far from it. His tongue is twisting with mine, curling, seeking, sucking . . .

The ache in my gut morphs into something else. Fear, I recognize. I pull back to brush his lips, and I wait, wait for him to push me away, to say something and stop this. I'm giving him his last chance.

He leans back, hand curving along the arch of my back, over my shoulders to linger on my chest. He takes a deep breath, and holding my gaze, grips my shirt and tugs me toward him. "Don't let go of me."

Chapter Forty-One

SAM

Eventually he has to let go of me, of course.

All the way back to his house, I miss his hands on me. I have no idea how we are going to make it through this dinner. I love the fact Jeremy actually has to cook—but right now, I'd even drop the whole grounded thing if he'd just go off and take his soccer buddies and Mum with him.

Luke has a dazed expression as he locks his truck and we move to the front door. He fumbles with the keys, almost dropping them. "Slippery buggers."

Through the closed door come voices and laughs, and the sound of running feet.

"Sounds like they're having far too much fun in there," I say. "We'd better put a stop to that."

"Or,"—the look Luke gives me, dark and half-lidded, has my toes curling—"they can take their good time and move it to your place."

The lock clicks open and I still my hand over his on the handle, keeping the door from swinging in. I press my lips at his ear. "How is it you always manage to read my mind?" I touch my other hand to his waist and creep up to the middle of his chest. "I'll fake a sickie. You sweep 'em out."

I let go of my hand from his on the handle. The door opens, and I clutch my belly as we hobble inside. There's the hammering of teenage feet at the other end of the house.

"We're—"

The back door slams, and then it's quiet.

"—Back," I finish, straightening. "That's strange."

I waltz into the kitchen, surprised that it's so clean in there. It's almost as if no cooking happened, except for the warm, comforting smell of food.

Luke gives a small *huh*, and moves toward the dining room. I hear him **1**, maybe **2** seconds later. "Sam? Christ. Come in here."

I stride to the dining room, stopping short in the doorway just behind Luke. The table set for **2**, lit by **3** fat candles in the center. Sitting on a wooden board is a casserole dish of Shepherd's Pie. The boys must have just put it out, because it's steaming. Next to that is a bottle of red wine tucked behind an opened card.

I fold my arms, not sure if I should be shaking my head or grinning wildly. I decide on both. "It was a set-up. The game, everything."

Luke's shoulders rise with a deep breath and he moves to the table and picks up the card. I sneak up beside him. He glances at me, and with a twitching lip, reads aloud.

"Staying at Mum's. Yes, she was involved too. How else could I get the wine? Later, Jeremy."

He rests the card back on the table. Turning, he takes my hand in his and links our fingers together. He squeezes, pulling me a step closer. "So, Sam, would you like to have dinner with me sometime?"

"Yeah, yeah, I'd like that."

He inclines his head toward the table, flickering with candlelight. "Now good for you?"

"Well, I wouldn't want to waste the potato-peeling labor that went into this meal."

"Then it's set. A date." His thumb caresses the back of my hand. "I hope this is the first of many to come." His gaze drops to my mouth.

"But—"

"No," he pinches my lips lightly together. "Don't say we've been on a date before. That time was you wanting to have fun and me wanting to give that to you. But this," he draws me tight. His chestnut scent tingles my tongue as if I could taste him, "this is for real."

He drops his fingers from my lips and leans in to kiss me, but I shake my head softly. "But Luke, you're wrong. It's all been real. The whole last seven years of you and me.

"You know me better than anyone, I trust you more than anyone—that doesn't come out of nowhere. It came from all the times we spent together, all the dinners we shared, all the trips we had. If the definition of a date is going out with someone to get to know them better, to get to see how well you'll work together . . . then by my count, this will be one of over a hundred dates we've been on.

"The only difference between our dates and traditional dates is that it's taken me over a hundred of them to get to the making-out part." I grin at him. "You're one very patient man, Luke."

My lips meet his and my tongue darts out to gently pry his mouth open. His tongue touches mine, and heat floods between us. It's so much, and so strong, I'm kinda not sure I even want the food part of the date anymore. "I really think I'd better start making up that time to you."

He nuzzles his face into the crook of my neck. "Say this is true," he says. "Say I'm not dreaming this."

I press my head against the side of his and kiss his neck. The ground gives way from under my feet again as the falling feeling rushes through me. I grip Luke, and he tightens his hold. And this time, this time I'm not afraid of slamming hard and breaking. Against his skin, I tell him, "I love you, Luke. I'm *in* love with you."

WE EAT DINNER WITH OUR FEET LOCKED TOGETHER. AND other than the gentle presses we pass back and forth, the rest of our meal is much like any other. We banter, laugh, roll our eyes . . .

It's only once we've cleaned up and deposited ourselves on the couch that my stomach gets this uncontrollable fluttery feeling. It's a feeling that seems to pull at me from every angle, and I want it to stop.

I glance at Luke, stretched out next to me. His feet rest on the messy coffee table, covered with sport magazines, newspapers, and his landline phone. His hands twitch on either side of his lap and I follow them.

His hands on you will make it better.

When I look up, I find Luke already watching me. "I want —I want . . ." my voice fails me, and I bite my bottom lip.

Luke drops his feet to the ground and faces me. Lifting his thumb to my mouth, he eases my lip free. He leans in and sucks it gently into his mouth, his eyes closing. Goosebumps prickle at my neck, arms, legs, *everywhere*.

"Luke," I whisper, sinking my hand into his hair. "Can we shower first, and then go to bed?"

He stands up and pulls me with him.

In the bathroom, he turns on the shower. I watch him, back against the door, though I'm itching to move over, to have him touch me again.

"You go in here on one condition," he says, as the room starts filling with steam.

"What's that?"

"Stay in there longer than five minutes."

I push off the door, and stand in front of him by the sink. Our shorts and T-shirts are touching, and I slowly lift my chin up to meet his gaze. One more inch and we'd be flush. His arm curves around me and clamps us together at the legs, hips, groin. He's hard and I can feel the outline of his cock on my lower stomach. I'm hard too. I have been most of the evening.

"What'll happen if I can't wait that long?"

Something sparks in his eye. "You can wait that long, I'm not going anywhere."

I raise my arms above my head. "Undress me."

His fingers are warm as they slide over my sides and push off the T-shirt. My feet are already bare, so the last pieces of clothing that need to come off are my shorts and boxers. Teasingly, he skims the skin at the waistband. "I'm sad to see the nipple ring is gone."

I hiss at his light touches. "That one I can put back in."

His mouth comes down on my nipple and he bites; at the same time his touch turns from feathery-light to pinching. Then he hooks his thumbs into my pants and pulls them to my ankles. I step out of them, nervous suddenly at how exposed I am. I want to cover myself, but Luke cuffs my wrists and keeps them at my sides. He presses a kiss to my jaw and a few more to my neck. "You're beautiful, Sam."

Reluctantly, Luke lets go of me and steps back. "Shower," he says. "I'll get a fresh towel for you."

I step past him and into the shower. The water is hot, but

just the right hot, and it drums heavily on my back and shoulders. Soap, shampoo and conditioner are all there, and I complete the cleaning processes in a few quick minutes. I'm aching to be with Luke again—and not just in my cock, but somewhere deeper.

I turn off the taps, and step out—

Luke is there, sitting on the closed toilet seat with towels on his lap. He shakes his head and stands up, placing the towels on the toilet. "I said I'm not going anywhere."

"I just . . . I really couldn't wait that long. Can I have a towel?"

Luke peels off his T-shirt. "No." Next, he's chucking his shorts and underwear.

My cock jerks at the sight of him, all the strong planes of his chest, stomach, legs, ass . . . I swallow, and I'm thinking of the moment on his couch after that one date. *He'd filled your mouth, he'd pumped and you'd sucked him in.*

What will it feel like when he's filling me in other ways? My ass clenches at the thought.

"Longer shower." He grips my shoulders and steers me back into the shower. My back hits the plastic wall, and I'm pinned in place by Luke's slightly larger body. He works the taps with one hand, not flinching when a jet of cooler water hits him.

I jerk though, and it makes our chests rub and cocks hit against each other. His palm moves to caress my cheek. "I want you to have everything I can give you," Luke says. "Everything you've never had and want."

Fine sprays of water coming off the main shower jets rain over us, and as I blink, drops of water roll off my eyelashes. "You've been doing that all along." I slowly raise my hips, pushing our cocks closer together. My voice drops to a shy whisper. "All I want now is you." I glance at him, to the showerhead, to the water hitting his ass. "Can you show me how I can have that?"

He trembles, and drops his hands to mine at our sides. Linking our fingers, he pins the back of my hands against the cooler wall, and tilts his head to kiss me. As his tongue explores my mouth, he slides my hands up the wall until they are just over my head. He squeezes, unwinds our fingers, and crossing my wrists, he cuffs me with one hand.

His other hand traces over my arm, elbow, to the shoulder, and over my chest, pausing at my nipple before trailing off my skin.

He reaches to the hanging rack in the corner of the shower, and picks up a bar of half-used soap. Against the wall, he snaps the soap lengthwise in two. One piece drops to the floor, and Luke shoves it aside with his toes.

With the remaining piece in his hand, he draws over my skin. The tip of the soap is hard, but smooth as it circles my nipples in a figure eight that gets tighter and tighter until finally it rubs over my nubs.

I gasp and jerk to get my hands free, but Luke tightens his hold. And I think he has the right idea, because if I get free, I'm going to melt into one big puddle.

He brings his nose to touch mine and as soon as he does, I'm pressing my arms back, and silently begging him to keep going. To keep touching me.

He speaks instead, words whispering over my mouth and chin. "What do you want?"

I let out a nervous breath. "I want you inside me, Luke, in the only way you aren't already." A whimper escapes him. I add, "What do *you* want?"

His gaze holds mine. "I want to move, Sam."

In a moment of panic, I pull to free myself. Luke's got me strong though and his weight is heavy against me. "Trust me, Sam. Listen."

"But I thought—"

"I want *us* to move. I want us to buy a house. I want us to share a kitchen, a bathroom, a lounge, a dining table . . . a bed. I want to take care of the bills while you study, and when it's your week with Jeremy, I want him to be coming home to the both of us." A tremor shudders down my arms, and it's coming from him. "I want us to be a family."

The falling feeling intensifies and I'm lost to the sensation. I don't even realize I'm crying, until Luke's voice cuts through. "Hey, love. Are you okay? Is this going too fast for you?"

The endearment snaps everything in me, and I sharply shake my head. "Not too fast. I need more of you."

His kiss has a dominant streak in it, and it calls to my senses. My cock gets harder, and everything feels more intense.

Then Luke, soap still in hand, draws it down my chest, over my treasure trail until it hits the head of my cock. I jerk at the sensation, and then jerk some more as Luke traces the soap around the tip.

Arranging the soap in the center of his palm, he grips my shaft.

I suck in a breath, and when he starts a slow tortuous pumping, I throw my head back against the wall, groaning. I see my hands locked in his, and a shiver races through me— one that is multiplied when Luke begins stroking his thumb over the inside of my wrist in time to his strokes on my cock.

Just when I think I can't take anymore, that I'm about to explode, Luke stops. His thumb presses against my wrist, and I lower my head to look at him. "You're so incredibly sexy," he says, and the lust dripping off him is as clear as the rivulets of water gliding over his skin.

I shiver at the words. No one has ever said that to me before, and it's a rush to hear it come from Luke. Luke who has such a perfect male body. "I'm nothing as amazing as you. I've always wished for a body like yours."

I blush, because thinking back on that, my physical attraction to him seems so obvious. But I'd not allowed myself to see anything past the bro-gap. "Though maybe," I say slowly, "maybe I meant that differently."

Luke comes in for another kiss, his free hand steers his cock so it runs against my heavy balls. I clench my ass and stretch my fingers as I arch against him.

The tip of the soap works circles on my thigh, coming higher and inching toward the curve of my ass. Luke draws away from the kiss, and he reaches further around with the soap. Over my ass cheek, he runs the soap in strong, long lines from the base of my back to the very top of my thigh.

Luke's gaze probes mine, asking. He loosens his hold on my wrists, and I answer by turning for him. I rest my forearms against the wall, leaving a gap from it and the rest of my body. I want Luke holding me again, so I cross my wrists and hope he understands.

He does, because no sooner than I'm in place, he's gripping me again. Soft kisses sweep across my shoulder blade and up to the nape of my neck. The soap follows his trail and then slides with aching slowness down my back.

His toes grip the back of my right heel, clenching and releasing. Warm water dribbles from him and onto the backs of my thighs.

"Are you cold?" he asks.

I'm not. "Far from it."

His soft laugh has the hairs on the back of my head prickling. "Tell me if you don't like anything. Tell me if you want me to stop."

"Trust me, stopping is the last thing from my mind. And I'm no flower, Luke. I can handle a bit of pain—"

The soap slips down my crack, and Luke skates it over my hole to my balls. My cock pulses, and I buck my ass toward him. "Yes, more of that."

Luke runs the soap back up, creating a thick slickness between my cheeks. He pauses at my entrance and when I moan, he gently twists the soap. The tip slips inside me, teasing, and it's wonderful and not anywhere near enough.

Luke's thigh comes up against the back of mine, his hard length resting at the side of my ass cheek. He kisses my shoulder, lightly nipping me with his teeth, and drops the soap to slip a finger inside me. My cock jerks, and I wish I was closer to the wall that I could thrust against it.

Up and down, up and down, Luke works his finger.

After the next *up*, he pulls it out all the way. And then Luke breaches me with two fingers. I cry out at the depth they plunge, but it's not a cry from the tweak of pain, it's a cry of feeling so good, so right that Luke is touching me this way. It's a thousand times my *thank you* for making me feel so much, so intensely, like I never have before.

With each thrust of his fingers, I'm lost to sensation, but blurring in it are images of that house of ours, of coming home to him making dinner and asking me how my day was. Of us. As a family. Of waking up every morning to Luke's double-dimpled smile.

"There are no numbers," I hear myself murmur. "There are no numbers for how good this is. How good it will be."

Luke stops his fingers and the thrusts of his cock against my ass cheek. He withdraws and the dull tinkering of water dissipates to a drip.

Leaning his upper body against me, he whispers into my ear. "*Now* we've been in here long enough."

He tugs me with him out of the bathroom and pats us both dry with the towel. Clasping my hand in his, he leads me into the hall. It still smells of our dinner, and the feeling of being *home* pulses in my chest.

Luke draws me to his large bed. I sit as he grabs a condom from his side table and tosses it onto the bed. I stare from the foiled package to the expanse of bed around me. All the times I've been in Luke's bedroom before, his bed was just a bed— the brass headboard matching the lamp he has in the corner of his room and the chair beside it. It had style, and looked comfortable.

But now . . .

I swallow as I imagine curling my hands around the rods in the headboard as Luke takes me with everything he has.

My hand rushes to close over my cock, but Luke catches my fingers and tugs me to the middle of the bed with him. I roll over onto my stomach, making sure I'm close enough to those rods.

"When we move," I say as Luke straddles the backs of my thighs and rolls on the condom, "let's keep your bed."

There's a sigh, then something cold dribbles into the crease of my ass. Luke runs his fingers through what has to be lube, and he circles it at my entrance. Then he settles his weight on top of mine like he did in Stewart Island, his hands pushing, kneading their way up my back and down my arms as he brings himself flush against me. He shifts his hips so his cock sits between my ass cheeks. I can feel he's slicked himself with the lube as well. Our fingers link together, and he squeezes. "Is that a yes, Sam?"

"Yes. God, yes."

He stretches to kiss my lips, his cock sliding further into my crack as he does. He rocks against me, settling deeper and closer—

His shaft brushes over my entrance and I clench my cheeks around him to keep him moving along that spot. I push back and Luke groans long and hard as he slides against my skin.

I free my hands from his and reach under his pillows for the headboard as I spread my legs wide. Luke grasps the sheets on either side of me, balling them tight.

My fingers brush over paper as I push the pillows aside to hang on to the rods, stretching myself into an X.

I grip the bars as my focus sharpens on the worn paper. As soon as I see it, I know what it is. The lump in my throat is so tight, I can barely swallow.

The tip of Luke's cock runs over my entrance again. I arch toward him, needing him in me, needing him right—

Now.

The head of his cock enters me. It's thick and full, and the stretching burns—but not entirely unpleasantly. Luke is breathing raggedly as he holds himself still.

"It's okay," I say to him, looking at the paper again. "I want this. I want *you.*"

"I want you too. So badly." His body unfreezes, and he carefully pushes all the way inside me. He drops a kiss to the base of my neck, bordering my back, and then begins moving in short slow strokes, for me to get used to him and his size.

With each thrust, my cock rubs against the bed and I grip the rods harder as waves of pleasure and pain mingle together.

Soon the pain is much less, and my cock is weeping pre-cum into the sheets. "Use the force, Luke."

"Wisecrack." He lengthens his strokes and increases his speed. His arms are braced against the bed at my sides, lifting his weight, and his careful thrusts are edging to something carnal—and possessive.

His balls slap against my ass, and each of his thrusts is a mixture of light throbbing pain and this burst of deep sensation when he hits my prostate.

My feet brace against his and I push down on them as he pushes up with each thrust. Every part of my body is swarming with nerve-endings and I don't think I can hold out much longer. I turn my gaze away from the paper, and bury my forehead against the mattress, because that's tipping me over the edge. Love and sex is wrapping me so tight, my release is mere strokes away.

"Luke, I'm about to—"

"Fuck, me too." And he grinds himself all the way in, circling his hips and then pumps in a short, hard rhythm that ricochets through my whole body.

I let out a sharp gasp, and Luke follows. He tenses, and his cock pulses inside me, and I'm coming too, smothering my cries into the sheets, the edge of the paper touching my forehead as I spill.

Luke collapses onto my back, his body slick with sweat. His heavy breaths comb over my hair and down my neck. A soft kiss ends the last wave of pleasure. Luke is still full in me, and a part of me wants him to stay like that. If it weren't for the mess, this would be just perfect. Luke. In me.

"Beautiful and sexy, and together with me at last." He nips my shoulder as he withdraws himself, and I swallow a sigh.

I hear him dealing with the condom, and then his hand rests against my back. "Stay there. I'll get something to clean you up."

His fingers dance off my skin, but I can still feel the ghost of them there. I stay in the exact same position until Luke comes back, and then I roll over onto my side. The wet patch in the bed is large and sticky.

Luke comes around to the other side of the bed, sits on the edge and taps my shoulder for me to lie on my back. I do, and he wipes me down gently with a hot cloth. "The bed got the worst of it."

"No worries. Slide off the bed for a sec?"

When I'm off, Luke strips the top layer of the bed. The bedspread pools at our feet, and Luke starts to say something and stops. Something has caught his attention; I follow his gaze to the paper lying near the headboard.

His Adam's apple bulges in his throat, and he looks at me.

"I—it's just that I—" He fumbles for an explanation. But I don't need one.

I step on the bedspread so I'm standing in front of him. Raising a hand to cup the side of his face, I shake my head. "I understand, Luke. I wondered where I'd put the list, thought I'd lost it, but . . . you had it all along, didn't you? Even before I told you about it."

He turns his head to kiss the base of my palm. On it, he answers, "I've had it since before I left for Auckland. It's been on me almost every day."

I nod, and then hesitate. "Jeremy knew about it too, didn't he?"

"Just recently. He found it when he came over. When I was trying not to care about it anymore. As you can see, I failed."

"Then I'm glad. Is this list . . . why you kept asking me if I wanted to play taboo?"

Luke blushes. "At one point I was so high on hoping, I thought maybe if we did something together, you'd see what we could have. That's why I suggested us experimenting that first time. But at the same time, all along, I knew it was a bad idea. Knew I could get badly hurt."

"And you did. For a little while there, I really hurt you. I'm sorry for that, Luke." I pause, "But if it's any consolation, it did seem to work. I kept telling myself it was the thrill of doing something taboo, but it was really that I loved being with you. Close to you like that—like this."

Luke lowers my hand and links our fingers. He rubs his thumb over my skin. "Sam, I really don't want what we do together to be taboo for you. Not anymore. Not ever again. When I take you to our bed, when we explore each other's bodies, when we make love, or have sex, or just plain fuck, it never was and never will be taboo for me. It'll never be a sin. It'll just be *us*, and that's just *right*."

I squeeze his hand as I nod, too choked up to speak.

I lean in and kiss him. And then I let go, and crawl over the bed to get the list. On my knees, I shuffle back over to him, the sheets tangling under me. I read the list out loud. "Read the books I should have read at school—ticked. Stay up the whole night dancing—ticked. Have a hangover, wear shades, and eat mince pies—ticked."

Now I get how he'd known that was exactly what I'd wanted that day. *He made them for you. He gave you everything on that list.*

Well, almost everything.

I stop at the line in the middle of the list. The line that's ticked and shouldn't be.

I toss the list onto the bed. "It doesn't matter how much you want me to get everything on that list done, Luke. It's not ever going to happen now."

"What did you not . . ." His gaze searches for the clock. It's ten. "We've still two hours. Maybe—

I reach out, curl a hand behind his neck and bring him into a crashing kiss. "Not going to happen. Read the sixth line down. You'll know why."

He does, and there's that look again. The one that'd nagged at me that first evening Luke was back from Auckland.

Flirt, have fun, don't fall in love.

Chapter Forty-Two

JEREMY

We're at Dad's. By we, I mean me and my mum and Steven. Luke goes without saying. We've just eaten a big birthday brunch, and now I'm unwrapping gifts. Dad sits on an armchair and Luke is perched on its arm. They are lost in puppy-dog, lovey-dovey looks at one another—and it's about enough to make anyone feel nauseous.

Steven, sprawled on the armchair behind me, carefully leafs through one of the collector's comics Luke bought me, while I'm on the floor, staring at the wrapping paper of mum and dad's gift in my lap. I think they must have flipped a switch or something, because there's no fucking way that is funny.

But obviously mum thinks it is, if her light giggling behind her flute of sparkling wine is anything to go by.

I stare at the banana-covered wrapping, and shake my head. "I'm going to be traumatized the rest of my life for sure."

"What's that?" she asks, eyebrow arching.

"I'm not sure I want to open this one."

She picks up the discarded wrapping from one of my other gifts, screws it up and throws it at me.

I catch it, and chuck it back at her. She jerks and splashes sparkling wine over her front. Luke and Dad don't seem to have seen a thing. Whatever they're chatting about in hushed tones must be seriously gripping.

I shake my head at them, and grin at Mum. "That'll teach you for drinking wine at midday!"

"Hey, do I have to remind you that fifteen years ago to the day"—she checks her watch—"scratch that, to the *hour*, I was pushing you out of me."

Gah. Too much imagery.

Now Dad pipes up—and it's with a groan. "God, don't remind me."

The wrapping-paper ball sails over to ping him on the head.

"For all the bloody, hard work," she says, cruelly emphasizing so that it has Steven shuddering too, "I deserve this glass as much as you deserve all these gifts, Jeremy."

"Fine, okay. You can be a booze-hag on all my birthdays to come." I shake the banana-wrapped gift. "Do I really want to open this?"

She sighs, rests her flute on the small table where my gifts are piled, and clasps her hands together. "You're fifteen now, you're growing up. I . . . I have to learn to step back and trust you more."

"So . . . does that mean I'm un-grounded?" I batter my lashes and give her my most charming smile. Steven puts out his fist and I lift mine and bump it over my shoulder.

She laughs. "Good try. No. It means I'm not going to hassle you so much about the Golden Condom Rule." At this point, Steven gurgles something, and from the corner of my eye, I see him lift the comic high to cover his face. Mum continues, "You can consider the bananas in the fruit bowl nothing more than something to eat from now on, okay?"

Steven chokes on his suppressed laughter and murmurs, "You've been holding back on me, Jer."

I glare at him and his comic. "Seriously, you wouldn't want to know." Then to Mum, I say, "Considering 'tis the season, I'll thank you with: Hallelujah."

Luke barks out in laughter, and I'm glad I have his attention. Dad's not the only one with his birthday. Though, it's not an entirely fair thought. Dad pretty much told everyone to pretend like it wasn't his birthday, so he could keep the illusion of being twenty-nine.

Finally, I open the gift. It's a blue-spotted piggy bank. The piggy bank that has been sitting on Mum's bedroom dresser for years.

"Every week for the last year, your dad and I put five dollars each in there."

"Are you serious? That's like $520."

"Well, I'm glad to see you take after me when it comes to math."

Dad cuts her a mean glare that has Mum grinning. "Come on, it's the truth. Jeremy wouldn't even be here if you'd been better at math." She laughs as Dad goes a shade of red that really should be reserved for emergency services.

"Do tell us that story, Mrs. Carole," Steven suddenly pipes up, the comic book lowered to his lap.

"The night of our . . . misguided passion, we first tried to buy condoms from the supermarket. But your dad only counted two dollars and twenty cents in his wallet and we needed three. He shrugged his shoulders and said, 'Well guess that's not happening.' But of course, later that evening, our hormones got the better of us. And afterward, when we hopped on the bus, he realized he actually had four dollars after all."

Dad groans and scrubs his face. "I was hoping you'd forgotten that little error of mine."

Mum cocks her head at me. "That little error gave us a son. One that almost eats us out of house and home."

"*Hardly.* I never touch the bananas."

Mum and Dad laugh so hard that I can feel it flapping in my belly. I lift the piggy bank, pointing its nose toward mine, and sigh.

"Thanks guys, but, I mean, it's too much. Mum, Dad, you need this."

Dad laughs. "Actually, we both figure you'll need it. Well, now that you can get your driver's license, we figured you'll soon be wanting a car to go with it. You have to save up the rest of course—and anything you save, we'll double."

"I'm, like, flabbergasted." And I am. Seriously. I think I'm going to need Steven to kick my back to dislodge the lump in my throat.

I kiss the piggy bank. Hell, I'm so freaking psyched, I could kiss the damn banana wrapping.

"It's still a way off yet," Mum reminds me, "but we wanted to give you motivation to save yourself."

"Your parents are so freaking cool," Steven says behind me. "If I could choose, I'd choose yours. Mrs. Carole, Mr. Sam, and Mr. Luke."

"Of course," Luke says, "if any of us find you using that car for anything more than driving—"

Steven kicks me then and says under his breath. "Dude, he's talking about you and Suzy."

Well, duh.

Ohhh, but there's an idea. Me and Suzy in the backseat of a car . . .

"—then you can be sure we'll take your keys and throw

them in shark-infested waters." Luke shivers as he says it, and my Dad lifts a hand and pats his knee, smiling softly to himself.

Luke slides a hand on top of his and threads their fingers together. Steven must have seen it too, because he makes a sound like a sigh.

"You won't be catching me in any compromising position with Suzy in the car. You can count on that." Because I would be very, very careful not to be caught.

Mum's phone rings. She's just picked up her wine again and, startled, spills more over herself. "Well, darn it," she mutters and quickly knocks the rest of the liquid back before answering her phone. "Hello?" She stands up suddenly, smiling. "Oh, hey."

I'm guessing it's Greg. She tiptoes her way around wrapping paper as she moves out of the room. "Yes." She glances over to me. "I'll pass on your congratulations."

A sinking heaviness settles in my gut—and I don't like it a bit.

Luke clears his throat and keeping his hand on Dad's, reaches down to the floor on his side. Another gift is tossed over to me. "I'm thinking this one is entirely appropriate right now."

The gift folds easily in my hands, and I quickly unwrap to find clothing. A T-shirt.

I open it up, and damn if Luke isn't right. It's fucking perfect for the moment, and I'll do good to heed its advice.

I read the smaller, red version of one of Luke's T-shirts.

"Stay Calm, and Suck It Up."

Chapter Forty-Three

LUKE

I f Jeremy thinks he's the only one that can be a trickster, then he can think again. The Greg calling/T-shirt gift stunt is proof of that.

I've had it planned since our little heart-to-heart the other week. Before meeting Jack for lunch, I'd hunted around and found it, and a quick call to Carole had us sorting out the finer details.

The birthday brunch goes by so fast. Soon I'm going to have to leave to pick Mum up from the airport. I glance at Sam, who purses his lips when I remind everyone it's his birthday too by making them all sing happy birthday as I bring out the cake with thirty candles on it.

"Make a wish," I tell him.

"It's already come true," Sam says, and I tighten my grip on the board holding the cake, only to whip my head around and scowl when Jeremy snorts.

He's sticking a finger in his mouth, as if me and his dad are making him sick. Steven, the good boy, is shaking his head.

When I turn back to Sam, he's glaring at his son too. "You know what? I've changed my mind, I do have a wish." He blows out all the candles, and says to me. "That should teach him."

Sam takes the other side of the board and stands up from the armchair; our hands are brushing where they meet in the middle. "Let's cut this in the kitchen," Sam says.

And that's the moment it happens.

The moment I don't think.

I lean over and kiss him gently on the mouth. Just a short, soft kiss, before I take the board back and turn around.

It's only when I take a few steps toward the kitchen that it dawns on me what I've just done.

This time there's only a mild twist of my stomach as I turn to back to him.

Sam has a cute, dreamy smile on his face and two of his fingers are touching his lips. He looks so touched that I shove the cake into Jeremy's hands, move over, and gather him up in my arms.

"Is this allowed to be part of the deal?" I ask.

He glances over my shoulder at Carole and Jeremy and Steven, and then he makes me the happiest man in the world.

And he does it by touching his palm to my face and kissing me again.

~THE END~

Acknowledgments

Thank you first to my wonderful husband. Your support is what enables me to write. I love you for it.

Cheers to Teresa Crawford for helping me to structure this story. That Skype session was invaluable.

To editor Lynda Lamb, for going through and fine-tuning the text—and for working with a tight deadline.

Thanks to HJS Editing for proofreading for being so thorough and answering all my nagging questions. I hope to work with you again.

Natasha Snow—what lovely work you did for the cover!

Another cheers to all my betas readers, for reading and offering your valuable feedback.

Finally, thanks to all my friends—you know who and how awesome you are!

Anyta Sunday

HEART-STOPPING SLOW BURN

A bit about me: I'm a big, BIG fan of slow-burn romances. I love to read and write stories with characters who slowly fall in love.

Some of my favorite tropes to read and write are: Enemies to Lovers, Friends to Lovers, Clueless Guys, Bisexual, Pansexual, Demisexual, Oblivious MCs, Everyone (Else) Can See It, Slow Burn, Love Has No Boundaries.

I write a variety of stories, Contemporary MM Romances with a good dollop of angst, Contemporary lighthearted MM Romances, and even a splash of fantasy.
My books have been translated into German, Italian, French, Spanish, and Thai.

Contact: http://www.anytasunday.com/about-anyta/
Sign up for Anyta's newsletter and receive a free e-book:
http://www.anytasunday.com/newsletter-free-e-book/

Printed in Great Britain
by Amazon